From New York Times and USA Today
bestselling author Thea Harrison…

This book contains *Dragos Takes a Holiday*, *Pia Saves the Day*, and *Peanut Goes to School* (two novellas and a short story in the Elder Races series, previously published separately). All three stories focus on the Cuelebres, the First Family of the Wyr.

Dragos Takes a Holiday: When the Cuelebre family heads to Bermuda for some much needed R&R, it's no ordinary weekend in the sun. Between Pirates, treasure hunting, and a baby dragon… what could possibly go wrong?

Pia Saves the Day: The Cuelebres have moved to upstate New York where they finally have the space to indulge their Wyr side, and Liam can grow in safety. Their idyllic situation is shattered when Dragos is injured and stripped of his memory. Without Pia's taming influence, there's nothing holding back Dragos's darkest side.

Peanut Goes to School: Dragos Cuelebre is no longer the only dragon. At just six months of age, Liam has already grown to the size of a large five-year-old boy. In an effort to give him a taste of normality, his parents enroll him in first grade. But school has a surprising number of pitfalls, and Liam is fast becoming one of the most dangerous creatures in all of the Elder Races.

A Dragon's Family Album

Thea Harrison

A Dragon's Family Album

Table of Contents

Dragos Takes a Holiday

Thea Harrison

Chapter One

ONE EVENING AFTER a particularly brutal day at work, Dragos leaned against the refrigerator and watched Pia cook dinner.

They had personal chefs. They could order takeout from any restaurant in New York, but these days, more often than not, Pia chose to cook. Although she was a lifelong dedicated vegan, she had overcome her revulsion for handling meat for his sake. He loved to watch her pore over recipes with her tongue between her teeth, and he enjoyed every meal she cooked for him, which she often set in front of him with an air of triumph and relief.

After preparing a sirloin roast with carrots and potatoes in one pan, she placed a strange-looking lump in a smaller, separate pan and set vegetables around that too.

Dragos asked, "What on earth is that?"

"It's a vegan harvest roast."

He shook his head. "I'm sorry, lover, someone should have taught you this by now. The words 'vegan' and 'roast' do not go together in the same sentence." He eyed the unappetizing lump with skepticism. "What's it made of?"

Pia glanced at him, amused. "Seitan, different kinds

of flour, seeds, soy sauce, seasonings, sometimes nuts..."

He lost interest after the first ingredient. "In other words, nothing edible."

"You might not think it's edible, but I think it's delicious." She wiped her hands on a towel and gave him a cheerful grin. "You're welcome to try it after it's cooked."

He grinned back. "No thanks, I'll pass."

His grin faded again almost immediately. He'd had a bitch of a day, but every workday was a bitch these days. It had started last year when Dragos had lost two of his seven sentinels to mating with women who lived outside the Wyr demesne.

This year had not gone any easier. He had finally replaced Rune and Tiago with two new sentinels, but now all the older sentinels needed vacations. As Dragos's First, Graydon had insisted on going last. By the time Graydon came back from his vacation, Dragos would have been operating short-staffed for more than a year.

Dragos had a short temper at the best of times. Now he was liable to bite somebody's head off if they looked at him funny.

For now, he was glad the day was over. He leaned back against the kitchen counter, still wearing the suit he had put on for work at six thirty that morning.

Liam had awakened from his nap, and Dragos held him against his shoulder. Even though the baby was three months old, he was growing at an inhumanly quick rate and exhibiting abilities far beyond most babies his age. At his last checkup, Pia's physician, Dr. Medina, said he had grown twice the size of a three-month-old human baby.

He could already sit up easily. A few days ago, he had gotten to his hands and knees and rocked. Soon he would be crawling, and he understood far more of what people said than most realized. He was the first ever dragon child, and he was so full of magic his small body glowed with it. Nobody knew what to expect from him, not even Dragos.

Both father and son watched Pia move around the kitchen. She had used a hot iron and pinned up her hair so that it fell in loose, soft curls of pale gold. Dragos itched to sink his hands into the shining, luxurious mass.

Post pregnancy, her body had returned to its slim runner's build, except now her breasts and her hips were slightly fuller. After the first month or so of startled indecision, she had taken to wearing form fitting clothing that accentuated her new curves and drove Dragos wild.

Tonight she wore a saucy red-and-white halter dress with a tucked-in waist and a flaring, knee-length skirt. Large strawberries splashed bright circles of red on the soft material, accented with a touch of green at the stem. She had painted her toes the same shade of cheerful red and walked around the kitchen barefoot, and Dragos wanted to eat her all up.

Later, he promised himself. After they put Liam to bed, and the penthouse was shadowed and quiet,

Dragos would carry Pia out to the terrace, lay her down on one of the cushioned lounge chairs underneath the stars, and feast on every inch of her delectable body. He would raise that sexy skirt of hers and ease her gorgeous legs apart…

Liam fussed and knuckled his round little face. Dragos considered the baby with a frown. Normally Liam had a sunny disposition. It was unlike him to be so fussy. His silky tufts of white-blond hair wafted in the air around his head, and his dark violet eyes looked puffy and tired.

Pia opened the convection-oven door, set in the two roast pans and glanced at Liam too. "I think he's already teething. He's had a tough couple of days. He keeps wanting to nurse, and today he's been fussing and rubbing his face. When I coaxed him to open his mouth earlier, I could see white lines at his gums."

"Good." Dragos patted Liam's diapered bottom gently. "A dragon needs a healthy set of teeth."

Pia widened her eyes at him and grinned. "Yes, of course he needs them, but he's only three months old!"

He shrugged. "He's got quite a bit of growing to do, and he's going to need a lot of meat. It's possible his dragon form will end up as big as mine."

"He's not developing so much as he's exploding into reality." Pia shook his head. "I guess he's creating his own definition of normal. We just have to figure out a way to keep up with him."

Dragos smiled at her over the baby's head. "We defeated the Dark Fae King. We can cope with one precocious child."

"You always sound so confident." She walked over to the stainless-steel island where a bottle of red wine stood alongside two wineglasses. Dragos noted with pleasure that she had opened one of his favorites, a Chateau Lafite Rothschild Pauillac that had once in Versailles been dubbed "the King's wine."

"That's because I am confident."

"No doubt you're right." She concentrated on pouring the rich ruby liquid into the glasses. "I think his bunny is in the living room. It might make him feel better. Would you mind getting it?"

"Of course." He took the baby down the hall.

Liam's bunny was one of those things Dragos didn't understand. The stuffed toy was floppy, super soft and had big, dark eyes. Liam adored it, although Dragos wasn't quite sure why. In real life, a bunny that size would barely make an appetizer.

His iPhone buzzed in his suit pocket. He checked it. Graydon's name lit up the display. He could leave a message. Dragos pressed the ignore button as he scanned the living room. Most of the spacious area lay in shadows, but a few accent lights remained on. Liam's bunny lay on one end of the couch. As he strode over to it, a flash of gold caught his eye.

He turned, his attention sharpening.

The flash of gold came from the front jacket of a hardcover book. It sat atop a pile of several books on one of the end tables. Absently, Dragos scooped up the soft toy and presented it to Liam. Liam snatched at the bunny and hugged it while he laid his head on Dragos's chest. Dragos cupped the back of the baby's soft head, cuddling him, as he strolled over to get a proper look at the cover.

The book was lavishly decorated in rich, eye-catching colors. A treasure chest sat on a bronze background, underneath the title *Missing Treasures of the Seventeenth Century.* Old, gold doubloons spilled out of the open lid.

Dragos flipped open the book. It was from the public library. He read the inside of the jacket. The narrative focused on several European ships that had gone missing on voyages of exploration.

Pia walked into the living room carrying two glasses of wine. He said, "I don't know why you keep going to the library instead of buying any book that you want."

"Because going to the library is an experience." Pia set his glass on the end table and curled up at one end of the couch. "It's a fun outing away from the Tower, Liam enjoys story time and the other babies, and I like supporting the library."

While she talked, he made a mental note to write a large check for the public library system. If Pia and Liam enjoyed going, he would make sure the library could provide them with anything they wanted.

"Why don't I have this book?" He owned several books about treasure in his own personal library, but he knew he didn't have this one. He would have remembered the flashy gold cover.

"You've been pretty busy. It came out last November."

"Mm."

He set it aside and picked up the next one, a large, trade-sized paperback entitled *The Lost Elders*. This one was decorated with a heavy, glossed cover. He flipped it over to scan the blurb on the back.

"I don't have this one either." He frowned.

"I think that one came out in March. I've skimmed all your books about treasure, and they made me curious, so I only checked out books that you don't already have." Pia sipped her wine. "Didn't you say that you used to hunt for lost treasure?"

"Yes, I did. Of course, I had a lot more free time in those days." He hefted the paperback in one hand as his gaze went unfocused. "I remember when this happened."

"Really?"

"It was early in the fifteenth century. Isabeau, the Light Fae Queen in Ireland, and her younger twin sister, Tatiana, had been feuding for several years. Tatiana sent the ship *Sebille* to scout for a new land where she could settle with her followers. The ship was rumored to have been loaded with gold and all kinds of treasure, so that the captain could negotiate with indigenous people for land rights."

"Tatiana… Do you mean the Light Fae Queen in Los Angeles?" Pia asked.

"Yes." He set the book down and settled beside her on the couch. Liam had started to chew on one of the bunny's floppy ears. "Eventually she settled in southern

California, but the *Sebille* disappeared completely, and people have been looking for it ever since. Some even said that Isabeau caught wind of the expedition and sabotaged it, but I doubt that. From everything I've heard, Isabeau wanted to get rid of Tatiana as much as Tatiana wanted to leave."

Pia slid close to him and rested her head on his shoulder. Warmth filled him, and he put an arm around her as she rubbed Liam's back. "What do you suppose happened to the *Sebille*?"

Dragos thought back. "There were rumors that it sank off the southeastern coast of North America. I wonder if this book goes into more detail."

She lifted her head. "You mean it might have gotten lost somewhere around the Bermuda Triangle?"

"It's possible, although back then it wasn't called the Bermuda Triangle." Unwilling to reach for his glass and disturb either Pia or Liam, he took a sip from her wineglass and handed it back to her. "It was called the Devil's Triangle, and still is sometimes. The area wasn't very well understood at the time the ship went missing."

"I didn't know it was that well understood now."

He gave into temptation and sank his hand into her soft, luxuriant hair. "It's unpredictable, which is not quite the same thing. There's a tangle of crossover passageways all over the area. The routes loop around and over each other, and the shifting ocean currents make most of them virtually impossible to map, although some old legends say that pirates found passageways to Other lands where they lived in secret hideouts."

She shuddered. "You could get caught up in one of those passageways and get lost forever."

"Yes, theoretically, and it's possible that the *Sebille* did just that." He tilted his head and buried his face in her hair, which was soft like silk and scented with her floral shampoo. "But it's also not likely, either, because they would have needed to stumble onto the exact path of the crossover passageway. If ships stick to the established shipping lanes, they're safe enough. Probably the *Sebille* sank."

"Have you been to Bermuda?" She walked her fingers across his chest.

"No, I've only flown over it several times."

"Bermuda, the Bahamas, the Caribbean—I've never been anywhere like that. I bet they're beautiful." She sounded wistful.

His phone buzzed, and they both sighed. He pulled the phone out of his jacket pocket and checked the display. It was Graydon again. Dragos gritted his teeth. "How long before we eat?"

They had come to a mutual decision several months ago. Dragos would not take any business or sentinel calls during dinner. Pia told him, "We've got at least a half an hour. You have time to take the call."

He kissed her forehead, handed Liam over to her, and stood to walk down the hallway as he answered his phone.

"Sorry to bother you." Graydon always apologized when he called after work hours.

"Never mind, what is it?" Dragos asked.

After listening to a few sentences, he switched direction and walked back into the living room. He met Pia's gaze. "Would you mind keeping dinner warm for me? I'll be as quick as I can."

She nodded, looking unsurprised. "Of course."

He strode out and didn't make it back until after midnight.

When he finally returned home, the penthouse lay in deep shadow, except for the kitchen, where a light burned over the stove. Pia had left a note on the counter. *Your supper plate is in the fridge. Microwave for three minutes. Love you.*

He smiled. She had never lost patience, no matter how challenging this last year had become. He opened the fridge to locate his supper. She had plated the roast-beef meal beautifully and even garnished it with a sprig of parsley.

Too hungry to wait while the food heated, he ate it cold, standing at the counter. Looking forward to sliding between cool silk sheets, he walked down the hall to the heart of the place, the large bedroom he shared with Pia.

She had left another light on, her bedside lamp. Wearing dark blue cotton shorts and a thin, matching T-shirt with spaghetti straps, she had tucked her legs underneath the covers and sprawled across the bed on her stomach, fast asleep. The pile of library books lay strewn around her like abandoned toys. The fingers of her right hand curled around *The Lost Elders.*

Moving gently so he didn't wake her, he stacked the

library books on her nightstand. As he leaned to pick up *The Lost Elders*, the sound of Liam crying came over the baby monitor.

Pia stirred. "Unh."

"Stay where you are," Dragos whispered. "I'll take care of him."

"You sure?" Her voice was sleep blurred. "You've had such a long day."

"I'm positive."

"Is everything okay?"

"Everything is fine. Go back to sleep."

He pressed a kiss to her bare shoulder, pulled the bedcovers up and tucked them around her. Still carrying the book, he walked into the nursery.

The mellow glow from a nightlight lit the room. In the crib, Liam had come up on his hands and knees but sank back a bit, so that he sat like a frog as he cried. Dragos set the book on the side table by the rocking chair and gathered up the baby.

"What is this?" He kept his voice soft and gentle. "Life is not nearly half as tragic as you think it is."

Liam shuddered and hiccupped, blinking up at Dragos with violet eyes that swam with tears. He embodied innocence, his energy so bright, shining and new, and Dragos loved him with a ferocity he had never felt about anything or anyone before, except for Pia.

"Now, what's wrong?" Dragos asked. "Is it your mouth?"

The baby nodded, and his soft face crumpled.

He nestled Liam against his chest. "I'll make it better."

He walked to the large rocking chair, sat and whispered a beguilement until Liam's small body relaxed. The baby sucked his thumb for a while and fell asleep as Dragos rocked him.

Peace settled around Dragos like a warm blanket. He was tired, and he wanted to go to bed. He wanted to block out the rest of the world and make love to Pia. But this quiet, intimate time with his son was too perfect, and it would pass all too soon. He would not be too quick to turn away from moments like this.

He remembered the book and picked it up. Still rocking, Dragos opened it. He began to read, and lost himself in thoughts of ancient gold and lost treasure.

Chapter Two

"**Y**OU SURE YOU weren't too clever for him?" Eva asked. "Don't get me wrong, I know he's bright. He's Lord of the Wyr and all, but he *is* still just a man."

Despite Eva's skepticism, Pia remained unfazed. "Wait and see. It isn't a matter of 'if' we go on vacation. It's a matter of 'when.'"

Bright morning sunlight streamed into Dragos and Pia's bedroom, although calling it a bedroom was a bit of a misnomer. The room was massive, with the king-sized bed at one end, and a fireplace and white couches at the other end. When Pia had come to live in Cuelebre Tower, the room had been stark, but she had added bright patches of color with jewel-toned pillows and throws, a rich bedspread and rugs.

Pia stood beside the bed where she had piled things to pack. She swung her suitcase up and opened it.

Eva lay sprawled on the floor in front of the French doors with a thick, soft blanket spread out beside her for Liam to play on. Not that Eva was having a great deal of success keeping Liam on the blanket. He had started another new thing that morning. He was busily scooting backwards everywhere.

"You're so sure, you're already packing?"

"Yes. He needs a break, and he wants it. He just might not know it yet. He's so tired he fell asleep in the nursery last night when he was rocking the peanut. That's where I found them both this morning." She looked at Eva pointedly. "*Dragos* fell asleep. Normally he can stay awake for days if he needs to."

Eva scratched the back of her head. The sunlight gleamed gold on her dark brown skin. "I just hope you aren't counting your chickens before they're hatched."

"Mark my words, you should pack too." Pia wagged her finger at the other woman. "He's remarkably decisive when he makes his mind up about something. We could be on the plane as soon as tomorrow, or even tonight. I'm going to suggest that we only take you and Hugh with us."

Eva sat up straight. "Sweet."

Pia paused to watch Liam scoot backwards toward her, his little diapered butt in the air, and barely managed to keep from laughing out loud. He was sharp as a whip, and he might figure out she was laughing at him. She didn't want to hurt his feelings.

She told Eva, "We won't need bodyguards, but I do want to have babysitters so Dragos and I can go out by ourselves."

"I'll take it." Eva grinned. "Do we by any chance know where Dragos will want to go on vacation?"

Pia scowled. "No, of course not. But I wouldn't rule out Bermuda, the Caribbean, or Cape Horn."

Eva cocked her head. "Am I sensing a water

theme?"

"You're sensing a shipwreck theme." Pia shook out a skirt and carefully folded it. "Or maybe I should say a theme about lost treasure."

"You're talking about those books you got from the library the other day, aren't you? Dayum, you're good. Does Graydon know we're leaving?"

Pia blinked at her. "Know what? Nothing's been decided yet."

Eva laughed and rolled to her feet. "I'll go tell Hugh and pack."

As Eva left, Pia checked her toiletries bag. It was filled with miniature bottles of everything she would need. She set it in her suitcase and bent to pick up the Peanut.

She whispered, "We have to pack for you too, you know. I'm guessing we might be going to Bermuda, since your daddy read that whole book in the middle of the night."

The baby looked deep into her eyes and patted her face.

✧   ✧   ✧

MOMMY CARRIED HIM into his room. He thought things were going well until she set him on the thick, soft rug in the middle of the floor.

No, that wasn't what he wanted. That was very much not what he wanted.

He was tired again, and his mouth hurt, and he was

hungry all the time. Hungry for what, he didn't know. Hungry, hungry.

So he scowled and concentrated mightily on *something that he wanted.*

And the world shifted.

He felt better. Quite a bit better, actually. His new mouth didn't hurt at all, but he was still very hungry.

Mommy kept talking as she moved around his room. She pulled diapers out of drawers, set them on the changing table and turned to the closet. "...I want to take you to the beach and play in the sand with you, except I don't know that we should. Are you too young to play in sand, or to go into salt water? Peanut, you are such a statistical outlier, half the time I have no idea what we should do with you."

She turned away from the closet, her arms full of clothes. When she looked at him, she shrieked and dropped everything.

It startled him so badly he felt a burst of anxiety. He turned around to scoot backward toward her as fast as he could, but something flopped along his back, and his arms and legs weren't quite working the way they should. He stopped, confused, and stared down at himself.

Slender white forelegs stretched to the floor. He raised a front paw, staring at the strange talons. His back felt odd too, and he looked over his shoulder, flexing sleek, graceful wings. A tail trailed the floor behind him. He reached for it with one forepaw, tugged the end and his butt wagged. The tail was attached to him.

Mommy knelt in front of him and cupped his face. He looked up into her eyes. She had grown teary, and yet she was smiling. "You are the cleverest baby ever. You're so beautiful, and exactly how I first dreamed of you."

Pleasure washed over him, and he smiled at her.

Her eyes went very round. She beamed at him. "That's quite a mouthful of toofers you've got there, too."

She gathered him up in her arms. He tucked his snout into the crook of her neck, and it was so good, almost everything he wanted, except...

He was *so* hungry.

He fussed and whined, and she sat on the floor and rocked him, while she dug her cell phone out of her pocket and moved her thumb rapidly over the keypad. "Dragos, you have to come home right now."

Daddy's sharp voice came over the phone. "What's wrong?"

"Nothing's wrong exactly, but Liam has changed and he's upset."

"What do you mean, he's changed?"

The pace of Mommy's rocking picked up, but she spoke softly. "I mean he's in his dragon form, and I can't tell you how beautiful he is. He's also upset for some reason. Maybe it scared him? And you're missing all of it. You need to come see this."

"I'll be right there."

Mommy set the phone aside as Liam whined and plucked at her shirt. "Are you hungry?" she asked gently. He nodded. "I can't nurse you when you're like this, sweetheart, not with all of those razor-sharp teeth."

That was the saddest thing he had ever heard in his whole life. He lifted his head and looked at her, grief stricken.

"Oh, Peanut, I'm so sorry. Please don't look at me that way." They considered each other desperately. Mommy's expression turned firm. He folded his wings back and clung to her as she rolled to her feet and carried him to the kitchen.

She opened the fridge door and pulled out a pan that had the something he was craving. It smelled oh so good. His stomach rumbled and he arched toward it, reaching with both front paws.

"Hold on—let me get the plastic wrap off first."

As she slid to the floor, he struggled to get to the appetizing smell. She snatched off the plastic wrap, set the pan on the kitchen tile, and he fell on the leftover sirloin roast. Eyes closed, his whole body tense, he focused on gorging on the meat.

Running footsteps sounded in the background, but it was only Daddy, so he ignored it. A moment later, Daddy said in a quiet voice, "Well, damn. Look at that. Hello, little man."

A large, gentle hand came down on Liam's back, between his wings, and contentment filled him.

"I didn't know what else to do." She gestured to the pan. "He acted like he was starving, and he has all those teeth. Then I remembered what you said about how he was going to need a lot of meat."

"He gave you clues about what he needed, and you followed your instincts," said Daddy. "You did exactly what you should have done."

Liam finished off the roast. The hungriness had gone away, and his belly felt comfortably stretched and full. Sleepiness descended. Eyes drooping, he looked over his shoulder. Daddy and Mommy knelt on either side of him, both smiling.

He scooted backward toward Mommy. When she gathered him up, he turned to climb up her body until he lay draped along her shoulders.

"I'm telling you, this is just like my dreams." Mommy reached up to stroke his leg. He stopped listening to their conversation, tucked his snout in the neckline of her shirt and fell fast asleep.

✧   ✧   ✧

RELIEF HAD TURNED her leg muscles into noodles, so Pia shifted to sit on the floor, and Dragos joined her. He leaned back against the fridge while she sat forward with her spine straight. She didn't want to disturb Liam while he was resting on her.

She angled her head and looked at Dragos. "What are we going to do if he doesn't change back into his human form, and he keeps growing at this rate?"

He stretched his legs out, loosened his tie and scratched his jaw. Even though it was just midday, a new growth of beard shadowed his lean cheeks. He kept his inky-black hair cut uncompromisingly short, and the formality of his dark suit highlighted the richness of his copper skin and intelligent, gold eyes.

In the last year, Pia had gone from living at the edge of Wyr society to being catapulted directly to the top. She had met any number of Powerful creatures in the different Elder Races from all over the world, but none of them, to her mind, had Dragos's sheer physicality. Standing just under seven feet tall and weighing close to three hundred pounds, he towered over the largest of his sentinels, and his dragon form was the size of a Cessna jet.

His handsomeness had a brutality that never failed to cause her breath to catch at the back of her throat. Not even tiredness could dim the Power and energy that boiled from him. He was as strong as the earth, and whenever she laid eyes on him she felt her soul winging out of her body, arrowing straight toward him.

He sighed. "I should be able to coax him back into his human form, but I don't think he'll be able to stay that way. His human form has no capacity to eat meat. If he follows the pattern of other Wyr children with large animal forms, he'll need to shift back periodically to his dragon form in order to feed."

"We're going to need a bigger skyscraper." She rubbed her eyes with a thumb and forefinger. "Part of me can't believe I just said that."

Dragos's cell phone buzzed. His gold gaze flashed with irritation. Without glancing at the screen, he thumbed the phone on and said into it, "No." After he hung up, he looked at her, his expression turning rueful.

"I think it's time we talk again about moving up north."

Resigned, she nodded. Dragos owned a country estate just outside of Carthage, in northern New York. Well technically, since they were married now and nobody had breathed a word to her about a prenup, she supposed she was part owner, too. The mansion had fifty rooms, a separate house for an estate manager, and it was surrounded by two hundred and fifty acres of rolling, forested hills.

They had gone to the estate for their honeymoon and had stayed in the estate manager's house, which had four bedrooms, four bathrooms and a family room with a fireplace that overlooked a lake. She loved that house. She had given birth to Liam in that house. She didn't feel any affinity whatsoever for the palatial mansion.

Still, she knew she wasn't being entirely rational. Just the sheer size of the place had intimidated her when she first saw it, but she might like it more if she spent some time there. After all, she had once felt funny about Cuelebre Tower and the penthouse, and familiarity had gone a long way to making her comfortable here.

She sighed. "He's going to need the space, isn't he? Especially when he learns to fly."

"Yes, he will. The place up north is more private, with lots of greenery and open space." He paused thoughtfully. "We can make it more secure too."

"Two hundred and fifty acres would be a hell of a backyard for him to play in," she murmured.

Pia had always followed her mother's advice and stayed in the city, which was densely populated and easier to hide in. She had never seriously considered moving to the country, but now as she poked at the idea, she realized that two hundred and fifty acres would be a hell of a backyard for her to play in too, and her Wyr form approved. It approved most strenuously.

"We can get to the city in a couple of hours if we fly in." Dragos angled his head, considering it. "That's not so bad. When you're stuck in traffic here, it can take a couple of hours just to get across town. I could have a complete office complex built on the property."

She put a hand on his leg. His hand sewn Armani suit was made of lightweight woven wool that stretched taut over the thick, powerful muscle of his thigh. "We would need more than just the office complex. There will need to be living space for security and staff, and for the sentinels, because they'll be flying back and forth. As spacious as that mansion is, it's no Cuelebre Tower. We can't all live there, nor would I want to try."

He rubbed her back, his clever fingers following the curve and hollow of her spine. "We could build along the lake. There's plenty of space to spread out. None of us would need to feel crowded."

She broached another subject hesitantly. "I would want to redecorate the main house. Maybe even do some renovations."

"You should," he told her, smiling. "Hell, you can bulldoze the place if you want, and start over from scratch."

That thought was a little too overwhelming. "I don't know if we need to go quite that far."

Dragos stroked a loose strand of hair away from her face. "But do we both believe that we need to make the move?"

She looked down. The weight of Liam's body lay draped along the back of her neck and shoulders, and his slender, graceful white legs and tail curled around her, just underneath her collarbones. While it seemed like it might be an awkward position, he didn't appear to mind at all. In fact he seemed perfectly comfortable, and he was sound asleep.

He was not a perfect white, but more of an ivory hue. His hide had the same iridescent sheen that Dragos's did, but he had gotten his pale coloring from her. She wondered what people would think when they saw him. She put a hand lightly on one of his forelegs, and he stretched, flexing his paws, and sighed.

"Yes, we need to move. But we won't have time to start building or redecorating until July. First we've got to get through all of the inter-demesne functions surrounding the summer solstice, and Graydon needs his vacation."

"Agreed." He gave her a lopsided smile that eased his harsh features and banished the tiredness from his expression. "In the meantime, is it too much upheaval if we consider taking a long weekend away?"

She loved him so much, with all of her heart. She loved his harsh side and needed his ruthlessness, because she knew he would always provide for her and Liam, and protect them with every ounce of his considerable power. But when he smiled at her like that, everything inside of her brightened, until she felt like she floated in a sea of light, and she grew weightless and dizzy with delight.

She peeked at him between her lashes. "I don't know, Dragos, this is awfully sudden. Where would you want to go?"

He tugged at a strand of her hair behind her ear, and her gaze fell to his wrist. It had been a year since she had sewn a lock of her braided hair around his wrist, and he still wore it. He had done something to protect it, and it shone with an extra sparkle of Power.

"You said you've never been to Bermuda or the Caribbean." He angled his head, watching her expression. "How would you like to go there? I think it would be fun to do some treasure hunting. We can go swimming and soak up some sunshine, and go out to eat. I could use a break before we plunge into all of the summer solstice activities, even if it's a short one, and I'll bet you could too."

She smiled. "I would really love to get away."

"How soon could you be ready to go?"

She tilted her head, and her smile turned into a grin. "Is fifteen minutes soon enough?"

"Really. Fifteen minutes." His gold eyes narrowed suddenly. "Those books. That conversation. You little Machiavellian, you set me up."

She closed one eye and held her thumb and forefinger close together. "Maybe a teensy, weensy bit. Actually, I just presented you with opportunities."

He laughed. "Is that what you call it? I should know

by now to expect this kind of thing from the thief who stole from my hoard."

Her eyes rounded. "You're never going to get over it, are you? I only stole one time, and it was just a penny!"

"I can't tell you how glad I am of that," said Dragos. "Because you're pretty lousy at it. The gods only know what kind of trouble you would have gotten yourself into, if you had kept up your life of crime."

Her tone of voice turned aggrieved. "That is completely untrue. I was absolutely excellent at stealing *the very one time* I did it. I was not quite so excellent at the getaway."

"You have a point," he admitted.

She grew serious. "While everybody else has a vacation scheduled, you need and deserve a break more than anybody. But you're so driven, I knew you would have a hard time disconnecting from work unless you had something else to focus on, so I went to the library to do some research. When I found new books about ships that had disappeared, I thought if I could interest you in some treasure hunting, it would be a good way for you to stop and smell the roses—or, in your case, search for some shiny sparklies."

His eyes flashed with an acquisitive gleam. "It's been a long time since I've found a good stash of treasure."

"I know."

"And you are wiser and far kinder than I deserve," he said quietly. He leaned forward to kiss her. Her eyelids fluttered shut as his warm, hard lips caressed hers. "And so damn sneaky."

"That's one of the things you love best about me," she reminded him.

His whisper turned into a low growl. "Damn right."

"What do you have to do to get ready to leave?" She stroked his face.

"Pack. I've already talked to Graydon, and he's good with us leaving. The jet is in the hangar, so I just need to make a phone call. While we're getting ready, I'll have Kris find us a good place to stay. What about you?"

"I need to finish packing Liam's stuff, but that won't take more than five or ten minutes. I would like to take Hugh and Eva so they can babysit."

He cocked his head. "We'll go out to dinner somewhere by the beach."

She beamed at him. "You mean we'll go on a date?"

He smiled. "Just as soon as we can get out of here."

Chapter Three

S INCE LIAM RESTRICTED her movements, Dragos helped her pack the baby's things. While he changed out of his suit into khaki pants and a black knit shirt and packed, she called Eva and Hugh.

Eva laughed. "Girl, you got some scary mojo."

"I just know my husband." Pia felt too excited to be smug.

Eva and Hugh soon showed up at the penthouse.

They stared in shocked silence at the sleeping baby dragon draped around Pia's neck. Pia smiled as she held a finger to her lips and silently warned them to be quiet. Nodding and grinning broadly, they took charge of the luggage.

Dragos made phone calls, while Pia raided his supply of organic beef jerky in the kitchen. She wanted to have lots of snacks in her purse, in case Liam woke with the same kind of desperate hunger as he'd shown earlier.

Dragos strode into the kitchen and looked at her and Liam. "If people caught sight of him in his Wyr form, it would start a riot, and we would never get out of here. Let's take the private elevator down to the parking garage."

"Sounds good to me," she said with relief.

Liam never stirred as they rode down the elevator or climbed into the waiting limo with Eva and Hugh. Pia eased him off her shoulders and into the car seat, and after some finagling managed to get him strapped in. During the ride to the airport they talked in quiet voices. Dragos's phone buzzed, and Pia twitched. He wasn't going to get much of a break if he kept answering phone calls and text messages.

He checked the screen of his iPhone and smiled. "Kris found us a place to stay. It's a house on Cambridge Beach Bay."

He handed the phone to Pia, and she scrolled through the images. The rental was a historic, peach-colored villa with a veranda that faced the ocean, and it had eight bedrooms and five baths, private gardens and a barbeque pit. Two grocery stores were a five minutes' walk away, and restaurants, shops, and boat rentals were all in close proximity. Even better, it had a terraced path to the beach framed by flowering bushes and palm trees.

She caught a glimpse of the astronomical price tag on the webpage. The cost for renting the villa for a week was close to ten thousand dollars.

The number danced in front of her eyes. She took a deep breath and let it out slowly. There was no need to hyperventilate. Dragos deposited twice that amount each month into a personal account for her, just for incidentals. She bought herself and Peanut anything she wanted, and she still had serious money left over, enough to dump into a fast-growing, hefty savings account. The point was, they could easily afford the rental.

"Forget about me," she told Eva. "Dragos's assistant has some serious mojo." She turned to Dragos. "This is amazing. How did he get it at such short notice?"

A smile tugged at the corners of his lips. "Kris implied there was a last-minute cancellation."

Or Dragos paid the other vacationers to change their plans. She paused to listen to her internal radar. Did she feel funny about that?

Nope. Her internal radar felt quite serene today. The others would have gotten a deal they couldn't refuse, and Dragos got to take a much-needed break. Plus, beach! The water looked so lovely.

Dragos continued. "We've got the house for up to a week if we want it. The manager of the property will stock the fridge with plenty of food and drinks, and is setting up a crib for the length of our stay. We don't have to do anything when we arrive. We can just relax and do whatever we want."

Absorbed in looking at the photos, she said, "What I want to know is, why don't we have a private island?"

She had meant to be facetious, but Dragos's expression turned thoughtful. "Good question. I'll have to look into that."

Her head snapped up, and she stared at him with wide eyes. He gave her a completely serious look in return. Wordless, she faced forward.

Hugh's shoulders shook, and Eva snickered into her

hand.

Dragos gently eased his phone out of her lax hands. She watched him sidelong as he turned it off.

✧   ✧   ✧

THE FLIGHT WAS short, just over two hours long. Eva and Hugh sat at the front of the cabin, talking and playing chess. Dragos and Pia settled with Liam on one of the two couches toward the back of the plane.

Toward the end of the flight, Pia watched out a window. Her excitement surged again as land came into view in the limitless expanse of blue water. Liam woke up as the plane started to descend. The change in altitude didn't seem to affect him at all. The baby dragon joined her in staring out the window.

Pia divided her attention between the scenery out-side and studying her son's triangular head with the slender, graceful snout. He was perfectly formed, with every detail that Dragos's dragon form had, only in miniature.

She might have given birth to him, but he was such a mystery to her. His midnight-dark, violet, jewel-like eyes had gone wide with fascination. As a raptor, he probably already had the capacity to see minute details a mile or two away, but she wondered what he really comprehended of the scenery spread out below them. Right now the lines of his body were delicate rather than powerful, but if Dragos was right and Liam did reach his father's size, he would be a juggernaut.

The magic in him burned fiercely. While Liam's Wyr form was a dragon, her blood ran in his veins as much as his father's did. Liam's Power felt cooler to her than the molten corona of Power that boiled out of Dragos. How would that combination manifest in Liam's talents and abilities? All they knew at this point was that he had some of her ability to heal, for he had saved her life before he had ever been born.

She pressed her lips to the top of his head and whispered telepathically, *I love you.*

He closed his eyes and leaned against her cheek with a sigh.

"Come here, little man." Dragos held his hands out to Liam.

Liam's body tightened in protest around Pia's neck. She patted his leg while she bit back a smile. As much as he loved his father, at this stage in his young life he was definitely a mama's boy.

When Dragos spoke again, his dark, rich voice was soothing. "I will give you back to your mother soon enough. For now you must come to me."

While he talked to his son in a low murmur, Liam's body relaxed and his sharp, slender talons slipped out of her T-shirt. He offered no protest when Dragos gathered him up in gentle hands.

Pia stuck fingers in the new holes in her shirt. She muttered, "If this keeps up, I'm going to need a new wardrobe."

She watched Dragos cradle Liam against his chest. As the small, white dragon looked up, Dragos bent his dark head and whispered in Liam's ear for several minutes. Liam rested his head on Dragos's chest as he listened. She couldn't make out specific words, but she felt the effect of Dragos's words in snatches. Reassurance, praise and encouragement radiated from him.

The sight of father and son together never failed to affect her. Dragos was the most lethal and efficient fighter she had ever seen. He had a killing speed along with his immense size, and he had once pulled the crumpled metal of a wrecked car away from her body.

As Dragos held Liam, his hands seemed even more massive on the baby's small body. He had positioned his long, powerful fingers with utmost care at the base of the lacy wings.

The small dragon's body shimmered and changed, and the baby Dragos cradled against his chest had turned human again.

Pia's sigh of relief mingled with a sense of awe. Her father had been human, and she had only learned how to shapeshift into her Wyr form the previous year. Even then she had needed Dragos's help. It had taken Liam less than four months.

Dragos patted Liam's round, diapered bottom. "Well done. Now that you've learned how to shapeshift, you can change back again whenever you need to." He lifted his head and handed the baby back to her.

As she took Liam, she whispered to Dragos, "You win all the good Daddy points."

His eyes glinted with wicked sensuality, and his eyelids lowered to conceal it. Ever the opportunist, he murmured, "And what will that get me?"

"If you play your cards right, it might get you lucky later."

He traced the line of her jaw with his forefinger. "How about if I throw in dinner by the ocean?"

It was a good thing they were both sitting, because that slight caress made her go weak at the knees.

As their gazes connected, all the light banter fell away, leaving something pure and naked, a shock of connection that reverberated through both mind and body. As she stared into his intent gold eyes, the rest of the world fell away. She was caught in a beguilement that would never end, and she would go anywhere with him, do anything for him. She loved him so much, she couldn't breathe.

She fumbled for a good reply. After all, she didn't want him to get too cocky. "Dinner by the ocean might increase your chances a bit."

The sexy, cruel line of his mouth tilted up. He slid one hand to the back of her neck, his fingers pressing lightly. The rasp of calluses against her sensitive skin caused a ripple of sensation to cascade down her body. She licked her lower lip and watched as his gaze fell to track the movement.

Her unsteady lips shaped his name, as she said without sound or air, "Dragos."

Heat flashed out of his tense body, invisible and volcanic. Slowly his fingers curled around the hair at her nape and clenched into a fist. He held her trapped in a possessive, barbaric hold, but everything he did was possessive and barbaric, and she wouldn't change him for the world.

On her lap, Liam burbled companionably and tugged at her shirt. It broke the molten spell burning the air between her and Dragos. She blinked down at the baby. For a moment she couldn't remember why they were on the plane, or where they were going.

Dragos hadn't loosened his hold on the hair at her nape. He growled very softly, "Tonight."

She managed a shaken nod. She was going to get so lucky tonight.

No, she meant he was.

Sooo lucky.

The plane's angle of descent grew steeper, and nearby land magic began to tickle at her senses. Dragos gently disengaged his fingers from her hair as she turned her attention to the peanut. Liam remained sublimely unaffected by the change in air pressure in the cabin, so she nursed him and changed his diaper while Dragos walked toward the front of the plane to talk with Eva and Hugh.

The last few minutes of their flight raced by, and they touched down at the L. F. Wade International Airport. The airport was small and the runways short, so the plane braked hard and taxied briefly until it rolled to a stop. Within moments the ground crew had the mobile stairway wheeled into place, and they disembarked into hot, bright sunshine.

A Mercedes SUV rental waited for them in the parking lot. They brought their car seat and fitted it to one of the bucket seats. Once Liam had been securely strapped in, Eva drove while Hugh rode shotgun, and Dragos, Liam and Pia rode in the back.

The airport was located on St. David's Island, at the northeast tip of Bermuda. Their house was located on the northwestern tip of the main island, so they drove across the causeway and along S Road. Even though they were on the opposite side of the island, Bermuda was not a large place, and the trip went quickly.

Pia couldn't see everything fast enough and craned her neck to look around at the intense green foliage and palm trees, the colorful variety of buildings and the glimpses of ocean and sandy beaches as they threaded through the streets.

Dragos lounged at her side, watching the passing scenery too. "Did you know that Bermuda has more than five hundred shipwrecks in the shallow reefs that circle the islands, dating from the 1500s?"

Pia turned to stare at him. "Five *hundred*?"

He nodded. "And those are only the ones that have been identified. Some are even popular scuba diving sites."

"The ocean floor must be like a pile of cars in a junkyard. How on earth could you hope to find the *Sebille* in all of that?"

He rubbed his jaw. "Well, if the *Sebille* had wrecked in shallow waters, it would have been discovered a long time ago. If it's out there, it's going to be deep."

She blinked. If it had sunk in deep water, it was no wonder nobody had located the ship yet. "Does that mean you won't be able to find it?"

He shook his head. "There's no way to know. It does mean finding it will be a challenge."

She studied his hard features. The frown that had been a part of his visage for so many months had eased, and he looked relaxed, alert and interested in life. She didn't care about treasure hunting for its own sake, but she was delighted that it had caught Dragos's interest, and the history of the *Sebille* had begun to engage her attention almost in spite of herself.

"How are you going to try to find it?" Most professional shipwreck hunters and maritime archaeologists had highly sophisticated and expensive equipment, and a single expedition could cost hundreds of thousands of dollars.

He lifted one shoulder in a casual shrug. "The first step will be to quarter off the area surrounding the islands. Then I'll search it systematically by flying low over the water. My magic sense is highly developed. In isolated circumstances, I can sense magic from a couple of miles away. The *Sebille* might not have been carrying treasure, but with a voyage that important, it would have carried magic items—at the very least an enchanted sextant for navigating in deep water under heavy cloud cover. And if I sense a spark of magic, I can dive for it."

She tried to imagine diving so deep with all of that water between her and the open air. A shudder tried to take over her limbs. She sternly pushed it down. "Could you dive as deep as the ocean floor?"

He never bothered with machismo swagger, because

he didn't need it. He said simply, "Yes."

"What will you do if you don't find anything in the flyovers?"

He shrugged. "Dive anyway until I've thoroughly explored each area. I'll concentrate first on the most likely routes ships sailed from Ireland and expand my radius from there. At that point, if I get serious, I'll look for primary sources in local records. It would help to talk to Tatiana, but she may not be willing to talk about details of the voyage. There might have been secrets on the ship that she would rather leave unfound."

"It sounds like a lot of grueling physical work."

"It is." He sounded pleased at the thought. "It's a lot of flying and swimming, and time spent outdoors in the open air and sun."

She pursed her lips. Maybe while Dragos conducted the physical search, she could do some digging for local sources.

Eva slowed the Mercedes on the narrow paved road, until she pulled to a stop beside a thick, recently trimmed hedge in front of the large, peach-colored villa. A flagstone path cut through an opening in the hedge.

The peanut had fallen asleep in her arms, so Eva opened the car door for her to step out. While Eva and Hugh pulled out the luggage, Dragos joined Pia and they walked up the path.

The house was two stories high and built into a hill. Steps led up to a wraparound porch on the upper level and the main front entrance. As they started up the steps, an attractive human woman in her forties opened the front door. She wore a summer linen suit and ballet flats, her dark hair pulled back in a chignon.

"Welcome, Lord and Lady Cuelebre." She spoke with a crisp British accent and smiled at them. "I'm Leanne Chambers, the property manager. We're so honored that you've come to visit."

"Hello." Pia returned her smile. "This is a beautiful place. I'm in love with it already."

"Isn't it lovely? This is my favorite of all the rentals I manage." Leanne's dark gaze dropped to Liam, and her smile turned indulgent. "If you like, I can show you straight to the bedroom where I've put the crib."

"Thank you, but if I try to put him down in a strange place, he'll only wake up and fuss."

The other woman inclined her head. "If you'll allow me, I'll give you a quick tour and get out of your way."

She handed two sets of keys to Dragos and led the way through the house, keeping up a light patter of conversation. The house had been built in the late nineteenth century and used as a vacation home ever since. The windows were high and elegant in spacious rooms with hardwood floors, and decorated with simple, comfortable furniture.

Pia could easily picture people in Victorian and Edwardian dress gracing the large parlor room and the living room with the immense fireplace, or playing cards and board games on the veranda. The front lawn was just large enough to contain a croquet set. Pia caught a glimpse of the beach through the trees down the terraced path.

Despite its age, the house had been updated with every modern convenience. An outside shower had been installed so people could rinse off from the beach before stepping inside. The large kitchen had new stainless-steel appliances, and two of the five bathrooms had Jacuzzi tubs. There was only one bedroom that had an *en suite* bathroom, and Pia was pleased to see that it still had the original enameled tiles and claw-foot tub.

Leanne paused in the doorway of the master suite. "I took the liberty of setting the crib in the room beside this one. And because the house is so large, I bought a baby monitor to go with it. Along with filling the grocery order, I've stocked the fridge with four complimentary bottles of white wine, and a fruit-and-candies tray."

Pia smiled at the other woman. "Thank you."

"My pleasure. Is there anything else that you need?"

"I can't think of anything," she replied. "I love this place. Everything is wonderful."

She glanced at Dragos. He had turned on his phone and his head was bent as he studied the screen. Her shoulders drooped. He glanced at her and frowned.

He pocketed his phone and told the manager, "Thank you, that will be all."

"Very good." This time the inclination of Leanne's head was deferential. "I'll see myself out. Enjoy your stay."

Pia moved to look out the window at the sparkling water. The baby snored slightly. He sounded like a squeaky toy. Sleeping soundly had turned him into a dead weight, and her back ached from carrying him around.

Disappointment tried to darken her earlier excitement and pleasure. She had dangled Dragos's favorite hobby in front of him, and they had just arrived in a literal paradise, but he still couldn't keep his phone turned off. When she'd started a relationship with him, she knew she was going to have to share his time and attention, but she never realized how much of a problem that would be, or how much it might grow to bother her at times like this.

Mostly she was fine with it. That wasn't rationalization; she really was. Between the overwhelming demands of his corporate responsibilities and the Wyr demesne, he carried a heavy load, and it suited her just fine to play a supporting role for him. She wasn't as driven as he was, and she absolutely adored the fact that she had the luxury to concentrate on the peanut while he was so small.

Only occasionally, like now, it caused a heavy ache in her chest.

Dragos walked up behind her and put his hands on her shoulders. "What has dimmed that bright smile of yours?"

She tried to think of something positive and supportive to say. "Don't you love it here? This place is gorgeous."

His fingers tightened. He bent over her until his lips touched the thin, sensitive shell of her ear. He whispered, "I turned on my phone to search for a place to go to dinner."

She looked over her shoulder at him. "Really?"

"Really. I've already turned it off again."

The leaden feeling in her chest lightened. At the same time the back of her nose prickled and moisture flooded her eyes. Embarrassed at the sudden surge of emotion, she folded her lips tight and nodded.

His gaze was too keen and filled with understanding. He rubbed her back. "I wouldn't trade this past year away for anything, but it's still been hard on us."

She leaned back against his strong frame, and he wrapped his arms around both her and the baby. "I wouldn't trade it away for anything either."

"Things will get easier, I promise." He rested his cheek on the top of her head. "As soon as all of the sentinels are back at work, let's go upstate and stay for a couple of months."

"Are you sure you can take the time away from the city?" She rested her head against his chest, and he stroked her hair.

"Yes. We'll need to make plans for renovations and building, but we can take things at our own pace and go as slow as we like. If there's an emergency and I have to work, I'll make sure it takes no more than twenty-five hours a week. Kris has been my assistant for so long, he should be able to handle most things. We can take Liam hiking. It will be a real, extended break. How does that sound?"

She had to clear her throat before she could speak again. "I would truly love that."

"I would too." He pressed a kiss to her temple. "Consider it a date."

"Okay." She turned her head toward him, and he nuzzled her.

The baby stirred in her arms, and Liam lifted his sleep-blurred face to look around. His round eyes and soft, open mouth reflected his astonishment at the change in venue. Pia grinned. The last time Liam knew, they had been on the plane.

"Okay, Peanut, time to show you around. Then you get to play with Aunt Eva and Uncle Hugh while I change into fresh clothes, and Mommy and Daddy go out to eat."

"Do you want an upscale restaurant, or a beachside tavern?" Dragos asked. "Because if you want upscale, I have to turn my phone back on again to make a reservation."

She didn't hesitate. "Ooh, beachside, please!"

He grinned. "That's what I thought you'd say, which is why I had already turned it off."

She stood on tiptoe to kiss him. "You know me so well."

He put a hand at the back of her head and held her in place as he returned her kiss lingeringly, setting her body on a slow burn.

"Get ready." His voice was so low it was barely more than a vibration against her lips.

Feeling intoxicated, she nodded as he let her go. She caught the heavy-lidded slant of his glance as he turned away, and she knew he hadn't been talking about their dinner.

Chapter Four

P IA SHOWED LIAM the house, along with his room with the crib, his clothes and toys. She knew from past experience that it would be easier to leave him once he saw where he was, and she was right. He didn't fuss when she handed him over to Eva.

Dragos left the master bedroom and bath to her and carried a change of clothes and his toiletry kit into one of the other bathrooms. Pia opened windows, and the sound of the nearby surf washed in.

She hummed as she shaved her legs and washed her hair. After blow-drying her hair, she chose to leave it down and loose. She slipped on a simple, dark blue sheath dress that ended at mid-thigh and flat, silver sandals that complemented her slender feet and legs. She spent the most time on her makeup, enhancing her eyes with a dark, smoky eye shadow and stroking a cranberry-colored lipstick on her lips.

Wearing such rich colors brought an extra sheen out of her thick, light gold hair and made the most of her tan. After she was finished, she stared at herself. Anticipation made her eyes sparkle.

"Look at you," she whispered at the bright, vivid creature in the mirror. "You look happy."

Happy. A year ago she wasn't sure she knew what the word meant.

Sure, in a lot of ways the last year had been hard. Aside from all the other challenges she and Dragos had faced, she still wasn't completely accepted by the Wyr community, and while the peanut had gone a long way to softening everybody's heart, criticism about her unrevealed Wyr form continued to be harsh.

Despite that, her life was pretty damn close to perfect. She had more than she had ever dreamed she could have. She had a husband and mate who adored her with a kind of ferocity that should have been scary but somehow wasn't, and she had the most precious son imaginable. She had friends, good friends, and while they weren't close, even Aryal had abandoned her antagonism toward Pia.

A sudden, superstitious fear chilled her skin. She was too happy.

Happiness this intense couldn't last. Something was bound to happen.

As soon as she had the thought, she clenched her fists and shoved it away. So what if something happened? Something always happened. When it did, she and Dragos would face it as a team, just like they had everything else over the past year. They could handle anything life gave them as long as they were together.

She could handle anything, except for losing either Dragos or Liam.

Angry at herself for letting baseless fear ruin her happy mood, she dragged a brush through her hair one last time, slipped a few things into a small silver purse with a chain-link strap and left the bedroom.

As she walked down the hall, she heard high-pitched baby squeals. In the living room, Dragos tossed Liam into the air and caught him. Liam was giggling so hard his face was almost purple. Nearby, Hugh and Eva lounged on couches, their faces creased with laughter as they watched the pair.

Pia started chuckling too. Liam's paroxysm of delight was simply too infectious to resist. As she walked into the living room, she said, "If it were anybody else doing that…"

Dragos threw Liam into the air again. "I won't let him fall."

"I know you won't."

Dragos had dressed in a black silk polo shirt and cream slacks. His clothes were expensive, simple and lethally effective, as they highlighted the power and grace of his muscled body. While he wasn't much for wearing jewelry, he never took his wedding ring off. He also loved the gold Rolex she had bought him for Christmas, and both it and the braided length of her hair gleamed brightly against his dark copper skin. As he caught the baby one last time and turned to her, she saw that he had shaved as well.

He had made an effort to look nice for her. The knowledge curled into the pit of her stomach and intensified the tug of attraction she always felt for him. She watched him look down her body. When he met her gaze, sultry heat shimmered in his gold eyes.

"I'm hungry," he said, and she knew again he wasn't talking about dinner.

She had to clear her throat. Her voice was huskier than ever as she replied, "Me too."

"Shall we go?"

She nodded and walked over to kiss Liam. Dragos handed the baby to Hugh, and they left.

The heat of the day had begun to ease, and heavy yellow light slanted through the lush greenery as they walked to the Mercedes. She noticed how cleverly the area had been designed to maximize the privacy of the houses, with rows of hedges bordering the narrow road. Dragos opened the passenger door for her, and she climbed into the warm car.

He slid into the driver's seat a moment later. As he turned to her, she asked, "How far away is this beachside—"

The rest of her question disappeared in a squeak as, eyes glittering, he yanked her to him. He took her mouth in a hard, hot kiss.

Her skin flashed with the heat from his mouth, his hands, and her pulse exploded. Melting against him, she kissed him back as hungrily as he kissed her. His pulse raced to meet hers as he slanted his lips over and over on her, driving deep into her mouth with his tongue.

When he finally lifted his head, they were both shaking. He stroked the disheveled hair away from her face and helped her to ease back into her seat.

"I didn't put a comb in my purse," she said.

"Leave it," he told her, very low.

Laughter shook out of her. "I can't just leave it and walk into public like this. It looks like we've been making out."

One of his black brows lifted as he reached over her to pull her seat belt around her torso and click it into place. "We have."

He was no help. He loved any and all barbaric displays of his claim on her. While he started the car, she ran unsteady fingers through the thick mass until she had the long, tangled strands smoothed out.

The restaurant was on Ireland Island, just a short drive away. After doing her best to tidy her appearance, Pia rolled down her window to let a blast of fresh, ocean-scented air clear her head. The streets were more narrow and winding than she was used to, but Dragos seemed completely comfortable driving on them. He reversed into a cramped parking space that she wasn't sure she would have attempted.

Outside the car, he took her hand as they walked to the beachside restaurant, where music played over loudspeakers. The restaurant was open on the three sides that faced the water, and railings that ran the border all the way around except for the entrance. The fourth side, where the kitchen was located, was solid building. A bar lined the wall between the kitchen and the tables, and a dance floor was set to one side.

The place wasn't fancy. It had wooden tables and concrete floors, but the bar was packed, and so was the dance floor, and the food smelled fabulous. People spilled out onto the beach, drinking and talking together in groups.

Pia studied the scene curiously as she followed Dragos to the bar. There was quite a mix of clientele. Some people were well dressed, but more than not wore jeans or shorts and T-shirts, and many appeared to have just come from the beach. A few looked downright rough, such as the pair of men lounged at the bar.

Space opened up beside them at the bar. Dragos approached.

The two men eyed Dragos speculatively and turned their attention to Pia where their gazes lingered. One of the men was human. He had a wiry build, a beaky face, and long, graying hair pulled back into a ponytail. He wore gold earrings, and he looked at her out of the corner of his eye.

The other man was Light Fae. He was bigger, younger and broader. He was almost as large as Dragos. He, too, had long hair pulled back in a ponytail, only his was blond and curling. He was deeply suntanned, and he wasn't nearly as circumspect as his companion. He stared openly at her breasts and hips.

He thrust out with his hips as he said something to his companion in a language she had never heard before, and the other man laughed.

Their crudity was like a slap in the face. She ignored them, her expression turning stony, but Dragos didn't.

Dragos's immense body turned taut with sudden menace. He turned to face the bigger of the two men, slowly and deliberately, and he took a step forward until he stared down into the man's eyes. He looked hard as granite, his gold eyes flat and deadly.

People around them fell silent, some animal instinct warning them of possible danger.

Pia's breathing constricted. The other man stood his ground, with an arrogant, insolent stance. Although it was hard to believe, clearly the idiot didn't have a clue either who he had ogled, or who he had engaged in a pissing contest. Had he been living under a rock?

She tugged at Dragos's hand.

He ignored her. The tension between the two men ratcheted higher, hovering just on the edge of violence.

Pia wasn't sure what happened next, but the other man's stance changed. He shrugged, said something again in his strange language, and turned away to lean his elbows on the bar where he and his companion muttered together in low voices. Neither man glanced at Pia.

Dragos took a step back. She let go of the breath she had been holding. The crowd relaxed and conversation picked up.

She asked Dragos telepathically, *Was that really necessary?*

He looked at her. *Yes.*

She studied him with a frown. His expression and his body language had relaxed, but his molten gaze was still murderous. *They're just assholes*, she said gently. *Can you let it go, or do you want to go somewhere else for dinner?*

If anything his expression turned angrier at the thought of leaving. *Fuck, no.* He paused and his eyebrows knit together. *Unless you do.*

She smiled up at him. *Thank you for asking, but I'm fine.*

He considered the crowded space, eyes narrowing. *We can find somewhere else to wait for a table.*

I told you, I'm fine. You already backed them down. They're just two dumb jerks, and they're probably drunk to boot. They're not that important.

His expression lightened with approval. She wiggled around him, opposite the other men, and came up to the bar. Dragos came up behind her until his hard body pressed against her back. He slid an arm around her, and she felt totally surrounded, protected and at ease. She couldn't have been safer if she had been locked in a secret vault at Fort Knox. She leaned her head back against his chest to smile at him and finally felt him relax a little. The other two men ignored them as if they were in another room.

The bartender came up to them. Pia ordered a Mai Tai while Dragos ordered scotch, and they put their name on the waiting list for a seat at one of the tables.

She raised her voice to be heard over the music. "So when do you want to start your search?"

"I thought I'd get going first thing tomorrow morning," Dragos said. "Would you and Liam like to come with me for a little while?"

"I'd love to." She sipped her drink. It was delicious. "If you don't mind help, I thought I might check out museums and libraries to see if I can find any mention of the *Sebille*."

He smiled down at her. "I don't mind at all, but don't you want to spend some time on the beach?"

"Sure," she said. "But Bermuda is only, what, twenty miles from end to end?"

"Something like that."

She shrugged, enjoying the excuse to snuggle back against him. "I doubt there will be many places to do research on ancient Elder shipwrecks. I could look around in the morning, and Liam and I can go to the beach afterward."

"Sounds good to me," Dragos said. "We've got a plan for tomorrow."

Something snagged her attention, and she turned her head. The two men beside them had stopped talking. They both leaned against the bar and stared into their drinks, their bodies tense and still.

Her gaze narrowed, and she caught the bigger, younger male glancing at them. All sexual innuendo and crudity had left his expression, leaving him looking cold and hard.

She turned away again quickly. What the hell was his problem? The men might speak a strange language, but they could know English too. Was he listening to her conversation with Dragos, or was he still mad at the unspoken pissing contest he and Dragos had been in? She shook her head. He was going to live a very short life if he didn't either learn to be polite or to let things go.

A waitress came up behind them and took them to their table, which was right by the beach. Pia was so delighted, she put the unpleasantness from the bar firmly behind her and settled in to enjoy the rare treat— a date with Dragos, while he was on vacation.

She ordered a salad with mangos and artichokes. Dragos ordered steak and lobster, and a bottle of Pinot Noir. The server brought the wine right away.

Even before they got their meal, she started plotting.

Due to the inter-demesne functions they had attended over the last year, she had learned how to dance in a formal setting. The experience of waltzing with Dragos was something she would never forget, his power and assurance as he swept her around a ballroom while he looked down at her, unsmiling and severe in his black tie.

She had never seen him dance just for the fun of it, though.

She sighed happily as their server set a beautiful salad in front of her and gave Dragos his meal. When they were alone again, she told him, "I sure love to dance."

Dragos said, "No."

She almost burst out laughing. Instead she raised her eyebrows pointedly. "Don't you love to dance with me?"

Amusement creased the sides of his mouth. He cut into his steak. "What a talent you have for asking loaded questions. You made a political chore very enjoyable. It's important to present a united front and to demonstrate to everyone that we are a team."

"You don't have a romantic bone in your body, do you?" She grinned and thought about teasing him some more, but he had been so responsive about taking a vacation, she decided to take pity on him and relent.

"Never mind. I'll just have to enjoy those waltzes enough for the both of us."

They talked more about plans for moving upstate, and the decision became more real with conversation. While they had made the decision because it was best for Liam, by the end of the meal Pia started to look forward to the change.

After all, young parents move to the 'burbs all the time, for all kinds of reasons. To get away from crime, to get away from the noise and crowdedness of the city. To raise their children in greater peace and safety, and to give them greater freedom to roam.

Raising a magic baby dragon wasn't so *very* different.

She thought of the long, lone flights Dragos took periodically to relieve the stresses of city life.

She said, "This is going to be good for all of us."

"I think it will too. I'm starting to look forward to it." He took the last bite of his lobster and set his fork down. "Do you want dessert or coffee?"

While Dragos didn't have much of a sweet tooth, she did, and he often chose to have a cheese plate and port to keep her company. She shrugged. "I could take it or leave it."

"Then come on." He stood and held out a hand.

Obligingly, she slid out of her seat and slipped her fingers into his grasp. "We haven't paid yet. What are we doing?"

He slanted a black eyebrow at her. "We're dancing."

She went into delighted shock. He led her onto the dance floor.

Chapter Five

No, Dragos didn't have a romantic bone in his body, but Pia made it easy for him. Whenever he did something for her, she lit up with pleasure. Her midnight-violet eyes sparkled, and joy glowed from her skin. Canny businessman that he was, he invested in her happiness and reaped the returns in bright laughter, soft smiles, gentle touches and impulsive hugs.

His world turned grim when she was unhappy, and his thoughts became aggressive and bladelike. He grew intolerant and quick to slash out. He did not trust a world that had the audacity to hurt his mate. Her happiness filled him with contentment.

What was a little dancing compared to that?

They reached the crowded floor. Without the discipline and structure of a waltz, he wasn't sure what he should do. He stood, hands on his hips, as he studied the movements of the other dancers. Some of them looked like they had been tasered and were shuddering just before they collapsed.

That, he would not do. Could not.

Pia touched his biceps. When he looked down at her, her face brimmed with… Okay, that was more than just joy. That was laughter, too.

"Just move." She put her hands on his hips. "Don't overthink it. Listen to the music, do what you want and be natural."

Do what you want. Those instructions were easy enough to follow.

He tugged her close, and she came readily to him, wrapping her arms around his waist. However, she did more than just hug him. She rubbed her slender, curvy body against his rhythmically, twisting and swaying in time to the music, and Dragos's opinion about dancing underwent a drastic change.

He stared at the sinfully gorgeous woman in his arms. She slid along his body with such sensuous grace she set his skin smoldering.

"You know, Dragos," she said with an upward glance and a twinkle, "when two people are dancing, it usually requires both of them to do something."

At her words, his attention snapped to the music. The song was a popular one, bright, quirky and with a strong, tribal beat. He caught the rhythm of it and began to move, and it wiped the laughter off Pia's face.

Holding her gaze, he set his hands on her hips and guided her to move with him. They swayed and undulated together. After a year of living as mates, he was so attuned to her, he could anticipate what she did. Ever the aggressor, he bent forward, and she bowed back. She draped one arm around his neck, her gaze never leaving his.

The music changed, and the next song was darker, smokier. It wormed its way into his blood, and the rest of the world fell away. Their movements together, hip to hip and thigh to thigh, were as necessary and as elemental as sex. The connection between them was always present, but now it grew bright and taut like a bridge of fire.

Sometimes he grew afraid that he burned too hot, that the roar he felt in his blood for her would overwhelm or frighten her, but she never turned from him or backed away. Instead she met his fire with a fierce passion of her own, her cooler, moonlit energy burnishing under the force of his attention until she shone.

She straightened and tugged at the same time, and he bent his head. She whispered in his ear, "If you don't take me out of here, I'm going to come right on the dance floor."

Each word caressed his ear. Her lips were trembling.

It doused him in a sheet of flame. He took her arm and led her off the floor. Everything happened from a distance, on the other side of the urgency that pounded in his body.

To the exit. Someone came and bleated at him. Their server. He dug in his pocket and shoved cash at her without counting it. The server stepped back, beaming.

Away from the beach, toward the car.

The sun had set while they ate their dinner. White light from halogen street lamps threw pools of light along the streets and the beach, heightening the darkness beyond. Pia almost stumbled, but his tight hold wouldn't let her. She looked etched, the contours of her face marked with tension. His sharp predator's eye caught the subtle shift of her slender throat muscles as she swallowed. Her scent was feminine and musky at once, and he listened to the tiny friction of her silk dress against her skin.

They reached the Mercedes. As he looked at it he thought of the myriad, complex movements it would take to drive the machine. How mundane. How human. The dragon rebelled at the thought.

He wrapped them in a cloak of invisibility and picked her up. A muffled noise came out of her. It sounded stark and needy. She hooked her arm around his neck as he strode to the edge of the parking lot. A waist-high stone wall separated the asphalt from the sand. He leaped it and ran down the beach, faster and faster until the wind whipped through their hair.

Within moments they left behind the bright lights of the dockyard and the incessant chatter of humanity. The ocean murmured against the sand in a rhythm far older than any music. Lights dotted the dark shoreline, and a slice of moon curved in the dark blue, starred night, but the place he found was deep with shadows.

He walked into the deepest of the shadows, where the line of trees and bushes met the beach. Only then did he set her on her feet. Now her whole body trembled. He could hear her heart racing.

He did that. He caused her body to shake and cry out. He set her heart racing, made her laugh, created her happiness. He reached past the bone and sinew of her body and touched the invisible, mysterious core of her, the place that defined her.

That place. *That* invisible, mysterious place was his home.

He lived for it. He would die for it.

It did not define him. He was too old and too wicked. But if he were ever to believe in a place called Eden, paradise or heaven, that invisible place would be it. It had nothing to do with forgiveness. It was more necessary to him than redemption.

She could break him. Him. In their year together, the surprise had still not left him. He had lived through cataclysms. He had survived the undying enmity of Elves and the shifting of continents, but she held his old, jaded heart in her two slender hands.

"Here?" she whispered.

"Here," he told her. "Now."

He pushed her against the trunk of a tree and went to his knees in front of her. Sliding his hands up the taut, graceful line of her thighs, he made a startling discovery.

She wore no panties underneath that short—*very short*—thin dress.

Her audacity shocked a growl out of him. He cupped her round, silken-smooth ass and buried his face greedily in the soft, private hair at the juncture of her thighs.

She gasped, shaking all over, and leaned back against the tree while she hooked one of her fabulous legs over his shoulder, opening herself for his exploration. He licked and suckled at the velvety, succulent flesh of her sex. She was slick and inviting, and she tasted like arousal.

The sensation shot down his spine. His already hard cock stiffened further until he felt thick and swollen.

Gods, he loved to fuck her, with his tongue, his fingers, and his penis—anything he could use to get inside her most private place, and to feel how she responded to him. He inserted his forefinger into her gently, feeling how her inner muscles gripped him.

Her body vibrated with tension as her pleasure escalated. She cupped the back of his head with trembling fingers as he found the stiff little nubbin of her clitoris and licked. He inserted a second finger. She arched her back as she accommodated him, and her moisture coated his hand.

"You need this," he growled. "Say it."

"Yes." She stroked her fingers through his hair.

"You need me."

He knew what he sounded like. He sounded arrogant and demanding, and slightly ridiculous, but she didn't seem to mind.

"Yes!" she cried out.

He used the back of his knuckle to press her clitoris to his mouth, rubbed his teeth gently, gently across the delicate, delicious flesh and felt the shock waves shudder through her body. She shoved a hand against her mouth to muffle a cry.

His own need was growing urgent, and his pants felt too tight. Too civilized. He unzipped and yanked them open to let his engorged penis spill out, never once letting up from working on her.

The incantation he wove on her was his greatest enchantment. Each stroke, lick and thrust was a line that made a verse, each verse necessary and building on each other to create the final spell. She showed him the way the spell should be cast with every gasp and flex of her muscles, every tiny betrayal revealing the intensity of her pleasure.

Her tension escalated until it broke apart. She bucked against his hold and forgot to muffle her cry when she climaxed. The tiny shock waves rippled through her muscles. He felt it through his fingers as he stroked her deep inside, at the site of her second pleasure center, while he never stopped licking.

She was so hot, so tight. He was dying to sheathe himself in her, but he held himself under rigid control while he sucked hard and drove in with his fingers at the same time—and she convulsed again, sobbing.

That's it, he murmured in her head. *There you are. Give it to me again.*

She shook her head jerkily. "I can't—Those blew my mind. I can't—I can't stand up any longer."

Yes, you can, he told her. *I'm going to take you right up against that tree trunk. Right after you come for me one more time.*

"Good God, Dragos!" She clenched her fingers in his short hair.

He fucked her with his fingers while he never let up on the pressure with his tongue. The heat coming off of her body was unbelievably erotic. She made a strangled, mewling noise at the back of her throat, and the sound went straight to his cock. In that moment, he was absolutely sure he was going to die if he didn't get inside of her just as quickly as he could.

Swearing, she bent over and draped across his shoulder, and her inner muscles clenched on his fingers as she came one more time. He wrapped an arm around her neck while he cupped her until the orgasm eased.

He was breathing like he had raced a marathon, his own need turning his muscles rigid. As he loosened his hold on her, she slid into his lap. He yanked her torso closer, and she wrapped her legs around his waist as she reached between them.

The sensation of her slender fingers closing over his erection was delicious, agonizing. His head fell back, and he sucked in air through clenched teeth as she stroked him.

"Come here," she whispered.

He widened his thighs, spreading her legs as she raised herself up and rubbed the tip of his erection against her soft, drenched entrance. Slowly she sank down on him. It didn't matter how many times they had made love over the last year. The sensation of piercing into her body was indescribable. Every time it was like the first time, like new. A guttural groan broke out of his mouth.

He couldn't get inside deeply enough. He gripped her and thrust with his hips. The friction of sliding into her tight, wet sheath made him crazy, crazy. Her moonlit hair was tousled and shadowed her face. Watching his expression with wise, loving eyes, she flexed on him as she undulated her torso. She knew exactly what to do, and it sent him over the edge.

Gripping her tighter, he pumped once, twice, three times hard and fast. The climax ran through the muscles of his body, hitting him like a steamroller, and he felt himself beginning to pulse inside of her. The pleasure was so violent it was almost excruciating.

"Fuck me," he gasped.

"Any time you want," she whispered. She stroked his face and gave him a siren's smile. "Any time, anywhere."

The aftershocks were still hitting him, pleasure slowly spiraling him down to sanity once again. He pulled her closer, one hand at the back of her neck and the other arm wrapped around her waist. "Always."

She laid her head on his shoulder and pressed her lips to his neck. "Forever."

The mating frenzy that had gripped them last year was never too far away, and for a moment he wavered on the edge. He could take her over and over, passion blazing through the night like a comet. They had done it before, and no doubt would do it again.

For the moment, instead, peace stole over him gradually, until the dragon let go and eased back, and he could think more humanlike thoughts.

"I think I might be able to drive now," he said.

She snickered. "Are you sure?"

He smiled into her neck. "Pretty sure. When we

reached the car earlier, all I could think of was: Key. Ignition. Stick shift. Wheel. And then: No."

She laughed harder. "When you picked me up, all I could think of was: Yay!"

"Sometimes the single-syllable conversations are the most important ones." He kissed her and fell into the private, voluptuous world of exploring her soft, sensual mouth.

She murmured wordlessly, the sound filled with contentment, and kissed him back as she stroked her fingers through his hair. They both sighed with regret when his softening penis slipped out of her.

She said against his mouth, "I think I have sand burn on my knees."

He shifted immediately to help her stand. "I'm sorry."

"No, don't be sorry. If it had been really irritating, I would have said something."

Together they brushed the sand off her legs. "We should be heading back anyway."

"As long as you cloak us again on the way to the car. I'm not fit to be seen in public." She tried to straighten her dress while he zipped up his pants.

He paused to look at her with a private, possessive smile. While he liked displays of his claim on her—disheveled hair, lipstick gone, or even the slight evidence of marks on her neck—no, at the moment, she was not fit to be seen in public. The thin material of her dress was crumpled, and they both smelled like sex, and that was too private to be shared.

"Of course," he said. "Are you ready?"

She nodded. This time he took her hand and they walked back, enjoying the night and the breeze that blew off the ocean. When they got back within sight of the bright lights and busy dockyard, Dragos wrapped the concealment cloak around them again.

Pia said, "I am horribly in love with you, you know."

He put his arm around her shoulders. "As I am with you. Horribly."

Her sigh made him smile. It was such a happy sound. He pulled her closer as they strolled toward the car.

Chapter Six

E ARLY THE NEXT morning, Pia dressed in Capri cargo pants, a lemon-yellow tank top and her slender silver sandals. Dragos dressed simply as well, in jeans and a gray T-shirt that stretched across the breadth of his chest and biceps.

After a quick, cheerful breakfast, Pia slipped Liam into his baby carrier and strapped him to her torso. She and Dragos walked the path to the beach, where Dragos changed into his dragon form.

Liam crowed with excitement and craned his neck to look at Dragos. Pia turned so he could study his father, and he flailed his arms.

"This is one excited baby." She jerked her head back with a laugh as one of his chubby fists clipped her on the chin.

The dragon bent his immense head and nosed Liam, who shrieked happily and pounded the dragon's snout. Pia laughed harder as she imagined what they might look like to a total stranger. If she had witnessed such a bizarre sight without knowing any of them, she would have been absolutely terrified for the baby and the woman holding him.

The dragon's huge gold eyes danced. He said to Pia,

"Are you ready?"

"You bet."

Dragos scooped Pia into one forepaw with extreme care and twisted to set her on his back. With the familiarity of long practice, she scooted up to the natural hollow where the base of the dragon's neck met his shoulders. As soon as she settled into place, she patted his dusky bronze hide. "All set."

Her heart leaped as he crouched and launched over the water in a breathtaking surge of power. It never got old. Dragos's lunges into the air used to scare her, since for flights like this, she rode him without a strap or harness of any kind, but her confidence and trust had grown over time. Even in his dragon form, he was blindingly fast. Once, she had started to slide from her perch, and he had twisted in midair to snatch her up in one paw before she fell.

However, this flight didn't go as planned. When they went airborne, Liam gave another happy shriek—and shapeshifted.

Astonished, Pia stared down at him. Normally when he rode in the baby carrier, he was strapped snugly against the front of her body, but his dragon form was much longer and leaner than his human baby form, and now the carrier hung loose around his sleek body.

He began to crawl onto her shoulders. She threw her arms tightly around him. He wriggled to get away from her, his head turned and jewel-bright eyes fixed on Dragos's huge, flapping wings.

"We've got a problem," she called out.

Immediately Dragos stopped his ascent, spread his wings wide and coasted. He tried to look around, but he couldn't twist far enough to see what happened at the base of his neck. "What's wrong?"

"Liam changed again—he's trying to get away from me. I don't know if I can hold on to him!"

She grabbed Liam by one foreleg and wrapped her fingers around the base of one wing as he freed it from the carrier. Liam flapped his wing and smacked her in the face. Pain flared as he hit her in the nose. Her eyes watered.

Dragos said, "Let him go."

Pia blinked the tears from her eyes and looked around, her thoughts racing. They were already a couple of hundred yards out from shore. If she let Liam go and he tried to fly but couldn't, Dragos would to have to lunge to catch him. If he did, she didn't know if she could hold her seat, or if Dragos could catch them both if they fell.

But it quickly became clear that they might both fall anyway. Liam's strength in his dragon form was sobering. He wasn't even fighting with her. She could tell he was excited, not distressed, but he was so determined she could barely hold on to him.

Thank God they were flying over the water. She thought of hitting the surface at the speed they were going. It might hurt, but at this height, it wouldn't kill her. It would help if she controlled her fall and hit the surface in a dive.

"Okay," she said. "Ready?"

"Yes."

She let go of Liam. He pulled free from the carrier, balanced on her shoulders and launched into the air. Heart in her throat, she watched as he flapped his wings enthusiastically and...

Plummeted in an ungainly spiral.

"Watch out, he's falling!" she shouted.

Fear clutched her. Strong though he might be, he was still a baby. She might survive if she hit the water, but the fall could kill him.

Quick as a cat, Dragos twisted and snatched him out of the air. "Got him."

"Jesus wept." She hunched over Dragos's neck, leaning on one hand. "That sight aged me twenty years."

Dragos wheeled and flew back to shore. When he landed, he knelt so Pia could slide to the ground. She managed to do so without falling, which was a major feat since her legs were shaking so badly. She walked around to face him.

He held the small, white dragon in one cupped paw. As she joined them, he turned his paw upward and opened his talons. Liam leaped and flapped his wings madly, and fell in a sprawl on the beach. He rolled to his feet and crouched to spring into the air again.

Dragos put a paw on him. "*NO.*"

Liam froze.

Dragos picked him up, held him between two talons and regarded him. The small, white dragon hung meekly limp in his grasp.

Dragos offered Liam to Pia, who gathered him in

her arms. Suddenly sitting down seemed like a good idea. She plopped on the sand, crossed her legs and cuddled the baby. Liam rested his head on her shoulder, his expression thoughtful.

Dragos's Wyr form disappeared as he shapeshifted. Glancing quickly along the deserted beach, he walked over to kneel beside her and they both contemplated the graceful white form of their son.

Uncertainty chewed at Pia. She angled her head up to Dragos. "Are we terrible parents? I mean, who takes their baby up in the air like that?"

"We're excellent parents. What we did was natural and normal. Avian Wyr take their babies in the air all the time."

He sounded so sensible. She tried to calm down. "My heart almost stopped when I watched him fall."

"He was never in any danger." Dragos looked deeply into her eyes. "Neither were you. If you had fallen with him, I would have caught you too. This wasn't any different than me tossing him in the air and catching him in the living room. You just got scared. That's all."

She put her cheek down on top of the white dragon's head. "Avian Wyr really do that?"

"Yes, they do." He rubbed her back, his touch slow and soothing. "In fact, falling is part of learning to fly. Clearly Liam and I will need to go out and do some practicing. You're welcome to come up with us if you want."

"No, thanks. I think I'll stay on the ground for those lessons." She shook her head and rubbed the back of her neck. "He's going to be able to fly before he's a year old. We need to get a toddler leash and hire avian nannies."

"We will. It's all right."

Gradually her heart stopped its headlong pounding as she listened to him. She considered Dragos's expression. He was entirely calm. In fact, the only thing he evidenced was mild concern for her.

She came to the humbling realization that she was the only one who had panicked. "You weren't bothered in the slightest by what happened, were you?"

He managed to produce a vaguely apologetic expression. "I'm afraid not."

Blowing out a breath, she glanced down at Liam. He lifted his head and smiled at her. Good God, look at those teeth. Baby though he was, with those teeth and razor-sharp talons, Liam could do some serious damage to someone if he had a mind to, yet the only thing he had done so far is damage her clothes.

He was already being careful.

She stroked his head. "You're such a good boy. I'm so proud of you."

He leaned into her hand and sighed.

"I guess our morning flight is cancelled," Dragos said.

Liam's head popped up. His expression turned stricken.

Pia steeled her heart against the sight. The primary reason they had come to Bermuda in the first place was so that Dragos would get some time for rest and recreation.

"That's all right." She smiled at Dragos. "Why don't you start your search? We don't need to come with you. I'll start on the research." She turned her attention to Liam. "If you want to come with me, you need to change back into your human form. Otherwise you have to stay here with Uncle Hugh."

Liam's gaze slid sideways to Dragos.

Pia told the baby firmly, "No, you're not going with your dad. You can go flying with him soon, but not this morning."

Thunderclouds gathered in his violet eyes. He growled.

A thoroughly annoyed baby dragon was quite a sight. Her face compressed, and she bit both of her lips. She would *not* laugh.

Dragos tapped Liam's snout. "Stop that. Don't growl at your mother."

The peanut blinked and jumped. Giving her an apologetic look, he changed, and she held her innocuous, human-looking baby in her arms.

She cuddled him close. "That's better."

Dragos kissed the top of Liam's head then kissed her on the mouth. "I'm going to take off."

"Have fun."

"You too." He paused. "Don't do anything you don't want to do. If it gets boring, stop."

"Don't worry about me. We'll have fun and be fine." She shooed him. "Go. Be free."

He smiled and changed, stepped a few paces away

from them and leaped. Dragos had taught her some time ago how to see beyond the cloaking spell. She watched him soar, the dragon's huge wingspan conquering the air. No matter how long she lived, she would never get tired of that sight.

BACK AT THE house, she found Eva and Hugh drinking coffee and reading newspapers that Hugh had picked up earlier from the local grocery store. They both looked up as she entered the kitchen. Eva asked, "Did you have a nice flight?"

"Well, we had an eventful one." Pia told them wryly what had happened. Eva groaned but Hugh just laughed. Pia regarded him with a sour expression. "Do gargoyles really take their babies on flights?"

"Every chance we get." Hugh grinned. "In some clans, the parents toss 'em off a cliff."

She shuddered. "And there for a while I thought we were the worst parents ever."

"Not so," he replied. "Hitting the ground in our gargoyle form doesn't hurt us. If a baby gargoyle gets that far, he'll just bounce."

She thought of Hugh's hard, stonelike façade when he was in his Wyr form. Still, she said doubtfully, "If you say so."

Eva slapped her hands on her thighs. "Enough about that. Ready to go exploring?"

Pia bounced on the balls of her feet. "Yep. Let's go."

They headed out the door. Eva drove again while

Hugh took shotgun, and Pia rode in the back beside Liam in his car seat.

Eva glanced in the rear view mirror. "I poked around online while you guys were out to dinner last night. There's an Elder museum located in an old lighthouse on the west coast of Somerset Island. You wanna start there?"

"Absolutely." Pia smiled with satisfaction.

The drive took about twenty minutes, and a good section of the route followed the coast. After a brilliant rose-and-gold dawn, the late morning remained perfect, sunny and cloudless. Light sparkled off the intense blue ocean. Both motor and sailboats dotted the water.

The Elder museum was located in the Beacon Hill lighthouse, which sat on the edge of land that jutted into the water. The white-and-red lighthouse towered against a backdrop of blue sky and water. Slowing, Eva turned the Mercedes down a narrow lane.

Pia looked around with interest as Eva pulled into a small, half-full parking lot. A few picnic benches were scattered across a wide lawn, and a Dark Fae family sat at one of the tables eating ice cream. Across the lawn, two trolls sat side by side, their faces tilted up to the sun. They looked like boulders that someone had carved faces on. At the far side of the building, a tall man with a ponytail leaned against the corner.

Pia's eyes narrowed. The man stood in the shade, and it was impossible to make out his features from the parking lot. His hair was dark, not blond. Could it be the human male from the bar?

If so, it was a hell of a coincidence for him to be hanging out here, after their run-in last night. She thought of how the two males had gone silent and tense while she and Dragos had talked. What exactly had they discussed?

They couldn't have mentioned the lighthouse. She had only found out about it this morning when Eva told her. But Bermuda was a small place. "Eva, you didn't find anywhere else for us to do research, did you?"

"Nope, unless you want to check out the Bermuda Maritime Museum. That'll be focused more on human history, so I think you might want to call first before making a trip over there."

Pia stepped out of the Mercedes, shading her eyes. Moving quicker than his nonchalant attitude would have suggested, Hugh joined her. The man pushed away from the building in the other direction and disappeared.

Hugh asked, "What's up?"

"Come with me." She told Eva, "Watch the baby."

She strode across the parking lot with Hugh at her side. Hugh said, "If you saw something you think is dangerous, you'd better tell me."

"I don't know what I saw." Unsettled, Pia's gaze swept over the people at the picnic tables again. "Just a man leaning against the side of the building, here at the corner."

They reached the spot where they could see the far side of the building. A narrow path led alongside the building and down the hill. Pia rubbed the back of her head and tried to decide how paranoid she was, while

Hugh stood watching her patiently.

She started on the path but was brought up short by Hugh's hand on her arm. "You wanna see what's down this path, okay, but I'll go first."

Impatiently, she gestured for him to go ahead of her then followed close behind, glancing up once at the lighthouse that towered high overhead. They reached the farthest corner of the building that faced the ocean, and walked to the edge of a sharp drop where they surveyed the scene.

The path cut down a short, rocky bluff to a pier where a motorboat carried a single male occupant with a dark ponytail. The boat headed out to sea.

Hugh angled his head at Pia. His usual sleepy expression had vanished, and he looked alert and interested. "What now?"

She blew out a breath. "Now we go back to the car, and I'll tell you and Eva about what happened last night."

They retraced their steps along the path. Pia paused where the man had been standing as they pulled up. She caught a faint whiff of cigarette smoke, along with a male scent.

Hugh inhaled deeply. "I'll remember his scent."

"So will I."

He narrowed his eyes. "Does this guy have anything to do with what happened last night?"

She shook her head. "I can't tell. We were in a bar with cooking food and a lot of people packed up against each other, and I didn't get close to him. Come on, let's get back to Eva and Liam."

The Mercedes idled, engine running, in the parking space. When they approached, she heard a mechanical click as Eva unlocked the doors. She and Hugh climbed into the air conditioned vehicle.

Pia told them about the men at the bar. She frowned. "I'm pretty sure that Dragos and I talked about starting the search for the *Sebille*, but I can't remember what exactly we said to each other."

"And you feel like they didn't recognize you or Dragos." Eva didn't frame it as a question.

Pia shrugged impatiently. "I don't even know that the man today had anything to do with last night. I just saw a guy with a ponytail and remembered the men at the bar. Maybe I'm being paranoid."

"Paranoid is a lot better than stupid, sugar." Eva drummed her fingers thoughtfully against the steering wheel. "And we're gonna keep on being paranoid. Hugh, go scout out the museum before we head inside."

"Be right back." Hugh slid out of the SUV and ambled toward the building.

He returned in a few minutes. Eva rolled down her window as he approached the driver's side. "The guy's scent is definitely inside, but the museum's all clear."

Pia unbuckled the straps on Liam's car seat and lifted him out. "Let's take a look around."

Chapter Seven

I NSIDE, THE MUSEUM took the entire ground floor. Aged wooden floors, colorful posters and display cases lured the eye. One section of shelves, lined with books, was roped off and someone had taped a computer-printed CLOSED sign to the rope.

Normally Pia would have been interested in looking around, but at the moment, she was too focused. Flanked by a watchful Eva, she walked through the museum and looked for a curator or attendant while Hugh strolled through the displays.

After some searching, she finally located a dwarf sitting at a desk in a back office, and she paused. The dwarf was dressed in jeans and a T-shirt with the museum's logo, and had a beard, but that was no indication of gender.

The office also carried a distinct male scent, with a whiff of cigarette smoke. Pia told Eva telepathically, *The man from outside has been in here very recently, within the last couple of hours.*

The plot thickens. Eva looked happy, but then Eva loved a challenge, and she usually looked happy when something got complicated or went wrong. *I didn't even know we had a plot on this trip.*

Pia said aloud, "Excuse me, could you answer a few questions for us?"

The dwarf jumped, knocked a sheaf of papers and exclaimed in a clearly feminine voice, "Gods! You startled me."

"I'm sorry." Pia started forward. "Let me help."

"No, no, never mind." The dwarf waved Pia away without looking at her. She slid out of her chair and onto her knees to gather up the papers. "Whatever you want, you'll have to make it quick. I'm very busy today."

Pia said, "I just wanted to know if the museum might have any historical records or information about an old Light Fae ship named the *Sebille* from the early fifteenth century."

"No," the dwarf replied, her voice flat. She still hadn't raised her head. She stacked the papers together. "I'm afraid I can't help you. We don't have anything."

Something about other woman's demeanor seemed off, but her instincts had gone into hyper drive, so for the moment she reserved judgment. "Can you recommend anywhere else in Bermuda where we might research the *Sebille*?"

"None of the other island museums have anything." The dwarf's tone had turned short to the point of rudeness. She rose to her feet and slapped the papers on the desk.

Pia exchanged a glance with Eva and shook her head. That wasn't just her imagination. Something definitely wasn't right. "You sound very sure of that."

"I am very sure," said the dwarf. "This is the only

museum of Elder history in Bermuda."

"But you've heard of the *Sebille*," Eva pressed. "You know what ship we're talking about."

"Of course I've heard of it," the dwarf replied irritably. "Every couple of years some fool comes through, itching to learn everything they can about the *Sebille*, and they want to scour the records here for any mention of the ship. I'm going to tell you the same thing I tell all the others." She finally looked at Pia, and her small, dark eyes were anxious. "Don't waste your time. Go enjoy your vacation, and play with that cute baby. Stop searching for the ship."

Pia's gaze narrowed. She said softly, "Talking about it seems to bother you for some reason. Are you all right? You're not afraid of someone, are you? Because if you are, we can help you."

The dwarf drew in a quick breath and lowered her voice. "Wait a minute, I know who you are. Look, there are some men who have been looking for that ship for a very long time—since before I came to Bermuda and took over the museum. I'm not sure how many men, and I don't know where they live. I don't want to know. All I know is they spend time at the dockyards a lot, and they frequent bars, and their leader…he's not a nice man."

Eva and Pia exchanged another glance. Pia asked, "The leader wouldn't happen to be a big Light Fae male, would he? Long hair pulled back in a ponytail?"

The dwarf rubbed her chin nervously with the back of one hand and nodded.

"And one of his men was in here earlier to talk to you." Pia didn't ask it as a question.

The dwarf nodded again. "Years ago, I used to have a few records that mentioned the *Sebille*. There was nothing substantial, mind you, just mainly some stuff that has been retold so much it's turned into legend. A massive storm and strange lights in the sky, that sort of thing."

"Strange lights." Eva's eyes narrowed. "What kind of strange lights?"

The dwarf snorted. "It was probably just lightning in the clouds. A few people claimed that they sighted the ship from the north shore, and then it disappeared."

Pia felt a thrill of excitement. "So it was sighted here."

The dwarf threw up her hands. "Apparently so, and people have been looking for it ever since. Like I said, every once in a while they show up here, just like you did. They want to dig for clues. But something always happens to them. Their boats disappear, or they have an accident. Somebody always ends up getting hurt. So I got rid of the records. I burned them. And I tell people I don't have anything, and to stop looking." She sniffed. "Sometimes they don't listen, but I still try."

"What about the man who was here earlier?" Pia asked. "He didn't threaten you, did he?"

The dwarf shook her head. "No, they don't bother with me. I wouldn't hunt for that damn wreck if my life depended on it. He wanted to know if anybody had been in today to ask about the *Sebille*. He must have been on the lookout for you."

Eva said gently, "If they come looking for us, they're not going to like what they find."

✧　✧　✧

DRAGOS FLEW AWAY from the islands in a bright flood of sunshine. After a short while, he left the shallow reefs behind and soared over deep water. He concentrated on flying thoroughly over a section before going on to the next, searching in a circular pattern around the islands. He made a complete pass all the way around, then moved outward in greater concentric circles.

Most people would have found it tedious work, but he didn't. He reveled in the solitude and freedom as he soaked up the sun's brilliant warmth. The air smelled briny and clean over the ocean. It felt good to stretch out his wings and work his body, and good to truly let go of crowded city life. He put away considerations of politics, stocks and profit margins, and let the dragon take over his thoughts.

The vast, tangled mass of land magic that made up the Bermuda Triangle lay to the west. He considered it without much curiosity. A few of the crossover passageways came in quite close to land, but passageways in the ocean were easy to avoid. All he had to do was fly high enough overhead.

He grew hungry, dove for fish and ate while he flew.

He covered more than a hundred miles in an hour. Within a few hours, he grew convinced that the *Sebille* had not foundered anywhere near the edge of the shallow reefs bordering the islands, and he headed farther out in a wider circle.

Dragos? Pia said.

Like every other Wyr, her telepathic range was quite limited, but Dragos's telepathic range was much larger than the average Wyr's, and he heard her quite clearly.

Yes? he replied. *Are you having a good morning?*

We're certainly having an interesting morning. How about you?

I'm having a great time, he told her. *It's beautiful out here.*

Her mental voice warmed. *I'm so glad.*

He banked and wheeled toward the east to start another circuit. *Did you find out anything at the museum?*

Yes, we actually found out quite a bit more than we expected. Her voice sounded a little odd.

He cocked his head. *Tell me.*

Apparently the Sebille *was sighted off the north shore in a big storm, and then it disappeared again. At least that's what the curator told us was in old records before she destroyed them.*

His interest quickened. If the *Sebille* was sighted off the north shore, he could try narrowing his search area down by doing some calculations of the currents. He left the area he had been searching, whirled in a big circle and began to follow the ocean's current north of the island. *Why did she destroy them?*

Because there's a group of men who have been searching for the wreck for a long time, and they don't take kindly to competition, Pia told him. *They've been scaring off anybody who goes looking for it. The curator said the treasure hunters' boats sink or disappear, and somebody always got hurt, so she finally destroyed the records. She said their leader is a big Light Fae male, and he's not a nice man.*

Dragos did not bother to snort. He was not a nice man either.

He said thoughtfully, *A big Light Fae male?*

Yes, and when we got to the museum, there was a man hanging around the building. He left as soon as we arrived. She paused. *He had been inside the museum before we got there, and he wanted to know if anybody had been in asking about the* Sebille.

Was it one of the men from the bar? His thoughts turned dark and murderous.

I don't know, but it might have been. Who else would have known that someone would be showing up at the museum this morning? You and I talked about it last night.

I remember, he said. *What are you doing now?*

We're going back to the house, she told him. *I want to feed the peanut and put him down for a nap.*

Okay, let me know when you get there. I'll be back soon.

Don't hurry back for our sake, okay? We're not going to let some pissant local thug ruin our vacation. Eva and Hugh are on alert. We're fine.

All right, he told her. *I'll still be back soon.*

In a matter of minutes he had followed the current past the last of the islands and out to deep sea. Then he continued straight over deeper water.

Almost five miles out from the island, he felt a faint tickle of magic from below. He wheeled around the area.

A moment later, Pia spoke again. *We're back at the house, and Eva and Hugh have thoroughly searched the whole property. Everything is peaceful. Nothing is out of place, and there aren't any strange scents.*

Okay, good, he replied. *I followed the current that wraps around the north shore, and I'm about five miles out from land. I found something. I'm going to dive.*

That's fantastic! Good luck!

He folded his wings and plunged headfirst into the waves. This far out, the water was quite cold. He found it pleasantly bracing. He burrowed down, past where the sunlight penetrated, into frigid darkness.

The pressure increased, and he knew he had dived deeper than most creatures could have survived without protection gear. Soon he had passed the limit of most manned submersibles.

Except for submarine canyons, most of Earth's ocean floors were no deeper than six thousand meters. Still, that was almost 3.75 miles. Aside from the strange marina life that was bred to survive on the ocean floor, very few creatures could survive reaching such depths. The mysterious, powerful kraken could, and so could Dragos, but only for brief periods of time.

To conserve his energy, he swam in complete darkness, following the spark of magic blind, until he sensed that he had gotten close. Then he threw a simple spell and brought light to the dense water.

The light spell illuminated the area roughly twenty-five feet around him in a strange bluish green. The pressure was so intense, he felt like he was digging his way through the water, not swimming. He pushed farther downward, until the light touched on the greenish ocean floor. His lungs had started to burn. He wouldn't be able to stay for much longer.

He kicked his way along the ocean floor, still searching mostly by his magic sense. A few crustaceans scuttled away from the light.

When the wreck came into view, it did so all at once. It sprawled along the ocean floor with the supporting planks of the hull exposed like the rib cage of a dead animal.

By now, Dragos's lungs were on fire, but he was unable to pull away. This close, he could tell there were multiple sparks of magic coming from inside the hull. He kicked along the length of the wreck, searching as quickly as he could for some kind of identification. Going by the size and shape of the ruins, it had been a caravel ship, which placed it in the right historical era. The wreck was as long as he was if he included his tail, roughly forty feet in length.

He drew closer to the port side. The wreck had deteriorated a lot over the centuries, but enough remained that he could see a significant, jagged break toward the rear of the ship. Quite a bit of the hull had sheared away long ago, leaving only the ribs curving up from the base of the ship's spine.

He plunged both front paws into the sediment along the floor, searching for pieces of the hull. As he found fragments of wood, he turned them over and discarded them until he unearthed one piece, roughly a yard and a half in length, that had letters inlaid in silver at one end.

ille.

Triumph surged, but he didn't have time to savor it. He needed air too badly and couldn't stay underwater any longer. Black spots danced in front of his eyes. Carrying the fragment of wood, he kicked to the surface to suck in huge draughts of air. As soon as he caught his breath, he launched out of the water and flew back toward land.

In order to have enough room to change, he had to land on the beach just outside the house. Still gripping the hull fragment, he strode up the terraced path.

Pia had been keeping an eye out for him, because he had barely stepped out of the tree line and onto the lawn when the door opened and she hurried out. Her eyes shone with excitement. "What is it? What did you find?"

He held up the piece of wood, letters facing outward, for her to see. "I think I found the *Sebille*."

Chapter Eight

"**A**LREADY? THAT'S AMAZING." She touched the blackened letters on the wood wonderingly.

He grinned. "I would have found it eventually, but I got lucky. I used what you gave me and followed the current off the north shore. The wreck is quite a ways out and it's deep. It's no wonder nobody has found it before now. There's only a few submersibles in the world that can dive down that far."

Pia glanced at him with an inward smile. He always had a vital, powerful presence, but now his dark bronze skin looked burnished, and his gold eyes shone with radiance. "Come inside and tell me all about it. Liam's gone down for a nap. Eva and Hugh barbequed steaks for lunch, and they set aside plenty for you."

His expression flared with interest. He propped the plank beside the back door and followed her inside. The interior was much cooler than outside. They had closed up the house and turned on the air condition. While he washed up, Pia piled the steaks on a plate for him and set it on the dining room table in the large, sunlit kitchen.

He thanked her as he sat at the table and began to eat. Pia eased into the seat across from him, and Eva and Hugh came to join them while Dragos told him about his flight and the search in between large bites of the juicy meat.

"By the time I found it, I was getting tired and needed air, so I wasn't able to stay down for very long." He sprinkled salt on the steak. "I didn't have a chance to examine the wreck too closely, but I did notice there was a jagged break toward the back third of the ship, between where the main mast would have been and the rear mast. It would have been a hell of a storm to cause that kind of damage. Poor bastards never had a chance."

"So there is at least one magic item with the wreck?" Pia asked.

"Yes." He polished off the last bite with a satisfied sigh. "In fact there are several. I want to go back down, maybe first thing tomorrow morning, and see what I can bring up."

Pia nodded. "I wish I could come with you."

Pushing away his plate, he crossed his arms on the table and smiled at her. "You could, at least in a boat. You would have to wait on the surface, but if we took a boat out, I could make a couple of dives to bring things back up."

She clapped her hands. "Let's rent one!"

He grinned. "You bet."

Eva spoke up. "I looked through the brochures the rental agency left. You can rent a boat from them. I'll give them a call."

"Great." Pia looked at Dragos. "So that's tomorrow morning. What do you want to do this afternoon?"

"You relax, enjoy the sun." Dragos pushed away from the table and stood. His face turned sharp as a blade. "I'm going to go on the hunt for a big Light Fae male who is not a nice man."

Pia stood too, quickly. That dangerous face was so sexy it made her knees weak. Sometimes she still wasn't quite sure of her reactions to Dragos. "I'm coming with you."

His inky-black eyebrows drew together in a frown. "I don't think that's a good idea."

"Well, I do." She put her hands on her hips. "You know what's going to happen if we find him. He's going to be an asshole, and, Dragos, you can't kill him just because he's an asshole. You're not Lord of these islands."

He regarded her with a dark expression. "Fine. Come on."

Pia looked at Eva. "We'll be back later."

The other woman's face was full of suppressed amusement. "Have fun."

Dragos went out the back door to get the plank of wood, which he set on the floor of the backseat of the Mercedes. They took off.

That afternoon Pia developed a healthy respect for how many bars, restaurants, grocery and marina supply stores, and fishing shops could be found in the Bermuda islands. Dragos was single-minded and didn't tire, and she was determined to keep up with him.

They scored a hit with their perseverance in Hamilton Harbor a couple of hours later. After Dragos parked, they walked along the rows of shops and bars at the edge of the marina.

Almost immediately, Dragos's nostrils flared. "He's here. Hold on a minute."

Dragos had literally been in the Light Fae male's face last night, so he had to have gotten a good fix on the other male's scent. Thank God. Pia was hot, tired and thirsty. She just didn't have a hunter's drive or instinct. If it had been up to her, she would have quit searching an hour ago.

She stood waiting while he strode back to the SUV. When he returned, he gripped the plank in one hand. Then he led the way unerringly to a bar located at the end of the lane, pushed open the door and strode in.

Bracing herself for whatever came next, Pia followed.

Inside, the décor was sturdy rather than elegant. Wide windows faced the water. They had been propped open in the heat of the day. Wooden tables dotted the floor, and tall stools lined the bar against the interior wall. Loud music played, the place was crowded, and it smelled of alcohol and fried food.

Pia spotted the Light Fae male right away, leaning against the bar. This time he appeared to be alone.

Despite the noisy, crowded atmosphere, Dragos's fiery presence drew attention. People fell silent, and the clink of cutlery against dishes ceased.

At the bar, the Light Fae male turned. His eyes narrowed as he caught sight of Dragos and Pia. He straightened, and his smile was more of a sneer.

"Get out," Dragos said. The dragon was in his voice.

Except for the Light Fae male, all the customers rushed for the door. Pia barely had time to move aside. Within seconds the place was empty except for, Dragos, Pia, the Light Fae male, and the bartender and wait staff who moved to one side of the room as they watched nervously.

The scene should have been ridiculous, but somehow it wasn't. Dragos tossed the plank onto the floor in front of the other man, and the Light Fae male's sneering smile vanished.

"I located the *Sebille*." Dragos strolled toward the other man. "And I'm going to bring up everything I can from it."

The Light Fae male's gaze flared as he stared at the plank at his feet. When he looked up again at Dragos, his gaze had turned flat and ugly. He said in a strongly accented voice, "That wreck, and everything on it, is mine. You made a big mistake, and not a healthy one for either you or your pretty companion."

Pia heaved a sigh. He did not just say that, did he? To Dragos, of all people.

Dragos blurred. He took hold of the Light Fae male in both hands, lifted him in the air and twisted at the waist to slam him into a table so hard the table collapsed, with him on it. Dragos followed him down, kneeling to hold the other man pinned by the throat.

"Aaaand, that's assault and battery," Pia muttered.

Did officials in another country have the legal authority to throw the head of an Elder demesne in jail? She didn't know the answer to that. Not that it necessarily mattered, since the question was purely hypothetical. If it came to that, the authorities couldn't trap him long enough to put him in jail, and anyway, Dragos would demolish any building with jail cells in it. The whole thing would become a legal snarl that would clog up the Elder tribunal for months and years. No wonder Dragos's lawyers were so rich. He was a litigator's wet dream.

She pinched the bridge of her nose to stave off a growing headache. She noticed one of the waitstaff was on the phone, no doubt calling the local police.

The Light Fae male struggled, but he could gain no purchase against the iron hand that gripped him. "Your mistakes are getting worse, my friend," he hissed. "There are many more of us than there are of you."

"You dare to threaten me?" Dragos hauled the Light Fae male close to his hard, angry face. "My wife says that I can't kill you for being an asshole. She has a much kinder heart than I do. If you or any of your men come anywhere near us, I will take you apart. Slowly."

The Light Fae male's face purpled. He clawed at Dragos's hand and spat out a long string of words in the strange language Pia had noticed last night. She didn't have to understand what he said to know he wasn't apologizing.

Pia tried smiling at the waitstaff. They stared at her, frozen. She said, "We'll pay for the damages, of course, and for everybody's meal."

Dragos threw the Light Fae male one-handed across the room. He slammed into the wall and slumped to the floor. Then Dragos stood. He was so quick, so inhumanly graceful for his massive size, that just the simple movement of rising to his feet made the skin at the back of Pia's neck prickle.

It would set a very bad precedent if he had any clue how he affected her when he behaved so badly, so she tried to play it cool. "You've had your fun. Are you done now?"

Eyes still glowing with fury, he stretched his neck and nodded. He bent to pick up the plank and said to the bartender, "Send the bill to Cuelebre Enterprises."

The bartender nodded.

The Light Fae male lifted his head. His expression underwent a drastic transformation. "*Draco*."

Finally. Now that the other male had realized who Dragos was, maybe he would grow some sanity and leave them the hell alone.

Dragos reached Pia, his face like a thundercloud. She held the door open for him. Neither one of them said a word until they had walked back to the SUV. He unlocked the doors with the key fob and threw the plank into the backseat again while Pia climbed in the front.

Sirens sounded in the distance. They grew closer rapidly. For a moment neither Pia nor Dragos moved.

She didn't even try to hold back on the sarcasm. "I think it went well, don't you?"

Dragos angled his head and just looked at her. Then

he started the engine and drove them back to the house.

When they stepped indoors, Pia tried to shake off the tension that had bunched the muscles between her shoulders. Liam had woken up from his nap and was playing on the floor. As he caught sight of them, he squealed in excitement and crawled toward them.

Dragos scooped him up and sat on one of the couches. Smiling at the baby's happiness, she joined them.

It took the authorities forty-five minutes to find them. When the knock came at the door, Pia took Liam and grinned at Dragos. "We're going to go play somewhere else for a while."

His mouth twitched. Enough time had gone by to allow for his temper to lighten. "Have fun."

Eva followed Pia and Liam outside, carrying wine-glasses and a blanket to spread out on for the baby. They walked down to the beach.

Pia settled on one corner of the blanket. Seagulls hovered over silver-capped waves. The early-evening sun on the water was simply spectacular. She took a deep, satisfying breath of fresh air. "You know, a year ago, I would have stayed in the living room to talk to the police with him, and I would have been all twisted up and anxious about it. Then I realized this stuff doesn't bother Dragos at all. And I mean, not in the slightest. So why should I get wound up if he doesn't?"

"You shouldn't." Eva kicked one foot over the other and stretched out.

Liam pointed at the seagulls, crowed and flapped his

arms. Pia and Eva laughed at his round eyes and excited expression.

Twenty minutes later Dragos strolled onto the beach. He told Eva, "Why don't you and Hugh take the evening off?"

"You sure?" Eva climbed to her feet. "We haven't really done anything since we got here."

Dragos looked at Pia, who nodded. "I'm sure," he replied. "Just stay close, and stay aware. Let us know if you notice anything that seems off."

"Will do." Eva grinned. "Have a good evening."

"Thanks, you too," Pia said. Dragos stretched out on the blanket beside her. She handed him her glass of wine while Liam crawled energetically over to climb on his legs. "What did the police have to say?"

"Not much." He handed the glass back to her, stripped off his T-shirt and stretched out with his arms behind his head. "The Light Fae's name is Rageon Merrous, and he's been on their radar for some time. He started showing up on the islands around forty years ago. He's been linked to the disappearance of a few people and implicated in accidents involving others, but they haven't actually caught him in a crime, nor have they been able to bring charges against him for anything specific. He was gone from the bar by the time they got there. They're going to send a police car to patrol this neighborhood while we're here."

The sight of his bare chest never failed to bring down the level of her concentration. His physique was simply tremendous. A sprinkle of black hair arrowed down the heavy, powerful muscles in his chest. She laid a hand on the ridged muscles of his warm abdomen and looked out to sea so that she could gain some coherency of mind again. He placed one hand over hers and laced their fingers together.

She asked, "Why does he think the *Sebille* is his?"

He moved under her hand in a shrug. "Who knows? Maybe he's a family member of one of the ship's crew. Maybe he feels he's entitled to it because he's been looking for the wreck for so long. Treasure hunters are an obsessive lot, and they can get pretty crazy, especially if they've sunk any kind of capital into a serious search."

"If he's a family member, does he have a point? I mean, would he have a claim on anything in the wreck?"

"There's a difference in maritime law regarding salvage versus treasure hunting. Salvage involves recovering property where owners have the right to compensation or return of their property. Treasure hunting is a separate matter, because usually there's no owner to make a claim on the property." He shrugged again. "That gets more tangled in Elder law, since so many of us are so long-lived. In this case, though, it's fairly simple. The one with any potentially legitimate claim is Tatiana as the sponsor of the original expedition. The bottom line is, Merrous doesn't have a leg to stand on."

She contemplated that for a few moments. "What about Tatiana?"

"If she's interested in whatever is on that wreck, she can file a petition with the Elder tribunal." He yawned.

"But it's just as likely she won't care enough to pay the legal costs."

She had to smile to herself. Of course he knew so much about treasure rights in maritime law. "So that's it."

"Pretty much." He closed his eyes. "Unless you let me kill him."

"Oh, no," she said strongly, twisting at the waist to scowl at him. "You cannot put that on me. You know as well as I do, you can't kill somebody just because they're an asshole. We've heard some hearsay and a lot of suspicion, but we don't know if Merrous has actually done anything wrong. If he becomes a real problem, then one way or another we'll take care of him. Until then, all of this is just male posturing and hot air."

His smile was lazy and relaxed. "Fair enough."

Liam had managed to climb on top of Dragos's legs. Now he crawled up his father's torso, his small face determined. As Liam kneed Dragos in the crotch, Dragos jackknifed onto his side, laughing, and they dropped the subject for the evening.

After a while Pia went up to the house to collect snacks and another bottle of wine for dinner, and they stayed out on the beach to watch the sunset. She nursed the baby, who fell asleep on her. She, in turn, curled against Dragos's chest, while he put his arms around her. When she tilted her head back to smile at him, he covered her mouth with his and kissed her with a slow, leisurely thoroughness that never failed to heat her blood.

Happy, she thought. *I'm too happy.*

She banished that traitorous thought firmly and eventually fell asleep.

She woke sometime later to movement. Dragos had wrapped her and the baby in the blanket and carried them up the path to the house. She yawned and mumbled, "Stuff on the beach."

"We'll get it in the morning," he said quietly.

He carried them through the shadowed, empty house and laid them gently on the bed. Then he gathered up Liam's small, sleeping form to carry him to his crib in the other bedroom. Pia yawned again so widely her jaw popped and pushed off the bed to go to the bathroom, wash up and brush her teeth. On the way back to bed, she peeled off her clothes and let them drop to the floor. Those could be picked up in the morning too.

A few minutes later, Dragos joined her. She rolled toward him as he slid under the covers. He was naked too, and she sighed as she came up against his long, muscled body. The comfort of nestling skin to skin with him was indescribable. She needed it as much as she needed air, or food. She rubbed her face against the warm skin of his chest while he ran his hands down the curves of her body and caressed her breasts. He let out a quiet hiss when she stroked his large, hard erection and the tight, full sac underneath.

She gave herself over to languid instinct and slid down the sheets while he rolled onto his back and stroked her hair. By now they knew how this dance would go, but instead of familiarity breeding boredom, it fueled the excitement.

She knew what would happen when she put her mouth on him. She knew what he tasted like, and she craved it. She craved him. It was an incomparably sweet ache that leavened every part of her day. She lived her life in a state of constant questioning.

Where will he be next? When will I see him again? In the living room? In the kitchen? Will we have time to shower together in the morning?

How can I bear to be apart from him for an entire day?

Sometimes they didn't manage it, and they came together in a heated rush at lunchtime. Then they created a fire that burned so beautifully.

That was how she felt then, as she opened her mouth and took him in. She sucked on the broad head of his penis, swirling her tongue around the small slit at the tip. He swore, a low, rapid stream of unintelligible words, while his body turned rigid.

It hurts, it hurts, she wanted to tell him. But she had lost the capacity for telepathy. A tear slipped down her cheek from the ache of it. She opened her throat and took him all in. He pumped into her mouth, hips flexing. She could not get close enough, could not take him in deeply enough.

When he grasped her head in both hands and pulled her away, she made a needy sound and tried to pull him back to her. He refused, hauled her bodily up the bed and came between her knees. Then she understood what he wanted, and she welcomed him greedily.

"I can't ever get enough of you," he whispered against her mouth as he positioned the tip of his cock at her opening.

"Me neither. Hurry." She gripped the back of his neck.

He pierced her, drew back and pierced her again, and that was the thing she needed, as they came together in the most intimate dance of all. She lifted her hips to meet his thrusts, flexing inside in the way she knew would bring him the most pleasure.

He gasped, shook his head and quickened the rhythm. Then he leaned on one arm and slid a hand between them. She was so ready, she climaxed as soon as he touched her. A high, thin whine came out of her, and she shook all over as the exquisite ripples conquered her body.

He thrust harder and quicker, once, twice, and then he arched his back as his own climax came. She held her breath so that she could feel everything as the hard, thick length of him pulsed inside of her.

There. There. Such sweet, beautiful fire.

Chapter Nine

I N THE MORNING, Liam enjoyed a long, lovely cuddle in bed with Mommy and Daddy. Then he grew excited because Mommy and Daddy started getting ready to go somewhere. Often that meant he got to go somewhere too, and he liked exploring this new, sunny place.

They said things to each other like, "Do you have our sat phone?" And: "They're bringing the boat to the pier on the beach."

He would have preferred to fly, but a boat sounded promising. In fact everything sounded promising, but then Mommy started saying things like, "You get to have fun with Aunt Eva and Uncle Hugh this morning."

He tried to ignore her, because sometimes she changed her mind, but soon it became clear that Mommy and Daddy were leaving, while he had to stay. When they kissed him and left, he turned exceedingly cranky. But it was hard to stay mad for long, because Aunt Eva and Uncle Hugh *were* fun.

He was determined to stay awake until Mommy and Daddy got home, but despite his best efforts his eyes grew heavy. Hugh carried him to the bedroom and tucked him in the crib. He watched with sleepy interest while Hugh checked the room. Hugh tugged at the handle of the closed window as he looked outside, then he pulled the curtains shut and left.

Liam yawned, fell asleep and woke some time later.

Fresh air sounded nice—fresh air and wind, and flying.

Daddy had said *NO*, but that had happened quite a while ago. Surely by now *NO* had turned into a *YES*.

In fact, he was all but certain of it.

He was a very helpful peanut. Mommy and Daddy were busy on a boat, so he would take himself out to practice flying.

He shapeshifted, crawled out of the crib and climbed the curtains to the closed window. He tugged at the handle.

Over his head, the latch clicked and the window slid open.

Pleased, he climbed onto the sill. Each day his balance got better. He looked out happily at the hot, sunny day. Aunt Eva walked by underneath. He watched her curiously, then she went around the corner of the house, and he forgot about her.

A flicker of movement caught his eye, and his head snapped around. A bright green lizard wandered down the road on the other side of the hedge.

Hm, hungry now. That lizard looked tasty.

He spread his wings and leaped into the air. Flapping as hard as he could, he half-flew, half-coasted to the other side of the hedge and landed in a tumble on the gravel shoulder beside the road. It startled the lizard into running alongside a row of parked cars.

Instinct kicked in. Liam rolled onto his feet and ran after the lizard. When he flapped his wings again, he rose into the air and flew several yards. Excited, he ran some more, jumped and flew several more yards. They ran down the road like that until, in a final lunge, he managed to grab the lizard's tail.

The lizard struggled as he dragged it toward him. To his immense surprise, it pulled away from its tail and ran away again. Confused, he looked down at the tail he still held in one forepaw. Then he ate it. Um, delicious.

Now he really wanted the rest of that lizard. Where had it gone? He walked, looking around and peering under cars, but the lizard was nowhere in sight.

A car door opened a few feet away, and a man stepped out to walk toward him. He was a human with a long, dark ponytail, and he stank like cigarette smoke.

"Well, well, well," said the man in a friendly voice. He shrugged out of a jean jacket and held it in front of him as he drew closer. "What have we got here? Why, you look just like a baby dragon."

Liam sat back on his haunches and smiled at him.

The man recoiled. "*Christos!*"

The man threw the jacket at Liam. Darkness descended as it settled over his head. He struggled to get free of the heavy material, but the man scooped him up in his arms and held on tight. Then they were bouncing—the man was running.

Liam growled. He didn't like this game.

"Shut up." The man no longer sounded friendly.

A car door opened. The world shifted and swayed, and the man held him on his lap. The car door shut again. They were in a car. It accelerated.

"What have you got wrapped in your jacket?" It was another man's voice.

"It looks like a small dragon," said his captor. "I think it's his kid."

✧ ✧ ✧

PIA AND DRAGOS decided to take the boat out for a couple of hours, so they didn't bother to pack any food, just plenty of drinking water. While Pia watched the changing landscape, Dragos piloted the boat skillfully between all the other traffic on the water. It didn't take them long to leave land behind altogether.

The boat was a much slower method of transportation than Dragos in flight, but he knew where he was going so he could take them directly to the spot.

When they reached the area, Dragos killed the motor, and Pia turned in a circle, marveling in the sight of water all around her without any sight of land. He told her, "The anchor won't do any good out here. You're going to drift, but don't worry about it. You won't go far."

"Okay." She grinned at him. "Go on, don't worry about me."

He nodded. "See you soon."

They had brought one of their emptied suitcases along. He tossed it into the water, leaped overboard and swam far enough away so that he could shapeshift without capsizing the boat. Then the dragon appeared and gave her a huge wink as it hooked the handle of the suitcase in one talon. With a great splash, he dove.

How long would it take him to find the wreck? She had no way to know, so she relaxed in one of the seats and watched the waves.

The endless vista of sparkling ocean was remarkably hypnotic, and the sight had lulled her half asleep when she heard a great splash. She jerked upright and swiveled around to see the dragon swimming toward her with the suitcase clutched in one paw.

As he drew near, he shimmered into a change and became the man. The boat rocked as he grabbed the short ladder toward the rear on the port side. He held on, gasping. She hovered nearby. "Can I help?"

He shook his head. "It's really heavy. Watch out."

She stepped back, and he climbed up the ladder with the suitcase dangling from one hand. He heaved it into the boat, and it landed with a spray of cold water and a solid thud. Then he knelt beside the case, unzipped it and flipped the lid back.

Gold winked at them. There were also blackened objects that Pia couldn't identify, possibly tarnished silver items. There were coins, and a small chest, and something that looked mechanical and felt magical.

"Wow. Just, wow." She pointed to it. "Is that a sextant?"

He nodded, still breathing hard. He fingered a coin as he said, "This stuff was half buried and in leather bags that deteriorated when I tried to pick them up. There's probably enough to fill two more suitcases down below. Tatiana wanted to find a new land badly, and she was willing to pay for it."

"What do you want to do?" Pia asked. "You can dump out what's in the suitcase, go back down and collect the rest of it now, if you want."

He shook his head. "It's not going anywhere. We can go back, and I'll buy some containers to haul it all in."

"Well, if you're sure—" she began. The sat phone rang. She reached for it and clicked it on. "Hello?"

"It's Eva." Eva didn't sound like herself, her voice harsh and ragged. "Liam's gone."

"What?" The words were perfectly audible, but they came out of nowhere, and they made no sense. Pia shook her head. "I'm sorry, what did you say?"

"Liam is missing," Eva said, enunciating carefully. "He's *missing*, Pia. We put him down for a nap, and now he's gone. The house was locked tight. Hugh stayed inside, and I walked the yard outside, but the window in his bedroom is wide open and he is fucking *gone*—"

"Oh my God." Pia's world bottomed out. The sat phone fell from her nerveless fingers.

Dragos didn't need to ask what had been said; he had already heard it. His bronze skin turned ashen, his eyes stark.

Eva was still talking. The words sounded far away and small coming from the phone. As Pia reached for the phone, Dragos crouched and sprang into the air, leaping so hard the boat rocked wildly and knocked her back against the side. He shapeshifted in midair and snatched her up in one claw. He tore through the sky, his huge body straining as they arrowed back to the islands.

Pia went numb. She couldn't feel her feet, or her lips. "The phone!"

Dragos said tensely, "I'm talking to her. They found Liam's scent outside and followed it. It disappeared down the road. The man from the bar—not Merrous, the other one—his scent was at the spot where Liam's stopped."

"Oh God, oh God." This reality was outrageous, nightmarish beyond belief. She screamed, "Are you telling me those bastards have my baby?"

The dragon growled and flew harder.

A hollow, roaring silence filled her mind. Time stopped and started in fitful spurts.

They reached the island and slammed to earth. Dragos shapeshifted again, but only partially. He was gigantic, monstrous, his face and muscles contorted, his hands long with lethally sharp talons.

Occasionally Wyr went into a partial shapeshift in times of extremity. At other times, some could even shapeshift small changes like bringing out their talons, but Pia had only seen Dragos caught in the monstrous half-shift once, when they had mated last year. In spite of her shock over Liam and how much she loved him, she almost recoiled from the sight.

But he was her mate, and she had never needed a

monster more than she did right now. He snatched her hand, and they raced up the path.

✧   ✧   ✧

AS THEY NEARED the house, the dragon let go of Pia's hand and lunged ahead, his long legs eating up the distance. He slammed through the door so hard it tore off its hinges, and he bounded up the stairs to his son's bedroom. It looked serene, with nothing displaced. He scented everything carefully. Nobody had been in Liam's room except for him, Pia, Eva and Hugh.

The window was wide open, and Liam's scent was on the sill. He looked outside. Pia had run around the house and was talking to Eva and Hugh. The body-guards' bodies were tense, their eyes heartsick.

He leaped down the stairs and tore out of the house to join the others. Eva pointed to a spot in the road. "Liam's scent starts here."

He reached the spot and looked back at the house. He could see Liam's open window. He raced to follow Liam's scent to the place where it stopped, and he caught the human's scent and followed that to where it stopped.

After that there was nowhere else to go. Feeling a rare sense of impotence and terror, he stood with his taloned fists clenched. They had gotten into a car. By now they could be on a boat.

And while Liam could understand a great deal, his verbal skills had not caught up with his comprehension.

Dragos might be able to reach him telepathically, but he couldn't reply.

Dragos could telepathize with someone else, though.

Merrous, said the dragon in a calm, quiet voice.

After a moment, Merrous gave a telepathic chuckle. *Well, this is uncomfortable and unexpected, but surprisingly useful. I was going to send you a burner phone, but this works even better. I have something of yours.*

He said, *Prove it.*

What do you want, a picture or a body part? Merrous laughed.

He had quite a sense of humor for a dead man. The dragon flexed his talons, and nearby, Eva and Hugh blanched. His voice grew gentler. *Do you want the* Sebille? *Because you will never have it without me.*

Merrous's laughter vanished. He said venomously, *Yes, I want the* Sebille, *and I want everything that went down with it. I presume you want this rug rat back. We'll do an exchange.*

When? he asked. *Where?*

I'll let you know when I work something out. Now, stop talking to me, or someone is liable to get hurt.

Rage filled his body like burning acid. Dragos looked at Pia and the other two. They had been watching his face closely. "I just talked to Merrous. He says he wants an exchange, and he'll get back to me once he decides when and where." He paused as a sliver of rational thought sliced through the lava running through his mind. "He sounds too confident."

Pia grabbed his arm, her fingers biting into his skin. "What do you mean?"

He shook his head as he thought it through. Instinct settled into certainty. "He knows we're Wyr, so he has to have some idea of our tracking skills. Right now he thinks he can't be tracked, which means he's on a boat."

Pia's voice shook. "He can't have gone too far, but there are a lot of boats out there."

"There's only one boat that will have their scents, so we cloak ourselves and go hunting." He looked at Hugh. "I need you to fly out and check every vessel headed away from shore. If he's thought this through at all, he will be expecting us to do that. I think he's acting like someone fishing or on vacation. He'll either be moored somewhere or he's moving very slowly. He'll be hiding in plain sight. We've got to move fast."

"Right." Hugh shapeshifted and launched.

"I need a gun," Pia said. Eva shoved hers into Pia's hands then drew a backup gun from an ankle holster.

"Let's go." Dragos shapeshifted, and the two women climbed on his back. Then he launched into the air too.

Chapter Ten

L IAM WAS STARTING to feel sorry for himself.

It had been a strange and interesting day, and he had learned a lot. He had flown! Well, a little bit, anyway. And lizard's tails were delicious. A man had given him his jacket, and had taken him on a car ride. Now he was on a boat. The man took his jacket back only to shove him quickly into a cage and slam and lock the door.

Liam sat and waited for something else to happen. Maybe Mommy and Daddy were on this boat, and they would come get him.

Nothing happened. Mommy and Daddy didn't come, and the cage smelled like dog. The boat's engine ran for a while then stopped, and they rocked with the waves.

Nobody came to play with him or bring him food. He had woken up hungry, and he only grew hungrier. And more thirsty.

After a while he looked around the cage. No blanket. No food. No bunny.

He heaved a big sigh and pushed at the door of the cage. When the lock sprang open, he walked out.

He explored the room. It was filled with interesting

things like rope, metal tanks, boxes and tarps. Still nothing to eat or drink. He left the room and padded down a short hall. Voices sounded from another room. One of them was the man with the jacket. Liam didn't know the other one.

Smoke wafted out of the room. His nose wrinkled. He didn't want to visit with them anymore. He wanted Mommy.

There were stairs at the end of the hall. He climbed up, found himself on a deck and looked around. There were two more strange men in a cabin. He didn't want to visit with them either, and the shore looked awfully small. He eyed it doubtfully. It was much too far for him to fly. He started to realize just how far away Mommy might be.

His eyes filled. That was the saddest thing he had ever thought in his whole life.

Then another thought occurred to him. He had flown the farthest when he had been the highest—from the window of his room. Maybe if he climbed up to the top of the boat he could fly to shore.

He hopped and flapped and climbed. The boat had a motor, but it also had sails. He swarmed up the sail to the very top of the mast, and there he perched. He looked from the boat to land, and back to the boat.

Now he was very high in the air, but the shore still seemed awfully far away—too far away for him to fly. The boat rocked, and he flapped his wings to keep his balance on his small perch. He did not want to climb down and visit the men again. He couldn't fly away.

He wasn't sure because he'd only heard the word once before, but he thought he might be in a quandary.

✧   ✧   ✧

WHILE HUGH FLEW farther out to sea, Dragos swung to the nearest pier and dove low over each boat. Pia could feel the dragon's body straining to move as fast as he could while still covering every boat thoroughly before he moved on to the next pier or the next boat that moved at a leisurely pace over the water. They caught wafts of scents from each one—people, alcohol, cooking food, and occasionally cigarette smoke, which was particularly odorous. Dragos always banked and swung around to double-check each boat that smelled like smoke.

She clenched her fists. This search was an excruciating gamble, but the alternative was to do nothing and wait, and that was unthinkable.

Eva sat behind her. "Pia, I don't know what to say," she said, her voice low and shaken. "I am so desperately sorry this happened. We did everything we usually do. Hugh swore he checked the room when he put Liam down for a nap, even though nobody had been in there since you got him up this morning. I swear to you, the house was locked up tight."

Locked.

Pia's head came up. "Oh, shit."

"What?" Dragos asked sharply.

"I was just wondering yesterday what talents or

attributes he might have gotten from me." She pressed her fists against her temples. "No lock can hold him. He did it himself. He climbed out the window, and he must have flown to the road."

Dragos turned so sharply, both women rocked in their seats. In a burst of power, he drove away from the boats they had been circling and hammered through the air. "I see him."

Pia's heart leaped. Maybe there was a way out of this nightmare after all. "You *see* him—where?"

"He's perched at the top of a mast, half a mile ahead." A strange mélange of emotions threaded Dragos's voice.

She shaded her eyes, squinting against the bright light. His predator's eyes were much sharper than hers. She couldn't see him.

"A quarter mile away now," said Dragos. "Dead ahead."

Then she caught sight of him. He was a small, white figure and from this distance looked very much like a large seagull, flapping his wings every once in a while as the boat rocked. She didn't know whether to laugh or cry. "Oh, thank you, God."

Thank you, thank you.

"Quiet now," Dragos ordered. "We don't have him yet."

He slowed as he approached the boat, spread his wings and coasted. As they passed overhead like a mammoth ghost, he reached out with one forepaw and scooped Liam up with unerring accuracy. Pia caught a whiff of cigarette smoke as they passed.

Dragos put on a burst of speed. "Got him!"

The unbearable tension broke. She buried her face in her hands and sobbed.

"Hold on," Dragos murmured gently. She wasn't sure if he was talking to her, or to Liam. "We're almost there."

He flew straight to shore and landed on a nearby promontory. Pia fell off his back before he came to a full stop, and she landed jarringly on her hands and knees. She ignored the pain and shoved to her feet, turning to face Dragos as he opened up his paw.

Liam exploded out in a flurry of white wings. He arrowed straight toward her and slammed into her chest. She sprawled on the ground with the breath knocked out of her. She didn't care. She didn't need to breathe. She clenched him to her.

Hard, strong arms lifted her up, and Dragos held them both tight against his chest, his head bent over them. Liam lifted his snout and licked his father's face with frantic enthusiasm.

The moment was too painful to be a happy one, too full of the terror of the last few hours, and she embraced it with her whole heart. She stroked Liam's head, soothing him, and he voluntarily shapeshifted back into his human form and clutched her shirt with both hands.

After a few moments, Dragos lifted his head. His haggard face was damp. "I have a promise to keep."

"Go," she said. "Do it."

He turned a murderous expression toward the boat,

stood and walked away. Eva joined her as he shapeshifted into the dragon again and took off. The women watched the sun gleam off his powerful form.

Eva gripped her shoulder. "He isn't cloaking himself. He wants them to see him coming."

They were too far away to hear any shouts or cries, but the sound of gunshots cracked across the water. Even though she knew that bullets couldn't penetrate the dragon's thick, tough hide, Pia twitched at every one.

Dragos reached the boat, slammed into the mast, took hold of it in both forepaws and snapped it in two. Small, faraway figures leaped into the water as he tore the boat to shreds with a savagery that took Pia's breath. As the pieces sank under foaming waves, he rose to hover in the air and turn his attention to the men who swam away.

"Nobody threatens my family and lives." The dragon's deep voice rolled over the waves like thunder. "Nobody."

He plummeted down.

Pia turned her attention to Liam's wide-eyed, round little face. "Don't look, my love," she said gently. She put a hand over his eyes and turned away from the sight.

✧   ✧   ✧

LIAM WAS CLINGY when they got back to the house. Pia didn't blame him. She felt clingy too. He whined and indicated he was hungry. Dragos pulled a roast chicken from the fridge and set it on the kitchen floor so he could eat. She and Dragos sat on the floor beside him, while Eva and Hugh stood in the doorway and watched.

He gorged until his belly was visibly distended. Then he climbed into Pia's lap. She pored over every inch of his slender, white body to make sure he hadn't been injured in any way, and she pressed careful fingers against his rib cage and legs. He didn't evidence any sign of pain or discomfort. Instead he stretched under her touch, sighing with pleasure, and fell deeply, instantly asleep.

"The young are incredibly resilient," Dragos murmured. He put a hand lightly on top of Liam's head.

"For which I'm very grateful," Pia said. "I wonder if he's too young to remember what happened."

His gold gaze flashed up to hers. "I hope he remembers everything. I hope it scared him. He's got dangerous abilities, and he going to grow up in a world full of enemies. He has to learn discipline early and to not go off by himself."

"That sounds so hard," she whispered.

"It *is* hard, but I have faith in him," Dragos said. "He may be small, but he's already proven that he has a big soul. He can handle it. And in the meantime, we'll put bars on his bedroom windows."

"I want them installed before we get home." She rubbed dry, tired eyes. The thought of him possibly getting loose outside the penthouse, so high off the ground, made her feel physically ill.

"They will be. I'll make the call in a few minutes."

"My lord." Hugh spoke hesitantly.

Both Pia and Dragos turned to the other man who knelt in front of him. Hugh's plain, bony face bore an anguished expression. As he opened his mouth to speak, Dragos told him in a weary voice, "Just don't. It wasn't your fault. It wasn't Eva's fault."

"If anything, it was our fault," Pia said. "Liam's evolving so fast, we haven't seen in time all the implications of what that might mean. We have to start thinking faster and planning better."

Hugh didn't appear convinced, but at least he fell silent.

"Open up a bottle of wine," Dragos told him. "We've all earned a drink."

The other man's expression lightened somewhat, and he rose to his feet.

Dragos turned to Pia. He asked telepathically, *How are you doing?*

I'm tired. She looked down at Liam and stroked his back. *And so grateful. And you?*

The same. He paused. *Do you want to go home?*

Her head came up. *Hell, no. We are, by God, going to have our vacation. We had a really bad, bad day, but it's over with now. They were dumb jerks, and I will not let them be that important. Unless, of course, you want to go home.*

He smiled. *Hell, no.*

She suddenly remembered and said out loud, "There's a motorboat floating around with a fortune in treasure on it."

"And more sitting on the ocean floor," Dragos added.

Hugh handed them each a glass of wine. Pia clinked her glass against Dragos. "You've got your work cut out for you tomorrow."

Epilogue

L IAM SLEPT FOR a very long time. When he woke up, he was cuddled in bed with Mommy under warm, soft covers. As he lifted his head, she said, "Good morning, my love. Did you sleep well?"

He nodded and looked at the empty space in the bed.

"Daddy has gone to find the boat we lost, and to collect some treasure. You and I are going to spend the day on the beach. Does that sound good to you?"

He nodded again.

She dressed in shorts and a tank top and took him to the kitchen. He shapeshifted into his dragon form and she fed him a delicious breakfast of tender, sautéed pork tenderloin, which he gobbled up. He watched with interest as she ate her breakfast of cantaloupe and blueberries, until she noticed his attention and offered him bites of fruit. He gobbled that up too.

She looked delighted. "You're not a carnivore. You're omnivorous."

After breakfast they went to the beach. The sun felt deliciously warm. Liam stayed in his dragon form, ignored his other toys, wrapped his forelegs around bunny and fell asleep. He napped and woke, and napped some more, while Mommy read and occasionally frowned at him. Once she asked, "Are you okay, Peanut?"

He nodded and yawned. He was just tired.

Later in the day, Liam rolled to his feet as a motorboat chugged up to the nearby pier. Daddy stood at the wheel, looking satisfied. Mommy scooped Liam up and walked down the pier. Daddy lifted them both into boat, and Liam stared with interest at the soggy suitcase and two metallic containers.

Daddy kissed Mommy. When it was Liam's turn, he lifted his head for his kiss.

"Did you get it all?" Mommy asked.

Daddy nodded. He threw open the suitcase and the containers.

A bolt of pure love hit Liam.

"Wow!" Mommy said. "We've sure got a lot of treasure."

"Wait a minute." Daddy sounded amused. "What do you mean 'we'? I thought this was my treasure."

"Technically, I don't think that's possible anymore." Mommy sounded smug. "We're mated, married, and as I just realized the other day, we have no prenup."

"You just realized that the other day, did you?" Daddy laughed.

Liam couldn't stand it any longer. He wriggled to get out of Mommy's arms. As she bent to let him go, he scrambled over to the suitcase as fast as he could and dove into the gold coins. Picking up one coin after the other, he stared at them in complete fascination. Feeling giddy, he rolled around on them.

These were the best toys ever.

Now both Mommy and Daddy were laughing as they watched him.

Daddy said, "I'm not sure either you or I own that treasure anymore."

Liam clutched as many coins as he could in both paws and hugged them to his chest as he gave his parents his best, sunniest smile.

Pia Saves the Day

Thea Harrison

To all my wonderful, supportive author friends,
especially Courtney, Vivian, Bree and Libby,
all of whom have been so generous with sharing
their knowledge, opinions and experience.
And to my assistant Janine, who has embraced this crazy
lifestyle with such enthusiasm.

Chapter One

PIA FLUFFED HER new haircut as Eva turned their SUV onto the long drive that led up to the house. When Pia realized she was still distancing herself from claiming the sprawling mansion as her own, she made a deliberate choice to change the wording in her head.

Their house—*her* house—was located in upstate New York, nestled in two hundred acres of land that contained virgin forest and a lake with water so clean and clear, it sparkled like a blue jewel in the sun.

While the estate was beautiful, she found it surprisingly hard to stake an emotional claim to it, but hopefully that would change with all of the renovations, when the house truly became her home.

"Stop fussing," Eva said. "Or you're gonna mess it up."

"I can't help it," she muttered, even as she forced herself to drop her hands into her lap. "I've never had my hair cut this short before, and it feels weird."

The summer had been a whirlwind of activity, and it was still only July. After they vacationed in Bermuda—a trip that had been full of wonderful moments and unexpected stresses—they went straight into the annual political season that surrounded the summer solstice.

Amidst parties, meetings and other inter-demesne functions that were attended by representatives of all the Elder Races, Dragos and his sentinels had worked double time to make sure all the sentinels got their promised time off.

At the same time, he and Pia set in motion plans to move upstate, build personal quarters for staff and an office complex, and completely redo the large mansion on the estate.

Meanwhile, Peanut kept growing, growing, growing. Because both his parents held such rare forms of Power, Dragos said he was springing into existence in a way that was reminiscent of the first of the Elder Races, at Earth's dawning.

Peanut's journey was not quite the same—at the birth of the world, magic had been wild and prolific, and the first-generation Elders had not gone through any childhood phase. Still, it had become more than apparent their son would not live any kind of ordinary life. While he was only four months old, he had already reached the size of a very precocious toddler, and it took everything Pia had to try to keep up with him.

From one day to the next, her patience snapped with the upkeep involved in taking care of her waist-length hair. It had to go.

Now the bottom of her new hairstyle touched her shoulders, and it was layered throughout. She had lost so much hair, she felt almost light-headed, and the ends tickled her collarbones as she turned her head from side to side.

She was very pleased with how the feminine style suited her triangular face, and it felt so much cooler, she was already in love with it.

However, she hadn't told Dragos she was getting her hair cut, and now she was starting to feel nervous. There was no way she would ever ask him for *permission* to cut her own hair—the very thought was outrageous—but she also knew he loved her long hair, and … well, she wanted him to like how she looked.

"It's perfect," Eva told her.

She smiled. "Thanks."

As they followed the drive that curved around a copse of trees, the house came into view, surrounded by scaffolding, more than twenty vehicles, an array of heavy construction tractors, and piles of building supplies. The nearby town's single motel remained perpetually booked, and a hundred yards away from the main house, several trailers housed even more workers, along with providing temporary quarters for any of the sentinels who chose to visit the estate, which happened often.

The sentinels claimed any number of excuses for coming—the need to talk over business with Dragos in person, the desire to help out—but Pia suspected they were all just excited at the change in lifestyle, and they enjoyed the opportunity to get out of the city.

Once construction was completed, the sentinels would go on rotation, so that at any given time, two would be headquartered upstate. Dragos believed the new system would help prevent burnout and give the sentinels a chance to stretch their wings—or, in Quentin's case, legs.

For now, the scene looked bustling and chaotic, and it wouldn't calm down for at least another two months. Close by, sounds of construction echoed off the surface of the lake. In a series of small explosions, the construction crew was blasting through a stubborn shelf of bedrock to level the site where the office complex would be built. Periodically the low boom from the blasts rolled over the valley like cannon fire.

After Eva parked, they climbed out of the air-conditioned vehicle into the sultry heat of the day.

Another thunderous boom sounded in the distance. Pia felt it vibrate in her chest, and she sighed. "I can't wait for them to be done with that."

"Yeah, it got old fast, didn't it?" Eva swept the scene with her gaze. A haze of dust lay over the tree line in the direction of the noise. "At least they should be finished with the blasting by the end of the week."

As they reached the open front doorway, they met several workmen coming out. Pia stepped aside to let them pass, returning cheerful greetings and smiling when one of them complimented her new look.

When the path was clear, Eva left her to head to the kitchen for some lunch, and Pia went in search of Dragos and Liam. Stepping around ladders, cans of paint and drop cloths, she made her way through the house to the back.

While the rest of the estate was in upheaval, and construction dust seemed to coat everything, Pia and

Dragos had finished a few areas before they had ever made the trip upstate. Their bedroom suite, Peanut's rooms, the rooms for essential household staff, like Eva and Hugh, along with the back patio areas and the kitchen had been completely redone. With the basics of survival sorted out, Pia felt like they could withstand anything.

At the back of the house, French doors opened to the large patio. Comfortable outside furniture with deep cushions dotted the open expanse. To one side, wide shallow steps led to an area created for open-air dining, with a spacious brick grill, an outdoor oven and a dining table and chairs.

To the other side, steps led to a sparkling, inground heated pool and pool house, surrounded by a decorative, black iron safety fence. Pia had to smile as she looked around with pleasure and satisfaction. Blooming bushes and flowerbeds surrounded the patio areas, and beyond that, a massive green lawn rolled gently downhill to the bordering forest.

Next week, work crews would build a security fence around that lawn, along with a large wooden play set, complete with a sandpit. Of course, neither the security fence nor the pool safety fence could contain Liam if he chose to change into his Wyr form and fly over them, but after what had happened in Bermuda, he had only been shapeshifting when he needed to feed his dragon form or when he was taken on a supervised flight.

Still, none of them could predict how long Liam's obedient streak would last. After his adventures in

Bermuda, Pia and Dragos had hired two extra avian nannies to fill in for when Pia was needed elsewhere. Along with Hugh, his new caretakers, Sasha and Ryssa, watched him like the hawks they were.

Pia looked wryly at her precocious, magical son, currently curled on Dragos's chest.

In the sitting area on the patio, Dragos sprawled on a lounge chair large enough to support his powerful, six-foot-eight frame. He wore jeans, boots and a white T-shirt. As he wasn't the kind of man to stand back while watching others work, his current outfit had already seen some wear and tear. Since they had come upstate, he had already demolished several pairs of jeans and shirts. Stacks of papers, manila folders and a laptop lay on a table pulled close to the right side of his chair, and toys lay scattered on the floor.

Peanut was fast asleep, and his thumb had fallen halfway out of his small, slack mouth. Wisps of his white blond hair fluttered in the gentle summer breeze.

His father read aloud, quietly, his voice steady and gentle, while he pressed a hand to Liam's delicate back, supporting his position. The bracelet Dragos had made from her braided hair last year glinted gold on the dark bronze skin of his thick, strong wrist.

Whenever she saw Dragos with Liam, a tangled well of emotion overcame Pia—a great, fierce storm of love. This time the emotional storm was mingled with a thread of laughter, as she realized Dragos was reading the quarterly profit percentages from a stockholders' report.

A snort escaped her nose. It was a small sound, amidst all the bustle and noise of the day, but Dragos's head lifted, and he turned to look at her.

His expression changed drastically and he surged to his feet, all in one smooth flowing motion that never disturbed the sleeping toddler he cradled in one arm.

He demanded telepathically, *Where's the rest of it?*

She knew immediately what he meant. One fact of their life would never change—her Wyr form was unique enough, they must always be careful to destroy any trace of her blood, and both Power and dangerous information could be gleaned from hair and nail clippings.

Giving him a reassuring smile, she told him, *Eva swept the floor and made sure she got all the clippings. I've got it right here.*

Reaching into her purse, she pulled out a paper bag that held the hair she had lost with the new hairstyle.

Dragos's tension eased. *Okay.*

Then he tilted his head, lids lowering over gold eyes as he regarded her, and his expression underwent a subtle, sensual change. Strolling over to her, he slid his free hand underneath the hair at the nape of her neck. Gently, gently, he took a fistful and tilted her head back.

Hot and fierce arousal pooled in her lower body, sweeping inescapably over her like slow-moving lava. As she stared up at him, her lips parted, and her breathing changed and grew ragged. He did this to her every time, so effortlessly, like striking a match. He could claim her with a glance, a touch, a simple shift of his cruel-looking, sexy lips, and when he did, she went up in flames. Every time, everywhere.

Not too short. His telepathic voice was a mere growl of a whisper that swept over her nerve endings in an intimate caress. While everything they did together was sexy, there was absolutely nothing sexier than having him in her head. *I can still grab a good handful. I like it.*

I hoped you would, she said, her own telepathic voice unsteady.

Dragos bent his head and kissed her, softly because their sleeping son nestled between them. His firm, warm lips parted hers, and he dipped his tongue into her mouth in an erotic promise for later. Awash in the lava that burned through her veins, she steadied herself by gripping his bicep. With obvious reluctance, he pulled away.

In the fourteen months they had been together, the desire had never changed. Elemental, as necessary as breathing, it dictated the rhythm of their lives. They orbited around each other, always looking, always reaching for the other, but it never ceased to amaze her that *he* looked at her this way.

His brutally handsome face could be so hard, so ruthless, but his need for her always won through. She never doubted what he felt for her. She could see it in everything he did.

You want me, she breathed.

She'd meant to say it in a cocky and flirtatious way, with a wink and a saucy Marilyn Monroe wiggle of the hips. But she forgot to wink, the hip wiggle turned into a slow, needy roll against his, and the words came out breathless and awed.

He rubbed the calloused ball of his thumb across her soft, moistened lips. A dark flush stained his high cheekbones, and his gold eyes glittered. *I'll die before I stop wanting you.*

Me too. She closed her eyes at his touch.

They were both immortal Wyr. Maybe, just maybe, that would be long enough to express the depth of what she felt for him.

He kissed her forehead. *Here, take Liam.*

Coming back to herself, she held open her arms, and he gently transferred the sleeping boy over to her. Liam half roused, gave her a sleepy, confused look and smiled. "Mama," he remarked happily. "Mamamama-mama."

So far, it was his favorite and only spoken word. Patting her with a small hand, he laid his head on her shoulder and fell back asleep with the abrupt abandonment of extreme youth.

Dragos took the paper bag that held her hair and strode over to the dining area. When he reached the brick grill, he set the bag down on it and his gold eyes flared with incandescence. Cradling Liam as she watched, she felt the small, hot surge of his Power from where she stood. The paper bag, along with its contents, burst into flames.

Dragos didn't move until the flames had burned out. Afterward, he blew on the white flakes of ash until they had dispersed entirely. Only then did he walk back to her.

"How was your trip into town?" he asked.

Located a short drive away from the estate, the town boasted a main street and three stoplights. At the moment, the largest nearby store was a Walmart, which lay fifteen minutes in the other direction. Local inhabitants regarded the influx of income that the Cuelebres brought the local economy with varying degrees of disconcertment and delight.

She grimaced. "Apparently some of the city would like to move upstate with us. Several people made a point of telling me that new shops and businesses were going to open up soon, including restaurants, clothing stores, a gourmet food store, a delicatessen and a more upscale hotel."

He frowned. "Some of that will be good, but we don't want it to get out of hand, or we could lose the reasons why we wanted to move in the first place. I'll talk to the town trustees about ways to limit the expansion."

"I think that's a good idea." She glanced down at the top of Liam's head and said softly, "I'm going to tuck him into his crib."

Dragos nodded, his expression softening as he looked down at Liam too. "Now that you're back, I'll head out to the site. I want to see how much headway they've made in the blasting today."

"Okay." She smiled at him. "See you later."

He answered her smile with a slow, wicked one of his own. "But not too much later. I fancy an early bedtime tonight."

She watched him walk away, thinking happy, comfortable thoughts. Dinner then bed, and who knew when they would finally fall asleep? They could take their time tonight. They had all the time in the world.

Less than half an hour later, she would give anything to call him back to her again. Anything to keep him from walking away.

Oh gods, anything.

✧　✧　✧

SHE TOOK LIAM upstairs, to his bedroom in the right wing of the house.

The right wing held their master suite, which included a wide balcony, a massive bedroom, a sitting room decorated with simple, elegant cream-colored furniture, a giant plasma television and a glass-fronted fireplace with a beautiful, streamlined slate mantle set against floor-to-ceiling windows that faced the Adirondack Mountains. They also had walk-in closets and a bathroom that rivaled the one in their New York penthouse for size and luxury.

Liam's nursery lay adjacent to their suite and included his bedroom, a bath, and a playroom with a small kitchenette set in one corner so that snacks could be made quickly and easily for the growing boy, and everything was decorated in bright, happy colors. Other bedrooms in the wing were available for Liam's caretakers whenever they were on duty watching him.

The left wing held the guest rooms, while downstairs there was a large library with an office nook for Pia, a massive, state-of-the-art office for Dragos, a formal receiving room, the more private, informal sunroom that led to the back patio area, the kitchen and breakfast dining area, and a dining room that seemed, at least to her, to be half the size of a football field.

The lower level held a giant recreation room with TVs, a pool table, and a wet bar that any New York restaurant would be proud to own. Also included below were an extensive wine cellar and a long-term larder, and security specialists had installed a panic room known only to Dragos, Pia, the sentinels, and Pia's bodyguards.

Sometimes Pia felt like she needed a GPS just to get around the place. Still, she reminded herself, the house was in no way as huge or complex as Cuelebre Tower in New York, and despite the construction, in some ways it already felt more intimate. She could see glimpses of the beautiful home it was becoming, filled with her favorite colors and hand-picked pieces of furniture, and she loved the personal spaces they had created for themselves and for Liam.

When she entered Liam's bedroom, he didn't even stir as she kissed his forehead lightly and eased him into his crib. As always when he slept, he had turned into a little furnace, and she was grateful to get some fresh air against her skin after she put him down.

She turned on his baby monitor and went into their suite to shower and change into a knee-length, lime green and yellow summer dress, along with flat sandals. Her new haircut and pretty outfit made her happy, and she hummed underneath her breath as she stroked on some eye shadow and lip gloss.

A knock sounded on the suite door. When she called out an invitation, Eva opened the door and sauntered in. The other woman's dark brown skin and bold features were accentuated by a saucy red, bustier-style top and jeans, and while she was armed—she always went armed—she looked as relaxed as Pia had ever seen her.

"Just wanted to know what was up for the rest of the day," Eva said. "You want to go out again?"

She shook her head. "Nope, we're going to stay in toni—"

As she spoke, another low boom like thunder rolled through the air.

A lightning bolt of pain struck her in the head. Her vision whited out. Dimly, she felt the container of lip gloss slide from lax fingers as she staggered and fell in an ungainly sprawl. More pain flared as she struck her knee against the corner of a nearby dresser.

Almost immediately, her vision cleared and the pain in her head eased, leaving behind a sense of dread so strong, it came in a wave of nausea.

Swearing, Eva dropped to her knees beside Pia and gathered her up in strong arms. "What the righteous fuck—Pia, talk to me. What's the matter?"

After the wave of dread came panic.

Pia had experienced that kind of panic before. It

was the kind you felt when you were staring at the end of your life.

And she knew. She knew.

Shoving Eva away, she scrambled to her feet. "Something's wrong." Her voice shook. It was something bad. Killing bad. "Something happened to Dragos. Watch Liam. Don't leave him."

Almost as quickly, Eva sprang upright too. As she switched to bodyguard mode, her expression changed and became deadly.

She made the mistake of taking hold of Pia's arm. "Stay here until we can find out what happened. You can't go running into an unknown situation. It could be dangerous."

The panic rode Pia harder than any devil could have, and she rounded on Eva with a wild animal's ferocity. "Oh, can't I? You fucking watch me. *Stay here and guard my son.*"

Eva's eyes widened. Her grip loosened, and she fell back a step.

Pia had nothing more to say. She had used up her words, all but one. The wild animal that had taken over her body whirled and sprinted down the hall. She flew down the stairs, burst out of the house and raced down the path to the construction site. She had never run so fast in her life.

As fast as she ran, it wasn't fast enough to stop what had happened to her mate, and the only word she had left inside of her was his name.

Dragos.

Chapter Two

BURSTING OUT OF the tree line, she reached the construction site bordering the lake.

The scene looked strange and wrong. It took her a few heartbeats to realize why.

The dimensions of the clearing had changed. A section of bedrock had collapsed, and at the pile of rubble at the base of a bluff, people swirled in a melee of urgency, the yellow of their hard hats bobbing through a growing haze of dust.

Others stared, their expressions aghast. She grabbed the nearest worker by the front of his shirt. "Where is he?"

He didn't ask whom she meant. Wordlessly, he pointed at the rubble.

Letting go of him, she raced toward the group who were digging frantically at the pile of rubble and shifting the heavier rocks. Leaping over obstacles, she landed beside the man shouting directions at the rest of the crew. He caught sight of her and fell silent, abruptly, and the expression in his gaze carried the same weight of horror as everyone else on the scene.

"Tell me he's not here," she said between her teeth.

Snatching off his hard hat, he shoved it onto her

head. "He's here, along with the shift foreman and another man."

She had already known it, but still, the stark words struck her like a punch to the stomach. Blindly, she turned toward the rubble and started to dig like the others, bare-handed in case a vulnerable body lay close underneath the surface.

He had to be okay. He had to. Even in his human form, he was unbelievably strong.

Last year, when they had been in a car wreck—before they had really mated—he had *pushed* out with his Power to keep the car from crushing them. He could bend metal with his bare hands. He…

He had always said he'd seen the car wreck coming, and he'd been able to brace himself. What if he hadn't seen this coming?

She only became aware she was sobbing under her breath when strong, dark hands came down on her shoulders.

"Hugh's watching Liam," Eva said in her ear. "I couldn't leave you to come out here on your own."

She glanced over her shoulder, took in Eva's sober, compassionate expression and her snarl died in her throat. Blinking rapidly, she nodded.

Eva glanced down at Pia's hands, which were scraped and bleeding. "I'll find you some gloves."

Not bothering to answer, Pia turned back to the rubble and started digging again.

"I found Jake!" a man shouted, to her left.

Instantly the focus of attention shifted, and several

men converged together to quickly dig out the unmoving man. At some point EMTs had arrived. Pia saw uniformed paramedics racing to the spot carrying a stretcher and medical bags.

As they lifted the man's limp body onto the stretcher, she looked away. Maybe she should care that they had found someone alive, but she didn't. Maybe she could care later. All she cared about right now was that they hadn't found Dragos yet.

He couldn't be dead. Just the thought of it made her world stop, and she had to struggle to breathe.

Come on, she said telepathically. *Where are you? COME ON!*

The pile of rubble exploded.

Dragos's mountainous dragon form appeared in front of her, his iridescent bronze hide dulled in a coating of dust. The sheer size of his body knocked aside rocks, equipment and men alike.

Something hit her in the chest, and she tumbled backward. Ignoring the hail of debris that fell on her, she climbed to her feet, joy and relief bringing tears to her eyes.

Oh, thank God, she told him. *I've been so scared....*

The bronze dragon's immense, triangular head swept from side to side as glaring gold eyes took in the surrounding scene.

As he did so, hot, wet droplets of moisture splattered her in the face and chest.

It was blood. Her gaze focused on a jagged gash that ran along the dragon's brow. Bright liquid crimson streamed down the long arch of his neck.

It's okay, she said to him. While virtually everyone else scrambled to get out of his way, she climbed over the rocks toward him, hand outstretched. *I'm here. You're going to be okay….*

The dragon mantled gigantic wings, strewing more debris and throwing a shadow over the clearing. Snapping his head back around to her, he bared wicked, razor-sharp teeth as long as her torso.

Face upturned, she stood motionless as his massive, monstrous head snaked toward her.

The dragon's jaws opened wide, and *he snapped at her.*

Hot breath blasted her hair back from her face. The edge of the dragon's teeth tore through the front of her dress, and Eva slammed into her from the side, tackling her to the ground.

It knocked the breath out of her. Even as she coughed and struggled to take a wheezing breath, her gaze never left Dragos as all her emotions and beliefs vaporized. Like the collapsing bedrock, they crumbled to dust.

All the terror and dread of the last several minutes, and all the joy and relief.

The unshakeable foundation of her faith that he would never, could never, hurt her.

Tail lashing from side to side, the dragon roared. The gigantic sound shook the earth, and fire boiled out of his massive, parted jaws. Spraying fire in a circle, he sent people screaming as they ran away.

His wings hammered down, and he launched.

As she watched the dragon climb in the air, wheel and wing away, she didn't know she could exist in such a cold, barren place.

She watched him until he had shrunk to a small speck in the sky and disappeared.

Come back, she whispered. *Come back.*

But her whisper was small and uncertain.

A million miles away, Eva rolled off her body and yanked her up by the shoulders. The other woman seemed to be shouting at her. She focused on Eva's lips as they shaped words. Are you hurt? Did you get burned anywhere?

One side of Eva's face was blistered, her dark eyes wide.

Pia looked around the clearing. Other people were burned and stumbling to help each other, some standing still as they stared up at the empty sky. Glancing down at herself, she fingered her dress. The bright material was torn, sheared by the edge of the dragon's teeth.

The immense distance between her and the rest of the world started to dissipate, and pain intruded. Her chest hurt, and her legs and back felt scraped and bruised from landing in a sprawl on the rocky, uneven ground.

Her ability to think returned as well, but thankfully all her emotions stayed away. Glancing down at her scraped, raw fingers, she laid her hand gently against Eva's burned cheek and watched as the other woman's burns faded away.

She said, "I need a phone. Now."

Eva nodded and whirled away. When she returned a few moments later, she held out a cell phone wordlessly.

Taking it, Pia dialed a number she knew by heart and listened to ringing.

A moment later, the call was answered.

Graydon said, "I don't know this number. Who are you?"

"Gray," she said. "I need you."

"Pia? Is that you, cupcake?"

In her mind's eye, she saw again the dragon's teeth approaching.

Snapping at her.

"I need all the sentinels," she told him. Her shoulders shuddered, as if her body wanted to sob again. She shut that down hard. She didn't have time to cry. "You'd better bring the demesne lawyers with you."

His voice sharpened, all the mild good humor falling away. "What happened? Where's Dragos?"

She lifted her head and stared at the empty sky. "We're not talking about it over the phone," she said softly. "But I think you should bring some treasure too. Lots and lots of treasure."

ONE SMALL BLESSING had occurred.

Everyone had already been scrambling to get away from Dragos, so the dragon's fire had caused only light burns. There was only one casualty from the construction site accident—Ned Brandling, the shift foreman.

Back at the house, Eva told her about Brandling's death while she took another quick shower to wash away the dust and grime. The scrapes on her fingers had already healed, and the bruises along her back and legs were fading.

Neither of them had mentioned Dragos's name since he had disappeared. Pia could tell by the quick, nervous way Eva spoke that the other woman was scared, but she had nothing to offer as reassurance or comfort.

After her shower, she dressed in sturdy clothes, knee-length jean shorts and a T-shirt, and tennis shoes. She moved fast, because she could hear Liam crying over the baby monitor, along with Hugh's gentle attempts to comfort him.

As soon as she had yanked on her shoes, Eva straightened. "What now?"

Pia said, "I'm going to take care of Liam. Go clean up."

Scowling, Eva flexed her hands. "I'm not leaving you."

The other woman was still covered in dust from the site. Pia glanced at her and shook her head. "You're not going into Liam's nursery like that. God only knows what he can sense of what's happened, and he already sounds frightened enough as it is. I don't want you upsetting him any further."

Looking abashed, Eva ducked her head. "Sorry," she muttered. "I didn't think. I'll get cleaned up and be right back."

Without further delay, Pia went into Liam's nursery. Hugh was cradling and walking him. As soon as Liam saw her, he wailed louder and tried to throw his body forward, reaching for her.

A sharp sliver of feeling wormed its way into her frozen heart. Gathering Liam close, she walked over to the rocking chair and pulled his favorite blanket around him.

Looking up into Hugh's worried expression, she said, "See that we're not disturbed until the sentinels arrive."

"Yes, ma'am," he said, his voice soft and careful. "I'll keep watch outside the door."

"Thank you."

As he eased the door shut behind him, she turned her attention to Liam. The toddler had clenched both fists into the front of her T-shirt. As soon as her eyes met his, his small face crumpled. The sliver of feeling in her heart grew larger until it was a hot, agonized pain, and she fought back tears of her own.

"Shh, my sweetest darling," she whispered, stroking Liam's silken head.

He put his cheek against hers in a gesture at once so mature and loving, it broke the tension in her spine, and she wrapped around him tightly. He clung to her, and neither of them moved until the door opened some time later, and Graydon strode in.

Graydon was the biggest of the sentinels, a burly, mild mannered giant almost as large as Dragos in his human form.

Just like Dragos, as always when Graydon entered the room, the available space seemed to shrink, due as much to the potent force of his personality as to his size. He wore the sentinel's usual outfit of black T-shirt, jeans and boots—clothing that was sturdy enough for a rough, often violent lifestyle and easy to discard when damaged—along with a Glock in a holster clipped to the waist of his jeans.

As soon as he saw her and Liam in the rocking chair, he strode toward them, went down on one knee and would have taken them into his arms if she hadn't stopped him with one hand pressed against his chest.

She couldn't bear to be hugged at the moment, or she might break down. And she didn't have time to break down. She had too much to do.

One look into Graydon's darkened, sober gaze, and she could tell that he had already heard at least some version of what had happened.

She patted him on the chest in silent apology for rebuffing his hug, and he took her hand. He told her telepathically. *Everyone else is downstairs, except for Alex, who drew the short straw, and Aryal, who went down to the construction site to try to find out how the accident occurred.*

Unsurprised, she nodded. Whenever a situation was serious enough to call for the full strength of the sentinels, they always left one of them behind in New York to handle whatever might arise while the rest were gone.

The lawyers are here too?

His jaw tightened as he nodded. *Them too. And I*

wasn't sure what you meant by treasure, but I brought rough, uncut jewels and gold.

That's fine, she said.

His rugged, weather-beaten face looked tight with worry. *What do you need right now?*

Steeling her spine, she told him, *I need for the sentinels to find out where Dragos has gone. Just track him down. It's important you keep your presence cloaked. Don't approach him, and don't try to talk to him. He took a blow to the head. He was bleeding profusely, and—and—Graydon, he's not himself right now.*

His hand tightened on hers. *What do you mean? The stories we heard have been pretty confused. What really happened out there?*

Cupping the back of Liam's head, she met his gaze. *I mean the only reason he didn't kill me earlier was because Eva knocked me out of the way.*

His eyes dilated in a quick reaction to her words. *That's impossible. He would die before he ever hurt you.*

Of course he would, she snapped. Her mouth worked as she fought to keep her face from crumpling as Liam's had earlier. *If he remembered me, he would.*

Graydon's indrawn breath was sharp and audible. *Okay, we'll find him. I swear it.*

Do it fast, she said tightly. *There's only so much I can heal. When Quentin and Aryal were so badly injured in the spring, I could help them, but only to a certain extent. Too much time had passed, and they both ended up scarred.*

Also, much of her Wyr nature still remained a mystery to her. She had no idea if the healing properties in her blood would help Dragos's mental state, or if she could only heal physical wounds.

That was assuming she could coax the dragon into letting her close enough to heal him. If Dragos had suffered some kind of traumatic amnesia, there was a possibility he might never recover his memories.

And he had snapped at her.

Snapped.

Closing her eyes, she tightened her jaw against the memory.

Wyr mated for life, but nobody fully understood why. It was a complicated process involving emotions, sexual attraction, timing and opportunity.

What if Dragos couldn't remember that he was Lord of the Wyr? That she was his mate? What if he *never* remembered? Could he live as though he had never mated before?

The thought made her feel physically ill. Maybe he could. Maybe… theoretically, he could even fall in love and mate with someone else, but if that happened, where would that leave her?

That was the panic talking. Forcing herself to breathe evenly, she backed away from the hectic questions hurtling through her mind.

We won't rest until we locate him, Graydon told her. He clenched her hand so hard, her fingers ached. *If he's that badly injured, he won't have flown far.*

I hope you're right, she muttered.

As they fell silent, she pressed her lips against Liam's forehead. If Dragos was her heart, this precious boy was her soul. She would do everything in her power to safeguard him, but she couldn't protect him from what was happening to them now.

Keeping her voice calm and gentle, she said, "Peanut, my love, you have to be a big soldier now."

Lifting his head from her shoulder, Liam looked at her with absolute trust in his eyes, and she thought, I cannot believe I am saying these horrible words to that small, sweet face. Swallowing the thought, she smiled at him. As he tried to smile back, the crazed animal inside of her wanted to howl and rip down the walls of the house.

Stroking Liam's cheek, she told him, "You need to be good for Hugh and Eva, while I need to talk to some lawyers about some boring legal stuff."

Boring things like power of attorney, and line of Wyr succession. Sorting out the legalities of inheritance had been high on their to-do list, but they had been so busy since Liam had been born in the spring, they hadn't yet gotten to it, and immortality had a sneaky way of lulling one into a false sense of security.

If the absolute worst came to worst, Graydon would make an outstanding father and a steady regent in the Wyr demesne until Liam came of age.

But she had no intention of letting the worst happen.

"After I finish dealing with all of that," she told Liam softly, "I'm going to go get Daddy back."

Chapter Three

THE DRAGON HAD a splitting headache, so he didn't fly down immediately to kill the fool who approached from below. Instead he stretched out along a shelf of rock near the top of a low mountain and basked in the afternoon sunshine while he waited for the fool to hike to him.

After all, he could always slaughter the fool with a minimum of effort once she drew close enough.

He could tell she was female from the snatches of her scent that wafted toward him on the hot summer breeze.

He could tell she was a fool, because it had become clear some time ago that she climbed toward him, not by accident but with intent. She was a small, slender-looking creature, and alone, and he didn't think she was armed with any weapons. And really, he couldn't fathom why any lone person would approach him without weapons, so she had to be suicidal as well.

Her scent bothered him, and he shifted the bulk of his body restlessly as he drew in great breaths of air. Strange, feminine and evocative, it tugged at something deep inside. He could almost recall what kind of creature she was, almost grasp at a tantalizing something that lay just beyond his reach….

Each time he came close to it, the tantalizing something slipped away again.

She wasn't Elven. He hated the Elves with a passion born of long-ago, shadowy memories of war. No Elf would approach him for any good reason, and if she had been Elven, blazing headache or no, he would have flown down from his perch and torn her to shreds for daring to encroach upon his space.

Flexing his talons at the murderous thoughts, he crawled forward to lap thirstily at the bubbling spring of cold water that ran down the steep mountainside beside his ledge. The spring was one of the reasons why he had chosen this place to rest. In this remote spot, the dragon had water, sunlight and a high vantage point to watch for enemies. He could rest here until his headache eased and his vision improved enough so he could hunt for food.

Windswept clouds danced overhead in the bright, aquamarine sky. It would almost be peaceful, except for the pain in his head and the nearing fool.

Who wasn't Elven.

Who was, somehow, both like the dragon and yet dramatically unlike him at the same time.

As her scent grew nearer and stronger, it evoked images of cool, wild moonlight, a fantastic Power pouring over him like a benediction for the damned, and a sense of a unique treasure more precious than anything the dragon had ever seen before or comprehended.

So. That was more than reason enough to let the fool live for the moment. The dragon's predatory thoughts wound like a serpent coiling on itself.

He would let her get close enough so he could discover for himself what kind of creature she was, but most importantly, so he could find out where she had hidden that fantastic, unique treasure and claim it for himself.

Still, the pain made him cranky and inclined to be vicious.

It was a good thing for her continued health and well-being that she approached him slowly, making a certain amount of polite noise—not too loud, but enough that they were both fully aware that they knew of each other's existence.

He waited until she reached the edge of the clearing surrounding his ledge. When he heard the sound of a small rock shifting underneath one of her shoes, the dragon said, "That's close enough."

Dead silence, as she froze.

The dragon lifted his head and glared at the fool out of his one good eye. She wasn't Elven, and although she looked human enough, she wasn't human either.

Like, yet unlike him in some fundamental way.

She was suntanned and slender, with long, bare legs, and she carried a heavy-looking, sturdy pack on her back. Her hair was the color of sunshine, the color of precious gold, and her eyes... he hadn't been prepared for the impact of her large, wary eyes. They were a beautiful rich, dark violet, and they embodied the very essence of cool, wild moonlight.

Her eyes confused and agitated him.

The dragon growled, "You disturb me."

Ducking her golden head, the female averted her gaze. "I apologize."

She was soft-spoken, her voice gentle. He had dreamed of such a voice whispering to him brokenly through the night. *Come back. Come back to me.*

The memory of the dream made him shake his head. Pain flared at the movement, and he bared his teeth in defiance against it. "Why do you dare bother me, and why should I let you survive it?"

"I brought you gifts."

Gifts?

Nobody brought the dragon gifts. The very idea was laughable.

While there was fear in the female's expression as she spoke, she watched him steadily without backing away, and her fear was not gratifying to him.

In fact, her fear disturbed him in a deeply profound way. He couldn't think clearly enough to puzzle it out. Leaning his aching head against the side of a boulder, he snapped, "What kind of gifts?"

"I would be glad to show you," she said in her soft, gentle voice. "But I'm afraid you might not be able to see them properly. It looks like you have dried blood in one of your eyes."

As soon as she said it, he realized it was true. Raising one forepaw, he rubbed at the eye on his blind side, which made the pain worse.

"Perhaps you might be able to see better if you could rinse some of the blood away," the female suggested. "I would be glad to help you, if you like."

Snapping his head up, he hissed, "Stay back."

She recoiled, the fear flaring again in her wide gaze. "Of course. I only meant to help."

The dragon could hear the truth in her voice, and once again, her fear disturbed him at some deep level. He growled, "Stay exactly where you are. I will deal with this myself."

"Yes, all right," she whispered.

He shifted closer to the spring, and, craning his neck, he managed to angle the injured side of his head under running water. The icy wetness cascaded over his hide, washing away the blood. It also helped to ease the pain somewhat, and he heaved a sigh of relief.

He stayed like that for some time, until his thoughts came with more clarity, and he was able to work his eye open. Lifting his head, he shook off the water and turned back to the female.

She had eased the pack from her back and taken a seat on the ground, resting her bright head in her hands. Her posture was at once both weary and so dejected, the sight tugged at him.

Troubled by his mysterious reactions to her, his crankiness returned. He hadn't asked for her to climb up his mountain and inflict her unwanted presence or emotions on him. "Now," the dragon said in a silken tone of voice, "what is this nonsense about you bringing me gifts?"

Her head came up. "I did. Can I show them to you now?"

Enjoying the way her hair glinted in the sunlight, he relaxed back against the hot stone ledge. The only reason why she would have brought him anything was because she wanted something from him. The more value there was in her gift, the more she would want from him. There was something wily about this female, and he meant to get to the bottom of why she had come.

"Very well," he told her.

He watched her from under lowered eyelids, as she opened her pack and drew out cloth-wrapped packages tied with twine. Taking the largest and clearly the heaviest, she set it on the ground, untied the twine and pulled back the cloth to reveal several bricks made of gold.

While he didn't abandon his relaxed posture, inside the dragon grew tense. Valuable gifts, indeed. He said, "Show me the rest."

She appeared eager now, as she did as he ordered. The next package she bared for his sharp gaze was much smaller and contained a handful of clear, shining rocks that reflected shards of light as icy as the mountain spring. Diamonds. The third package she opened held stones of such rich, deep violet-hued blue they had to be sapphires.

For a long moment, the dragon looked at the rich array of offerings spread on the ground. He could tell by the bulk of her pack that it wasn't empty, but what she had offered him was more than enough. Gold, diamonds and sapphires, all of which he loved. She had brought his favorite things.

When at last he looked up, his gaze had turned cold and deadly. "Who are you, and what do you want?"

At one side of her tense mouth, a delicate muscle flexed. Taking a deep breath, she said with quiet deliberation, "My name is Pia Cuelebre. What's yours?"

Cuelebre.

He knew that name. It meant winged serpent.

As soon as she said it, hot agony flared in his head again. There was a well of knowledge that lay just on the other side of that wall of fiery pain, something vital to his existence, but he couldn't access it.

He could access her, though.

Shock flared across her face as he lunged at her and pinned her to the ground underneath one outspread forepaw. She was so fragile he could crush her with a shrug.

So fragile.

She had climbed all this way to confront him, and she lay without weaponry or defenses of any kind. Not even her cool mysterious Power had flared to strike back at him. He held the bulk of his body tense, as he stared down at her in confusion. Gripping his talons on either side of her slender neck, she stared back unwaveringly at him, her body trembling.

He hissed, "You are no winged serpent."

"No, I'm not," she whispered. "But that's still my name. What's your name—or do you have one?"

The dragon had a name. He had chosen it for himself. He reached for it and ran into that wall of fiery pain again.

The female's gaze darkened and filled with moisture. One droplet slipped out the corner of her eye and streaked down her temple. "You don't know, do you?"

"Be silent," he ordered. Serpentine coils of thought writhing, he struggled to reach past the fiery wall in his head.

Agony drove him back, defeating him.

A hint of calculation flashed across her expression. She said, "I have another gift for you."

He bared his teeth. He didn't trust her gifts. "What?"

"Knowledge," she told him.

Carefully, he dug the tips of his talons into the ground around her prone body. Carefully, so that his threat was clear while he didn't hurt her. Not yet. He reserved that possibility for later.

"Why do you think your knowledge is of any use to me?" He let the possibility of her death darken his voice.

She swallowed. "Answer two questions, and I'll try to show you."

He paused suspiciously, suspecting a trick, but she could only trick him if he chose to answer. In the meantime, he might learn something valuable in the nature of her questions. "Ask."

The breath shook audibly in her throat. She whispered, "How many nights have you spent on this mountain?"

His gaze narrowed. If there was some kind of trick in such a simple question, he couldn't see what it was. "One. And your next question?"

"Where were you yesterday morning?"

Even as he tried to think back to the answer, he slammed into the fiery wall. His vision glazed. Rearing away from her, the dragon released his frustration and pain in a bellow of rage aimed at the sky.

When he could focus again, he discovered she had scrambled to the tree line at the edge of the clearing and crouched with her back pressed against the trunk of a tree.

Frankly, he was astonished she hadn't taken off running down the mountain, and he glanced back down at the array of gold and jewels at his feet. "What do you want from me in return for all of this, along with your precious knowledge?"

She scrubbed her face with the back of one hand, leaving a smear of dirt behind. Her voice shook as she told him, "You're the only one who can help me find my mate again."

Drawing in a deep breath, the dragon let her scent fill his lungs, and he realized something that had lain in the back of his mind for some time.

Like, but unlike.

He didn't know what kind of creature she was, but she was no predator. If she had been, he really might have killed her once she had dared to reach his ledge.

He realized something else, as disjointed images ran

through his mind.

An explosion of pain, the first pain. Crushing weight and darkness. Shouting from a distance.

And a voice in the darkness. *Her* voice?

Where are you? COME ON!

"Yesterday," he said. "You were one of the people who attacked me."

Dismay bolted across her features, and she straightened with a jerk. "No—that's not what happened!"

The dragon regarded her cynically. Wyrm, he was called. The Great Beast. Traps had been laid for him before, and he had been attacked, but no one had ever brought him down. "It wasn't? Then what would you call it?"

Rubbing her forehead with both hands, she said tightly, "I would call it a horrific misunderstanding." She dropped her hands and looked at him, and either anger or desperation flashed in her eyes. Or maybe both. "If you can recall anything at all about yesterday, try to think back to what I said to you. I said, 'It's okay. You're going to be okay.' Do you remember that?"

He tilted his head, eyes narrowing. He had no recollection of what she said, only the voice in the darkness, but once again, there was no hint of a lie in her voice.

He said, "No."

Her shoulders sagged. "I know your name," she told him. "Your name is Dragos."

A thread of recognition ran through him, like a jolt of electricity.

Dragos.

Yes, that was his name, but the rest of what she said… he strained to think back.

The female—she said her name was Pia—was continuing, her words tumbling rapidly over each other as she stepped forward. "You're obviously in pain. I don't think you realize how seriously you're hurt, but if you will only let me look at your wound, I swear I can help you."

She pushed him too hard, too far. The only things he could recall were the pain, being buried under a heavy weight, a heavy cloud of dust covering the scene like a shroud and people shouting.

"Stop," Dragos said. "I'm done talking. I need to think."

Alarm filled her expression. "No, you have to listen to me. This is more important than you can possibly understand—"

"Enough." He growled it with such intensity, the ground behind them vibrated. "I have listened to you enough. I have never needed healing from anyone before, and I will not tolerate you trying to convince me that I need it now."

She stared at him in astonishment and the beginnings of bitterness. "That's not true," she said, her voice clipped. "You've needed my healing before. You just don't remember it."

"If I don't remember it," the dragon said, "how can I trust you're telling the truth?" He spread out one forepaw to indicate the gold and jewels. "You bring me convenient gifts of all my favorite things. Do you think

I've never seen a trap baited with such as this before?"

She stared at him, breathing heavily, but remained silent. Then her chin came up. "Fine. Maybe bringing the treasure was a mistake, but I'm not leaving."

"As you wish," Dragos said.

He glanced dismissively once more at the treasure lying on the ground between them, then turned his back on her, gathered himself and sprang into flight.

The last thing he wanted to do was go hunting, but he needed food to heal and time to think. Either the female would be waiting for him when he returned, or she would not. If she truly wanted to find her mate again, she would wait.

If he returned.

Chapter Four

P IA STARED UP at the sky, watching Dragos leave. Normally she loved to see him take flight, but now watching the dragon fly away gave her a sick feeling in the pit of her stomach. How far would he go?

How could she be so stupid?

The satellite phone in her pack rang, and she dug it out to answer it.

Graydon demanded, "Are you all right? He didn't hurt you did he?"

She looked in the direction of the low, nearby peak of a neighboring mountain, where the gryphon hid, keeping watch from a distance. It said something, didn't it, that Graydon would even ask such a thing. A week ago—a day ago—the question would have been unthinkable.

"No," she said dully. "He didn't hurt me." At least, he hadn't hurt her anywhere that was visible. Inside, she felt like she was slowly bleeding from some vital artery.

"I'll follow him."

"No! Leave him be for now." Unable to stand still, she paced through the clearing. "It's my fault he left. I panicked and pushed him too hard. The gold and jewels—they were a bad idea. He doesn't remember me.

He doesn't remember, Gray, and of course he was suspicious. I'd brought all his favorite things, and he thought I was baiting some kind of trap."

"Take a deep breath," Graydon said gently. "You didn't do anything wrong. It was a good idea, as far as it went. Are you sure I shouldn't track him? What if he doesn't come back?"

Scrubbing at her face with the back of one hand, she tried to think. Where would he go? What would he do?

She was excellent at predicting what Dragos would do and where he would go, but she had no idea what this strange, frightening creature might decide. The thought of the dragon prowling unchecked through the countryside made her stomach tighten even further.

But she had roused the dragon's suspicions, and if he sensed Graydon following him, Dragos might attack him. Graydon could get hurt, or worse, killed. Dragos would never forgive himself if that happened, and she would never forgive herself either. Graydon's kind, steady presence was one of the reasons why she had made it through such a dark, awful night, and she couldn't bear the thought of losing him.

"No," she said again. "We can't risk it. Maybe I raised enough questions in his mind that he'll come back on his own for answers. He said he needed to think. For the moment, we're going to have to trust him, and wait to see if he returns on his own."

Those were some of the toughest words she'd ever had to say. They ranked right up there with telling Liam *you have to be a big soldier now*. The panicked animal inside her wanted nothing more than to chase after Dragos, but the thought of trusting the dragon who was even now acting without Dragos's memories was almost insupportable.

"I want to join you," Graydon said. "It's going against all my instincts to leave you there alone."

"Well, you can't," she replied flatly. "If he comes back, and he smells your scent, he'll be even more convinced this is some kind of trap." She glanced once more up into the sky. "For now, we'll just have to wait."

"Call me if anything changes, or if you need me to come. In fact, call me every half hour," Graydon said. "I want to hear the sound of your voice, and know you're okay."

She knew what he wanted. Like Eva, he was scared, and he wanted reassurance. With the fact that Wyr mated for life, and with Dragos so critically injured, everything about their lives was unpredictable now, unstable.

But she had no more reassurance to offer Graydon than she'd had to offer Eva.

She said, "I'm not going to pretend to be fine. To tell you the truth, I feel pretty crazy, and I feel like I'm fighting for my life. But you're going to have to trust me, too. I'm dealing with it. I'll deal. And I'll call you if I need you."

He swore under his breath. After a moment, he said, "Okay, sweetheart."

Hanging up, she stuffed the phone back into one of the side pockets of the pack. She had to get her act together. She didn't know how long Dragos would be gone, and she was exhausted. Waiting through the long, terrible night as the sentinels searched for Dragos, dealing with legalities for both the Wyr demesne and for Liam's sake—just in case—and the long hike up the mountain, along with confronting the dragon, had all taken their toll.

She needed to refuel and rest, at least as much as she was able, because she had no idea what would happen next.

Moving to the spring, she washed her face and arms in the icy water then drank as much as she could hold. Afterward, she forced herself to choke down a couple of vegan protein bars, and she wrapped up the gold bricks and jewels and stuffed them back into her pack.

The heat of the afternoon was fading, and the shadows from the trees lengthened. Even though it was high summer, it got cold in the mountains at night. She pulled one of the last treasures from her pack, a sturdy, flannel-lined jacket. Wrapping it around her torso, she curled into a tight ball against the trunk of the tree and fell into an uneasy doze.

Come back. Please come back to me.

THE RUSH OF gigantic wings roused her.

Scrambling to her feet, she watched as the dragon wheeled overhead. Inside, relief and tension grappled for supremacy, but in the end relief won out.

He had returned, and he didn't have to. He could have just as easily left. He had no stake in this location. He came back because she was here, and he wanted those answers.

While she had dozed, afternoon had turned to early evening, and the sky overhead had turned vivid, framing the dragon's bronze body with jewel tones. Light and graceful as a cat, despite his massive size, he landed on the ledge.

His muzzle was coated with bright, fresh blood. She could smell it from where she stood. It was cow's blood. Somewhere nearby, a farmer was missing some cattle. If we survive this, she thought with grim gallows humor, someone is going to have to hunt that farmer down and pay him for his trouble.

Ignoring her as if she didn't exist, Dragos strode to the spring to rinse his muzzle and forepaws, sleek muscle flowing under his bronze hide.

She studied him thoughtfully. He seemed to be moving better, with more ease and surety. The jagged wound at his brow looked partially healed, but she didn't know whether to be relieved or worried about that.

All she knew was that she wasn't buying his act. He might pretend to ignore her but he knew very well, probably to a fraction of an inch, where she was standing.

Still without looking at her, Dragos said, "Where's my treasure?"

His treasure. She cocked her head, resting her hands

on her hips. If the situation hadn't been so serious she might have smiled. Even now, amidst all his suspicions, the dragon remained as possessive as ever.

"I apologize for what happened earlier," she said, keeping her voice as soft and even as she had before. Nonaggressive, nonthreatening. "I understand that you have cause to be suspicious of anyone who approaches you as I did, but I meant no insult by offering the gifts, nor was I baiting any kind of trap. I was only hoping to strike a bargain with you."

"Ah, yes," he replied, glancing cynically over his shoulder. "Because I'm the only one who can help you find your mate."

She hesitated. "Yes."

He finished washing, circled and stretched out on the rough, stony ledge with all the arrogance of an emperor assuming his throne. Only then did he look directly at her, the expression in his great, gold eyes confrontational and cold.

The impact was almost overwhelming. She had seen him give his enemies just such a look before, but he had never looked that way at her until now.

He said, "That doesn't answer my question."

Tucking in her chin, she leveled her gaze at him. While he might have chosen to return, the decision seemed to have put him in a pissy mood. "What difference does it make? You clearly didn't want it."

The dragon narrowed his eyes. "I've changed my mind. You will bring it to me."

Normally, her impulse would be to back talk to all

that monumental arrogance, but she curbed it. Now wasn't the time to sass him. There was no hint of indulgence in his current demeanor, or softness. This was all about establishing dominance. His entire attitude demanded that she prove herself.

Bowing her head, she knelt to open her pack and pull out the packets of gold and jewels. Gathering them in her arms, she walked toward him. About fifteen feet away, she slowed to a stop. When she made as if to kneel, Dragos said, "Bring it closer."

Obediently, she took a few steps closer. The force of his personality pressed against her skin. His Power boiled around his physical form like an invisible corona, and despite the gravity of the situation, the desperate animal inside of her drew comfort from his closeness and calmed.

"Closer," the dragon said again, watching her intently.

He was lethally unpredictable, easily the most dangerous creature she had ever known or met, and at the moment, he did not remember he loved her.

She was supposed to stay wary of him, but it was too hard to maintain when she was so tired and it went against every one of her instincts. With a sigh, she approached until she could set the packets on the ground between his outstretched forelegs.

When she straightened, he lowered his head until the large curve of his nostrils stopped a few inches from her hair. They stood like that for some time, breathing quietly. As she looked up into one immense, molten eye, she wanted very badly to stroke his muzzle, or to take out her small penknife, slice the palm of her hand and lay it against that terrible, half-healed wound on his brow.

That wound had taken everything from her. No matter how suspiciously or aggressively Dragos treated her at the moment, she never forgot—that wound was the real enemy.

But she didn't dare go quite that far, not without his express permission. If she made a mistake and pushed him too far, he could lash out at her again, and they would both lose everything.

"Now, tell me about this 'horrible misunderstanding,'" he ordered.

At a loss, she glanced around the clearing. How could she explain what had happened in such a way that the dragon could accept it? So much depended on concepts and relationships built over centuries.

He was Lord of the Wyr demesne, the head of a multibillion-dollar corporation, and a husband, mate and father, and yet earlier, the dragon didn't even know his own name.

Taking in a deep breath, she said in a cautious, low voice, "It wasn't any kind of attack. I swear it. You'll know that for yourself, as soon as you remember more."

"If it wasn't an attack, then what was it?"

"An accident," she whispered. She wiped her cheeks with both hands. "A terrible, terrible accident. You were helping with building a project, and you were all working together."

It was impossible to tell if he believed her. The dragon's face remained expressionless. "How did this accident occur?"

The evening before, she had asked the very same thing of Aryal, but she had only half comprehended the answer.

Now, she said, "I don't know all the details of what happened, but what I do know is that you were setting off a series of small, controlled explosions in a large section of bedrock that bordered a lake."

"Why?" He watched her closely.

"The site is where a large building is going to be constructed, so the area needs to be level in certain places. But there was a buried fault line in the rock nobody knew was there. It looked solid when it was inspected, but it wasn't. You—along with a couple of other men—you all thought you were safe where you were standing, around one edge of the bluff."

She paused, but he said nothing, his steady breathing stirring her hair. Lacing her fingers together, she twisted her hands and continued, "When the explosion went off, the force of it blew through the fault line, and blasted out where you were standing. They call that kind of accident 'flyrock' in construction and quarry blasting—it's material projected outside a declared danger zone. At least that's how it was explained to me. When the fault line was breached, a whole section of the area collapsed. You were all buried underneath it. One man died. The rest of you were badly injured."

After a moment, he said, "Your mate was at this

building site."

The question took her by surprise, and she had to swallow before she could reply. "Yes," she whispered. "He's disappeared."

"You think I know where he is."

She shook her head. "No, but I believe you can help me find him."

"And you claim you've healed me before." The very lack of expression with which he said that indicated the depth of his skepticism.

"That must sound pretty outlandish to you." She tried to smile. "I guess it is pretty outlandish. It's been an outlandish kind of a year."

If he had such a hard time believing she might want to heal him, just wait until he found out about Peanut. She could imagine how well that conversation would go down.

"I don't remember you," he said.

Her head drooped. Of course, she knew that, but the clinical, dispassionate way in which he said it was every bit as devastating as the actual reality. All the passion she felt for him, this tremendous, consuming storm of love...

None of it was returned. None of the need, or his own love for her, manifested in anything he said or did. Here he was, as strong as ever, living and breathing in front of her, and she felt as if someone immeasurably precious to her had died.

"I wish, so very much, that I could find some way to convince you to let me heal you," she said unsteadily. "I wish it for your sake, so that you can feel better, and maybe—just maybe—your memories might return to you. But most of all, I wish it for my sake, because I miss my mate with all my heart, and I would do anything or give anything to get him back again."

"The wound is already healing." He added deliberately, "I don't need you either."

Maybe he was only speaking the truth as he knew it, but that seemed unnecessarily cruel, and it took everything she had not to lash out at him because of it.

Her voice hardened. "Maybe you don't need me, or maybe you only think you don't. You still don't remember what happened to you last week, or the week before, or the week before that. You don't know which of your old enemies might be close by, or what new enemies you might have made. You're vulnerable, Dragos, in a way you've never been vulnerable before, and I'm the only ally you've got who's offering you any kind of help."

Silence fell between them, and it was just long enough for her to castigate herself again for pushing him too hard when she had promised herself she wouldn't.

He stirred, shifting his long, bulky body, and by his very restlessness, she knew she had scored a hit.

"What is this healing you would attempt?" Dragos tilted his head to watch her more closely. "Do you really think it would help my memories return? I will not tolerate any kind of spell."

The surge of hope she felt was almost as unbearable

as everything else had been in the last twenty-four hours. "I can't tell you how much I hope it will help you get your memory back, but the truth is, I don't know," she told him. Unable to resist any longer, she laid a hand on his muzzle and stroked him. "I can promise you this—I would never hurt you."

A part of her thrilled to note he didn't pull back from her gentle caress, but then he had to go and spoil it.

"Of course you wouldn't, not if you have any hope of me helping you find your mate," he said, the cynical tone back in his voice.

She nearly smacked him on the nose, as she snapped, "Of course."

"Do it," he told her.

For a moment she could hardly believe her ears. Before he could change his mind, she dug into the front pocket of her jean shorts and pulled out her penknife. Under his sharp, distrustful gaze, she sliced open her palm.

"There's no spell," she told him, her voice tight with nerves. "It's just my blood. Bend your head to me."

Slowly, still watching her, the dragon bent his head down farther. She laid her bleeding palm lightly against his wound.

Power flowed out from her palm. Dragos sucked in a breath and shuddered. After a long moment, she pulled her hand away and inspected his wound in the failing light.

It had already been half healed, and as she watched,

the wound faded into a bone white scar.

Dragos released a long sigh. She asked, "How do you feel?"

"Better. The headache is finally gone." The dragon met her gaze. "But I still don't remember you."

Chapter Five

A S HE SAID the words, Dragos watched the light that had brightened her eyes dim. Her eyes were quite beautiful, he realized. Large and expressive, they showed her every emotion. Her shoulders slumped, and her head bowed.

"Okay." Her voice had turned dull and flat, matching her dejected expression. "At least we tried."

She turned to walk away.

He frowned. He didn't like the sight of her walking away from him. The realization seemed to echo in his mind, almost as if he had thought it once before. "Where do you think you're going?"

"It's getting cold. I'm not like you. I don't have your kind of body heat. I'm going to gather wood for a fire." She didn't look around at him as she spoke. "I should have done it earlier."

His frown deepened. While his presence deterred other predators in the immediate area, the ground was rocky and steep, and the gathering dusk would make traversing it dangerous for someone who was so much more fragile than he.

He said abruptly, "I didn't say you could leave me."

Her stride hitched, and the angle of the back of her

head seemed to express… exasperation? When she replied, her words had turned edged. "And I didn't ask you."

At that impudence, he growled a low warning, but she paid no attention and walked into the tree line. How dare she ignore him?

A new realization sidelined his burst of anger. While it was true he didn't remember her, the lack of pain and the absence of the fiery wall in his mind allowed something to surface—a single word that carried a huge concept.

Wyr.

Certainly she was unlike him, as she wasn't a predator, but still, she was like him in a fundamental way. They were both Wyr, both two-natured creatures.

Like him, she had an animal form that was somehow tied to her cool, witchy moonlit Power, the Power that had cascaded over his hot pain, easing and healing it.

And, like her, he had a human form.

Instinctively, he reached for his other form. It felt like flexing a familiar, well-toned muscle… and he shifted.

After the change, he regarded his body. In his human form, he was still much larger than she, taller and broader, and more heavily muscled. He was clad in jeans and a T-shirt, and sturdy boots, all of which were grimed with dirt and blood—his blood.

On his left hand, he wore a plain gold ring. As he stared at it curiously, he realized there was something attached to his wrist.

Holding up his hand, he inspected the thing on his wrist in the fading light.

It was a braid of gleaming, pale gold hair.

He sucked in a breath. No matter how suspiciously he might inspect the braid, the only touch of Power he felt on it was his own, and that felt like a protection spell. The braid of hair was just that, a simple braid.

And he had wanted to protect it.

The gold hair looked quite familiar. In fact, it looked like the exact shade of hair on the head of the woman who was even now stubbornly climbing around the steep mountainside in the growing dark.

Galvanized, he leaped after her. She had managed to travel much farther away from the clearing than he had expected. His gaze adjusting to the darker shadows under the trees, he tracked her by scent and instinct.

She crouched beside some deadfall, stacking sticks into the crook of one arm. As he approached, she pointed one stick toward him like a sword without looking up.

"Stay back," she said. Her voice sounded strange, clogged with emotion. "Leave me alone for a few minutes."

Distress seemed to bruise the air around her, and he could smell the tiny, telltale salt of tears. Scowling, Dragos folded his arms. He disliked the scent of her tears, and he had no intention of going anywhere just because she told him to.

"You're wasting your time," he told her abruptly.

"Those little twigs you're gathering will burn to ash within a half an hour."

She snapped, "It'll be better than nothing."

Brushing past the useless barrier of the stick she brandished and bending over her, he closed his hand carefully around the tense curve of her slender shoulder. She shuddered at his touch, her head tilting sideways as if she might lay her cheek against the back of his hand.

He waited for her to do it, and in the process discovered he savored the anticipation, but she didn't follow through with the gesture. Disappointment darkened his thoughts.

"Go back up to the clearing," he said. "I'll bring firewood."

Carefully, she pulled away from his touch and straightened. Still without looking at him, she told him stiltedly, "Thank you."

He lowered his head, watching her shadowed figure as she climbed back up to the ledge, still carrying her useless bundle of twigs. If he didn't like her walking away from him, he liked her pulling away from his touch even less.

They would have words about that. They would most definitely have words.

For now, he turned his attention back to the pile of deadfall. The frame of the fallen tree lay underneath a scatter of forest debris. With a few strong kicks, he splintered the dry wood and gathered several sturdy pieces. When he carried his load back to the clearing, he found that she had gathered rocks into a circle for a makeshift campfire ring.

Wordlessly, he stacked his load a few feet away from the ring, and went back for another load. When he returned and added the second armful to the stack, he found her squatting in front of the ring. She had stacked the sticks she had gathered, and she worked at lighting a handful of dry leaves with a small, handheld lighter.

Folding his arms, he watched. Even though he could have lit the fire with a single glance, she didn't ask for his help, and he didn't offer it. If she wanted to do it by herself, so be it.

After a few minutes, she had a small fire started. Tiny flames licked eagerly at the sticks, and the growing circle of light contrasted with the darkness around them.

Only then did she look up at him. She appeared calmer, more composed. She said, "It's a good sign that you remembered your human form. It's promising."

"Is it?" He tucked his chin and considered her from underneath lowered brows. "I suppose it is."

A powerful cascade of emotions made his mood uncertain, and apparently she picked up on it, for her gaze turned wary. "Don't you think so?"

The delicate skin around her eyes was shadowed with dark smudges, and she looked exhausted. Still, the firelight loved her, burnishing the warm, healthy tan of her skin. The pale gold of her hair shone.

Her hair.

He didn't look at his wrist.

"Perhaps it is a good sign," he conceded. "I find I have more questions as time goes on, thus more frustrations."

Feeding another stick to the fire, she nodded. In profile, her expression was grim, settled. She looked as though she were set upon a long journey requiring endurance.

Deciding to test her, he said, "I'm surprised you're still here. Once you realized I had no knowledge of your mate, I would have thought you'd have given up by now and left."

Anger flashed in her eyes, a deep, pure sapphire violet. The very best sapphires had that same intense, almost purple blue. "If you think I would give up searching for my mate, just because I've had a bad couple of days and a few setbacks, you're badly mistaken. I didn't mate for those times when it was convenient or easy for me—because, believe me, none of it has been convenient or easy. Not since the very first day."

The fire in her response was delicious. He wanted to bask in it, to eat it all up. And not once, since she had arrived, had she ever spoken a lie. Everything she had told him was the truth.

Still standing with his arms crossed, holding himself at a distance, he heard himself ask, "Tell me of this time before, when you claimed to have healed me."

There was a slight pause, as she adjusted to his change in focus. She lifted a shoulder. "I don't just claim to have healed you—I *have* healed you, three times now. The first time, last year, you were poisoned."

He didn't know what he had been expecting, but

whatever it was, it certainly wasn't that. He drew in a breath between his teeth, on a slow hiss. "How?"

She paused, clearly searching for words. "It was a complicated situation, and I take a lot of responsibility for it. It was when we had first met, before we had grown to trust one another. Essentially, I provoked you into breaking some border treaties with the Elven demesne. They shot you with a poisoned arrow so that you couldn't shapeshift into the dragon while in their territory. You still have a scar on your chest where the arrow struck."

Reflexively, he rubbed the broad flat, muscled area of his right pectoral. Immediately, as if his fingers remembered more than he, they found a small indentation in the flesh. "And the second time?"

A dark expression shadowed her delicate, triangular face. "The second time you almost died. Again, the story is complicated, but basically you, along with some allies, fought a battle against an invader, one of the elder Elves who had come from a place called Numenlaur. You had several broken bones, and probably sustained other internal injuries. You couldn't defend yourself against the attacking army. Luckily, I was able to get to you in time."

The Elves again. Always, so many of his problems seemed to come down to the bloody Elves.

Going down on one knee, he added larger pieces of wood to the fire. The dry wood caught almost instantly, and the flames leaped higher, bringing light and heat to the cold night air.

"Now you've healed me again," he said. "It seems to have become something of a habit."

The shadow crossed across her expression again. "I wasn't able to heal you as much this time as I had hoped."

Lifting his head, he pinned her with his gaze. "What interesting stories you tell," he said softly. "But there is a notable lack of information in each one."

She lifted her chin. "Everything I've told you is true."

"I can tell that," Dragos said. "But what I want to know is, when were you going to tell me that I am your mate?"

Surprise visibly shook her, along with a resurgence of hope so palpable it was painful to witness. "You remembered?"

Earlier, when he'd looked at the gold ring he wore and the braided bracelet of hair, he had pieced the facts together. He was the destination, not part of her journey. He was the reason why she had climbed the mountain to face him.

He thought again of the broken voice in the night.

Come back. Come back to me.

That had been her voice, calling to him. Astonishment came over him. Realizing the truth had been a matter of logical deduction, but he hadn't counted on the depth of emotion that had driven her to confront the dragon. She carried so much passion, so much light.

For him.

I miss my mate with all my heart, and I would do anything or give anything to get him back again.

She had been talking about him. No one had ever given him such devotion before—no one that he could remember. Over centuries uncounted, they had given him fear and hatred, and sometimes obeisance, and he had considered all of that his due.

And she had brought him diamonds, sapphires and gold. He stared at the sapphire color of her eyes and the gold of her hair. His favorite things.

He didn't know he was capable of compassion, until that moment. He said, as gently as he could, "No, I still haven't remembered."

Her gaze widened and drifted away, as if not knowing where to land, because wherever she looked, all she saw was the same horror.

That look drove through him like a spike.

He stepped over the fire, commanding it not to burn, and obedient to his will, the flames drew aside. Crouching in front of her, he put a hand underneath her chin, forcing her to look at him. He asked, "Why didn't you say something before now?"

She put a hand lightly against his forearm, stroking him, and even amidst his heat and anger, the action soothed him.

"How on earth could I tell you something like that, and hope you would possibly believe me?" she asked. "I mean, think a minute—you had a difficult time accepting the fact that I brought the gifts in good faith. How do you think it would have gone down if a total stranger had walked up to you and said, 'Oh hi, sorry about your head injury, by the way, I'm your mate'?"

He had pinned her underneath one claw. He had been fully prepared to kill her as she drew close to him. He demanded, "When did it happen?"

"Last year. We've been together fourteen months."

"And the building that's under construction?"

She moistened her lips. "It's a—that's another complicated concept."

He growled under his breath. "That response is not acceptable any longer."

"Sometimes that response is all I can give you," she told him. "Your loss of memory is not just about me, Dragos. There is a lot you can't recall, and I can't just tell you in a sentence or two about things that are based on years of emotions, commitments, and understandings." She gripped his wrist. "You've lost memories of an entire life, involving a lot of people. Do you remember what I said about enemies earlier? Not only is that true, but it's also true about friends. You have friends. You have people who care about you."

He stared at her.

Widening her eyes, she lifted her shoulders in a shrug. "I know, go figure. It's hard to believe, isn't it?"

"We've built a life for ourselves," he said slowly, experimenting with the words.

"We *are* building a life for ourselves," she whispered. "And we're not going to give up on it, just because we've had a bad couple of days. Or when one of us loses his memories for a while and gets a little bitey."

His eyes narrowed. "What are you talking about?"

"Never mind," she muttered.

The whole conversation was bizarre, and part of him wanted to reject it out of hand. He was a loner by nature, and suspicious for many centuries-old reasons.

It crossed his mind again that she could still be manipulating him, somehow, for her own gain. Setting aside the question of why she would do so, he thought of how she could have done it.

Perhaps she had found a way to cloak all of her lies in some sort of truthspell. Perhaps she was trying to lure him into some kind of trap. Perhaps *she* was the trap.

His gaze traveled again to the braid of hair at his wrist, and the gold ring on his finger. As much as he loved owning jewelry, he had never worn any, until apparently now. And that ring was a wedding ring.

For any kind of subterfuge to be employed at this sophisticated level, she would have needed to slip both wedding ring and braid onto his human form before he had been injured, and somehow gotten him to put a protection spell on the braid.

Really, that entire scenario strained his credulity.

But on the other hand, so did the thought of having a mate.

A wife.

A life full of complicated concepts, involving friendships.

Letting all of those thoughts go, he concentrated on the reality at hand.

The reality was, he held her life literally in one hand, his long fingers resting against the warm, soft skin underneath her chin. Her pulse beat delicately against his hand, and there was no fear anywhere in her eyes, or in her scent. She leaned forward into his touch, as if she wanted his hands on her skin.

She had no weapons or barriers of any kind. She had no magic spells, just her own wild, inherent Power that brushed with such a tantalizing coolness against the heat of his own.

"So we were building a life together," he said in a husky voice into her upturned face, as he stroked his fingers along her petal-soft skin. "Fine. I want to see it for myself."

With a growing predatory hunger, he watched her lovely mouth shape her words. "What do you mean?"

"I presume we have a home somewhere. Take me there. Show it to me." Lifting one shoulder, he added a touch of persuasion to his voice. "Maybe if I see it in person, it could jog my memory."

The painful, excruciatingly bright hope came back to life in her eyes, along with a multitude of other, more complex emotions that he couldn't decipher.

Complex emotions, no doubt, that went along with their complex life.

He didn't care about any of it. He only cared about one thing.

The other Dragos—the one with his memories intact—had somehow won this remarkable creature's heart and soul. Perhaps it was more than a touch insane to be jealous of himself, but he was.

He wanted what that other Dragos had. *She* was the real treasure, more precious than sapphires, diamonds and gold.

At the core of his ancient, cynical heart, he was an acquisitive creature, after all.

Chapter Six

"**I** THINK GOING home is a great idea," Pia said slowly.

For such an unbearable nightmare, things were actually beginning to look up. Dragos had shapeshifted into his human form, and he was talking to her. Really talking, not growling or roaring (or biting), or barking orders.

Also, she was intensely relieved that he had figured out the nature of their relationship for himself. He didn't feel any of the emotions, and that hurt like a burning knife had been thrust into her chest, but at least she didn't have to try to find some way to tell him and watch any possible disbelief cross his expression.

Her lips were dry. She hadn't hydrated enough after her climb, and she moistened them with the tip of her tongue. His gaze dropped to the small movement and grew intent, although his hard expression remained closed to her scrutiny.

He was still so suspicious, and that hurt too. Her own logic scolded her. Of course he would be suspicious. Suspicion was part of the dragon's nature. He had been a solitary creature for so long, with a predatory nature and an ancient, primitive past, and he was quick to war. He had a history of enemies that went back millennia.

This present mess wasn't his fault. None of this was anybody's damned fault. It was just a random, horrible accident that had happened, but it was still hard for her not to take things personally.

She had to stay braced. Seeing their house might not help his memories to return, but it might just help him to relax and learn to trust her a bit more. Anything would be better than the cold, confrontational attitude with which he had greeted her earlier.

He still touched her, the hard fingers of his hand curled under her chin. She still touched him, her own hand curled around his muscled forearm.

He would never let an enemy remain in such intimate contact with him. The realization fed the stubborn hope of hers that refused to die.

She gave him a tentative smile. "When would you like to leave?"

He didn't return the smile. That fierce gold gaze of his never left her mouth. "Now."

Nodding, she stood and glanced down at the fire. "I guess we didn't need to build this after all."

He straightened when she did, with that quick, lithe grace of his that belied his muscular bulk. "That remains to be seen," he said shortly. He passed a hand over the fire, and his Power flexed, dampening the flames. "It will still be here if needed."

Clenching her muscles, she forced herself not to flinch. Of course, just because he wanted to see their home didn't mean he was committed to staying there.

At least, not yet.

Walking to her pack, she dug in the side pocket for the satellite phone. As Dragos watched, she punched in Graydon's number. When Graydon answered, she told him, "We're going back to the house now."

Graydon said carefully, "That sounds promising."

She could tell by the neutrality in his voice and words that Graydon knew very well Dragos could hear everything he said. Pia glanced at Dragos, who watched her every move with a sharp frown.

She told Graydon, "It's great news. I didn't want you to worry. I'll call when I can."

"Make it soon, okay?"

Dragos prowled close. He growled, "Who was that male?"

Was that a touch of jealousy? She didn't dare smile, but for the first time in almost two days, the heaviness in her heart lightened a little.

She also wasn't sure what to make of the fact that he didn't remember Graydon. She and Dragos had only been together fourteen months, but he had known Graydon for much, much longer. The damage to his memory seemed profound.

Meeting his fierce gaze, she told him calmly, "That was one of your best friends. He's been worried about both of us."

"I want to know his name." He gripped her upper arm.

She glanced down at his hand. The gesture was

possessive, aggressive, yet his touch was gentle on her bare skin. Thank God, he had lost the impulse to violence.

She covered his hand with hers. "His name is Graydon, and he loves you very much."

"I want to meet him." His jaw tightened, and so did his fingers. "But not tonight. Where do we go?"

"Do you remember how to get back to the scene where you got hurt?" She studied him, uncertain how he would take the information. "It's about fifteen miles from here. You were pretty disoriented when you left yesterday."

His expression closed down. "Yes."

She hated when he shut her out like that. She couldn't tell what he was thinking. Tightening her lips, she said, "The accident happened roughly two hundred yards away from our house, on the other side of some bordering trees."

He remained silent for so long, she started to worry. He had thought he'd been attacked there. What if he refused to go anywhere near the construction site?

Finally, he replied, "I'll take us there."

Before she could do much other than nod her consent, he shapeshifted into the dragon again, his Wyr form filling up the clearing. He didn't give her time to gather up her pack. Instead, he scooped her into one of his forepaws, crouched and launched.

Clutching at one of his talons, she narrowed her eyes against the warm summer wind. Telepathically, she said, *You left your gold and jewels behind.*

Along with her satellite phone, in her pack. While she didn't want to mention that fact, she fretted at losing the ability to call Graydon. Just knowing she had the sat phone with her had felt like a lifeline.

High overhead, Dragos's head arched on his long, strong neck as he glanced behind them. His reply was telepathic as well. *That mountainside is deserted. I'll return soon enough for it, before anyone else has a chance to find it.*

Discouragement crushed down on her. Bracing one elbow on the curve of his claw, she rested her forehead in her hand. He wasn't just leaving the door open for a way out. He was actively planning on leaving again.

When he left again, would he let her come?

At that, the focus of her questions shifted drastically.

Would he allow her to leave him? What about Liam?

Her anxious thoughts ground to a halt. She didn't have any answers, only questions.

They fell silent. The dragon's powerful wingspread made short work of the distance back.

As they had talked, the moon had risen and silvery moonlight illuminated the countryside. A scattering of lights crisscrossed the land, following roads and highlighting houses. The scenery reminded her of the artwork that hung in his offices in New York.

When they neared their land, he slowed and circled, approaching the area in an oblique fashion. She had no doubt he was searching the area with all of his considerable senses, but she already knew what he would find.

Nothing, and no one. The property had been abandoned the day before, and except for a few safety lights, their house lay dark and deserted. Patiently, she waited for him to arrive at the same conclusion.

Apparently he did, for in an abrupt change of course, he landed in the wide clearing in front of the house and set her on her feet. As she watched, he changed back into his human form and strode over to take her arm again.

"A lot of people were here recently," he said. "Where did they go?"

"We knew you weren't thinking clearly." *Snapped at her.* She closed her eyes, willing the nightmarish image away. "But we also knew the dragon might come back. I ordered everyone to stay away until I told them they could return."

She took him up to the house. As they approached, his glittering gaze took in everything—the darkened, empty trailers a short distance away, the few cars that were still parked to one side of the house, the piles of building materials, two Caterpillar tractors resting at the edge of the nearby tree line.

Pausing on the front step, he turned to look over the clearing again, and he made a low sound of frustration at the back of his throat.

"Why do I remember some things and not others?" he muttered. "Those are cars. Those two vehicles are bulldozers. This apparatus attached to the side of the house is scaffolding. You called your friend on a satellite phone. You lit the fire with a BIC lighter. All those details are readily available, yet I wouldn't know my own name if you hadn't told me."

Heart aching, she shook her head. "I don't know. The mind is a complicated, mysterious thing. We could consult with doctors who specialize in traumatic brain injuries. They might be able to help."

Other than giving her one quick, frowning glance, he didn't respond to her suggestion. Instead, he grasped the doorknob and turned it. The door was unlocked. He pushed it open.

Twisting her hands together, she followed him into the house. Inside, the renovating materials—ladders, drop cloths, cans of paint and various tools—had been stacked neatly to the sides of the open spaces.

Silently, Dragos strode through the ground floor. She followed, flicking on light switches as they went.

His pace picked up until she had to trot to keep up with him. He paused in the doorway of his large, state-of-the-art office, and she hovered at his shoulder. "My scent is all over this room."

She told him, "That's because this room is yours, and you spend a lot of time in here. It's one of those complicated concepts."

His jaw flexed. She thought of all the places he would want to explore, that room would be at the top of the list, but after one more sweeping glance, he left it and moved on, prowling through the rest of the house, his presence brooding and intense.

She followed him everywhere he wanted to go—out on the patio, through the palatial kitchen, downstairs to the lower level.

Once, he paused for long moments in the hallway just outside of the hidden panic room. Hope surged again as she watched him. It was an exhausting, out-of-control feeling, as if it was a creature that existed entirely separate from her own needs or wishes.

But he said nothing, and after a few moments, he moved on.

Nerves started to get to her when he took the stairway up to the second floor. She felt strung out, as if she had drunk too much caffeine for too many days. At the top of the stairs he hesitated and turned right. Her heart started to pound, and her hands shook.

She thought, I should say something. I need to warn him.

"You're afraid." He said it over one wide shoulder as he strode down the hall, past empty bedrooms with open doors.

"Not afraid, exactly," she replied tensely.

"Then what—exactly?"

With impeccable instincts, he paused at the closed door of Liam's nursery and assessed her expression.

She rubbed the corner of her mouth with unsteady fingers. "It's another one of those complicated concepts."

He opened the door and walked inside. And froze.

Wrapping her arms around her torso, she gripped her elbows tightly as she watched him from the doorway. The line of his back, from his wide shoulders arrowing down to narrow hips, was taut.

After one pulsing second, he tore through the rest

of the rooms. She rushed after him.

He stopped in Peanut's bedroom, staring at the bright colors on the walls, the crib, the dresser with the changing pad and diapers. Liam's favorite stuffed animal, his bunny, lay in the crib. Evidently, Hugh and Eva had forgotten to grab it when everyone evacuated.

Dragos picked it up and briefly buried his face in it. His hands clenched on the soft toy until the broad knuckles turned white.

The silence had turned deafening. She hurt everywhere. Her body physically hurt. She didn't know where to look, or how to hold herself in such a way that the pain would lessen.

He whispered, "This is a male scent. I have a son."

The words struck the room as loud as a shout. She swallowed hard, and her voice shook as she said, "Yes."

He looked in the direction of the changing table. "He's small."

Again, she said, "Yes."

He turned to her, his gaze incandescent and raw. "How is that possible? How could I not remember I have a son?"

"I don't know." She hadn't intended to say anything, but her words acquired a life of their own and wrenched themselves out of her. "I don't know how you could forget either of us. *You're in my bones.*"

He jerked toward her, Liam's bunny still gripped in one fist. "Where is he?"

She put her head in her hands. "He's in the city."

"Because of me," he said through clenched teeth.

He cut through the air with one hand. "Because I might have come back here to attack you. He was in danger because of me."

His violent emotions beat against her skin, an invisible force, until she felt bruised all over. She needed to lean on something.

There was nowhere to go that would be strong enough to brace her against the volcanic force raging in front of her—nowhere but forward. Blindly, she walked until she collided into his chest. "Please stop," she whispered. "You aren't the bad guy. There isn't a bad guy in this situation. It's just a bad situation."

His arms came around her. That was what she needed, more than air, more than water. She leaned on his strength, and he held her tightly.

Something came down on the top of her head—his cheek. It touched her briefly then lifted away. His arms loosened.

"I need to see the construction site," he growled.

Stiffening her spine, she lifted her head as she stepped back. The savagery in his expression took her aback until she realized what he really needed. He felt the need to fight, but there wasn't any enemy at hand, so he had focused on the only other thing available.

"All right," she told him. "Let's go. Let's do it now."

Pausing, he set the bunny on the dresser. His fingers seemed to linger on the toy's soft fur. Then he turned back to her, and they walked out of the nursery together.

There was only one other place in that wing that he

hadn't explored, the closed door at the end of the hall. Glancing toward it, he looked an inquiry at her. She said briefly, "Those are our rooms."

He hesitated. Conflicting emotions evident in his reluctant pace, he walked to the door and opened it.

A little while ago, she had been braced for him walking into their suite. Now after the raw scene in Liam's nursery, she could hardly stand it. It felt worse than stripping her clothes off in front of a stranger, more revealing, and she couldn't breathe as she waited to hear what he would say.

What if he disliked it? What if he rejected it?

He didn't step over the threshold, but instead flipped on the light switch and stared for a long time at the room inside. His hands had clenched into fists again. He muttered, "This is *his* space with you."

She couldn't have heard him correctly. Shaking her head, she asked, "Excuse me, what did you say?"

Turning off the light again, he closed the door. "Never mind," he said. His expression had shut down again. Shutting her out again.

Suddenly wild to get out of that hall, with all of its happy memories, she walked rapidly back to the staircase and took the stairs two at a time. This time he was the one who followed her. She walked out the front of the house, never bothering to shut the front door, and strode down the path to the construction site by the lake.

To the place where her life had vanished.

He stayed close on her heels. She could sense him, a

great inferno of heat prowling at her back. Within a few moments, they traversed the wooded area and walked out into clear air, at the edge of the site.

As she paused, Dragos came up by her side and they looked over the scene.

Nearby, the lake sparkled peacefully in the moonlight. This construction area was not neat, like the space around their house had been. Tools, hard hats and equipment had been abandoned, and across the clearing, the pile of rubble still lay strewn at the foot of the bluff.

She covered her mouth as she stared at the place, remembering the dread and panic.

Dragos took her by the hand, lacing his fingers with hers, and drew her forward until they stood together at the base of the bluff.

She fell into the past.

Digging bare-handed through the rubble. Hoping against hope.

She was so lost in the memory of her own nightmare, it took her a few moments to realize that the large, strong hand she gripped was trembling.

Pulled out of herself, she turned to face Dragos.

The frame of his body shook. In the moonlight, he looked drawn and ill.

"What is it?" Concerned, she rubbed his arm.

His bleak gaze met hers. He said hoarsely, "I snapped at you."

Of all the things she needed him to remember, that was the one thing she had hoped he never would.

She had a split second in which to decide how to

respond. In that moment, she made a private vow to never talk about the experience.

How she had felt—the shock, the despair—was none of his business. At least she could protect him from that. They would each need to cope with their own issues that had arisen from what had happened, but for now, there was nothing else to do but confront this head-on.

Keeping her voice calm and reasonable, she said, "Well, of course you did. How else would you act? You had just suffered a massive blow to the head, and you thought you were under attack."

In the short amount of time they'd had together, they had shared some tough moments, but through it all, she had never seen him look so injured. He looked like he wanted to vomit.

"I almost killed you," he said from the back of his throat. "I could have killed you. What kind of Wyr could do that to his mate?"

He was breathing raggedly, as if he had been running for a long time.

"You didn't." She put her arms around his shaking body and held him in her strongest, tightest grip, turning her head so that her cheek rested in the slight hollow of his breastbone. "*You* wouldn't."

He made an inarticulate noise that sounded crushed, and clenched her to him.

"I still don't remember you," he whispered.

A few hours ago, hearing those words had wounded her terribly, but now she knew better.

She rubbed his back soothingly. "Yes, you do. Somewhere deep inside of you, you do. We just have to be patient and give this some time." Tilting back her head, she gave him a gentle smile. "Because I'm in your bones, too."

Chapter Seven

RAGOS DIDN'T KNOW about that.

If she was in his bones, why did holding the delicate, feminine form in his arms feel entirely new? The perfumed scent of her hair was amazing. The trust she exhibited as she leaned against his body was revolutionary, life-changing.

He hadn't earned her trust. It was a gift, like her healing, and the gold and jewels. Her generosity of spirit staggered him.

The different aspects of his personality raged against each other. He felt torn, pulled in too many directions. Part of him strained for the memories that weren't there. He was shocked at so much evidence of his presence in this place, and furious that he could not feel a part of any of it.

Then there was the jealousy, which made him feel more insane than ever.

He hated the other Dragos, the one who had been a full participant in this rich, complex life. The one whom Pia obviously adored. He wanted to roar a challenge at that other dragon and tear him to shreds, until he was the only one left alive, the true victor and inheritor of all this bounty.

But there was no other dragon. There was only himself. The threat he sensed lay inside of him.

He was the one who had snapped at her. He could have killed her, without knowing, and then at some future date, he might have realized what he had done. He might have remembered that she was his mate. A cold nausea swept over him again at the thought.

"I'm sorry," he whispered into her. "I can't tell you how sorry I am. I didn't know. I could never have done it if I'd known."

She rubbed his back with one slender hand. When she spoke her voice remained as gentle and pragmatic as ever. "I know how sorry you are, and I knew you would be. What happened here—I never wanted you to remember that. All I want is for you to remember us."

Of course, she wanted her husband back. It seemed the time to say something reassuring, but he couldn't reconcile the warring parts of himself enough to verbalize anything that didn't sound completely crazy.

Things like, you are not his. You are mine.

I'll kill anyone who tries to take you away from me.

Forget the time you had with him. Be with me, here and now, not some image of who you think I am supposed to be.

Growling in frustration, he gave up on words entirely, tilted up her head and covered her mouth with his. Her body softened readily, eagerly, against his, and her lips parted for his invasion.

This response should be his, but he couldn't trust it. The things he felt were dark, tangled, and edged in violence. She thought she was kissing her husband. Instead she was kissing a savage creature. One who might kill anyone, or do anything to have her.

He wrenched his mouth away, and she made a soft sound of protest that went straight to his heart and groin alike. For a moment he thought she might tug on him to coax his head back down to her, and a greedy, ravenous part of him needed her to do it, to show him that she wanted him.

See me. Choose me.

Instead, she let him go and stepped away.

"Do you need more time here?" She sounded breathless.

"No," he snapped. He watched her recoil, and part of him wanted to rampage through the night in a rage.

Cautiously, she peered sideways at him as she suggested, "Would you like to go back to the house?"

Back to the house, with the silent, empty nursery for an absent child, and the beautiful, serene suite of rooms *the other Dragos* shared with her.

Clenching his fists, he pressed them against his thighs. This was too volatile, even for him. He had to get in control of himself. How could he expect her to continue trusting him, if he didn't trust himself?

"Go on back." His tone was too short, and he fought to soften it. "I need a few minutes alone."

She hesitated, her face tilted up to his like some rare flower that only emerged in moonlight, and while she tried to hide her anxiety, he could still sense it running through her slender form. "Are you sure?"

With a sudden flash of intuition, he realized what she was worried about. He touched her face. The softness of her skin was addicting. This time, when he reached for gentleness, it came to him readily. "I'm not going to leave," he murmured. "I only want a few minutes."

Her fingers curled around his, and she pressed her face into the palm of his hand. She said quietly, "Okay. I'll see you back at the house."

Some predatory instinct had him gripping the delicate angle of her chin, carefully to avoid bruising that soft skin. He said into her face, "I didn't want to stop kissing you."

The tiny sound of her indrawn breath brushed over his heated skin. Her heartbeat pulsed against the tips of his fingers. She whispered, "I didn't want to pull away."

I'm not who you think I am.

I am not the man you so badly want me to be.

He didn't say it. Instead, he brushed her soft mouth with his lips, and never mind that he really was *the other Dragos*—this impulse to sensual intimacy was all new. It was the first time it had ever existed in his world, and trapped in a tangle of his own devising, the dragon had no idea how to tell her that.

Letting go of his hand, she stepped back, pivoted on her heel and walked back to the house.

He stared at her retreating form, his muscles tightening instinctively as she disappeared underneath the shadow of the trees. Once he was truly alone, he gave in to the savage, jealous creature inside, shapeshifted back into the dragon and prowled over every inch of the construction site.

He didn't care what he looked at. He wasn't searching for any kind of evidence of wrongdoing. That suspicion had been thoroughly laid to rest. The dragon simply picked through the rock and various items for something to do while the real activity happened inside his massive, convoluted mind.

He hadn't left the gold and jewels back up the mountain for safekeeping. He had forgotten about it, and he'd only remembered when she had brought it up.

Which, he would have said, was rather unlike him. He never forgot about treasure. Never. Except for this time, when all of his attention had been focused on the real treasure in front of him.

There was only one creature he'd ever heard of who could heal with her blood, a creature that had long ago disappeared into myth and legend, and yet he knew that must be her true nature. He knew it like he knew how to make the fire respond to his commands.

Leaving the construction site, he leaped into a short flight that took him over the barrier of trees and landed in the clearing on the other side. Once grounded, he cloaked his presence in case she watched for him and prowled around the massive house.

Look at the scene, so civilized. So pretty.

The lights she had left on for him twinkled in the darkness.

His tail whipped back and forth as he bared his teeth at the house. He did not fit in that civilized, pretty life. He fit out here in the night, where the moon created a world filled with shadows, and other predators knew to slink away at the first sign of his presence.

Dragos.

Cuelebre.

Those were his names, and they said what he was. No more, no less, yet everywhere in that house he had seen the evidence of a civilized man, the man she had mated with, the man who might never return to her.

The man he hated and would kill if he could. The man he did not want to be.

But he did want to take that man's place in those soft, serene rooms upstairs. That private place, filled with cream furniture and jewel-toned colors, and all the sensual evidence of her nesting. The perfume she wore. The scatter of feminine clothes, and shoes, and jewelry.

Most especially, he wanted to take that man's wife for his own.

So he would put up with the rest of the civilized life. He would figure out the complexities in that office of his and learn to make peace with the many other creatures who seemed to be part of the total package. Tilting his head, he shapeshifted back into his human form and strode toward the house.

A better man, perhaps *the other Dragos* she had fallen in love with, might warn her of what he had become.

But he wasn't a better man. He wasn't a good man at all.

And unfortunately for her, he was the one who wore her ring on his finger.

Entering by the front door, he tracked her to the back of the house, where he found her in the kitchen, sitting at the table and eating a bowl of cereal.

She had showered, and her damp, combed hair followed the curve of her shapely head. Her sturdy hiking clothes were gone, and she wore thin, soft-looking pajama pants along with a matching sleeveless top that was a deep, ruby red that highlighted the golden tan of her skin. She was barefoot also, he saw, her pink-painted toenails peeping from underneath the hem of her pants.

Glancing at him self-consciously, she said, "If you're hungry, there's plenty of food in the fridge."

He was on fire with hunger, but not for food. He watched her ravenously as she spooned the last bite of her cereal into her mouth. The way her plump, naked lips slipped around her spoon as she took the last bite of food gave him an incredibly painful erection.

Clenching, he fought for self-control. She had undergone a lot of stress, and to the best of his knowledge hadn't eaten anything for a long time. "How about you?" the dragon asked, striving for a solicitous tone. "Is there anything else you would like to eat?"

Her large gaze slid sideways to him, and he could tell by her guarded expression that he wasn't acting quite right. "No, thank you. I've had enough."

As she slid out of her seat and carried her bowl and spoon to the sink, his gaze dropped to her shapely ass and thighs, the tight glide of toned muscle sliding sinuously underneath the thin material of her pants.

Abruptly, he said, "I know what you are. I knew when you healed me."

Setting her bowl in the sink, she turned to face him, her teeth worrying at her lower lip. "I wasn't really trying to hide it from you, although you should know—we hide it from everybody else."

He wasn't surprised. In her Wyr form, her horn could dispel any poison. She could heal with her blood. She could only be captured by unfair means. No cage could hold her. Her life sacrificed could bestow immortality. If word got out about what kind of creature she was, she would be hunted for the rest of her life.

He stalked across the room toward her, slowly so as not to frighten her. Cocking his head, he studied her closely. "You're cloaking yourself somehow. I didn't notice it before. I know how to cloak my presence, but I have never seen someone with the ability to cloak as subtly as you do."

While she might not have realized it consciously yet, some deep, animal part of her sensed that he had gone on the hunt, and she shifted her body restlessly as she leaned back against the kitchen counter. "My mom always said our cloaking was the most important thing we could do for ourselves. That, and knowing when to run and how to hide."

He would like to see her run. Not in fear, or because she felt she was in danger—those thoughts were as distasteful to him as the scent of her tears. But the thought of chasing her down a dark forest path as she tried her best to elude him... that was a game that appealed to every hunter's instinct he had, and his erection hardened.

Stepping in front of her, he trapped her against the sink by putting one hand on the counter on either side of her torso. This close, he could hear how her pulse picked up and her breathing shortened. Of all the many revelations in this long struggle of the day, the fact that he could smell her arousal for him was one of the most amazing.

The warmth from her body was a gentle heat that bathed the air against his skin. "Take the cloaking spell off," he said, in a voice that had turned low and husky. "I want to see you for who you really are."

A small smile tugged at the corner of her lips. "You never have tolerated any barriers between us."

He frowned, not sure how much he liked the comparison between himself and *the other Dragos*, but before he could decide how to respond, that elegant, subtle cloaking spell of hers fell away.

Pale, delicate illumination shone from her skin. He lost every other impulse and stared. The glow was so much like the moon's silvery glow, yet it was exponentially more precious, as it was drenched with her cool, witchy magic.

He lost himself in awe. The dragon couldn't remember the last time he had ever felt awe. Perhaps he had felt it once at the morning of the world, in that first, bright dawn. Gently taking one of her hands, he lifted it to his mouth, marveling in the effortless symmetry of the movement in her graceful wrist and arm.

She adapted to his action and took it for her own, as she raised her hand to cup the side of his face. That magic, the immediacy of her presence, sank into his skin and found its way into his old, wicked soul. Forgetting to breathe, he closed his eyes and soaked her in greedily.

"What do you need now, Dragos?" she asked softly. "Do you know? Do you need space, or your own place to sleep? Or do you want to go back to the mountaintop?"

The swiftness of his internal reaction jolted him, an immediate whiplash of denial at the thought of taking his own space, but when she mentioned going back to the mountaintop, he had to pause.

He couldn't deny it. He was tempted. The stone of the ledge would still be radiating heat from the day's sun, and the gigantic canopy of the night sky would arc overhead, stars gleaming like diamonds. The wildness and solitude of the place called him, and he knew she would come with him if he asked.

Yet, while he wanted to return at some point to collect the small pile of treasure—his gifts—going back there now would not be conquering the alien landscape of this place, and that was what he was most determined to do. He needed to invade that private place upstairs, the nest she had shared with *the other Dragos*, and to claim it for his own.

He needed to claim her in that space.

Holding her gaze, he said deliberately, "I need to take you to bed."

The sense of her arousal deepened, and the light that came into her face in that moment had nothing to do with her own magic, and everything to do with the magic they were creating between them. She whispered, "I'm glad."

Keeping hold of her hand, he turned and they walked through the silent house together.

Chapter Eight

P IA DIDN'T KNOW what to think of Dragos's deliberate, sensual approach, or the way they journeyed upstairs hand in hand.

It should have felt like a sedate pace. It didn't. It felt like a slow burn that crawled underneath her skin and set her on fire.

As they passed Peanut's nursery, he glanced at the closed door, and the expression in his eyes turned moody. "I need to see him too," he said. "But not yet. First, I need to be more settled in myself."

After a pause to think it over, she replied, "That's an excellent idea. The accident was only yesterday afternoon—it's been barely over a day. Much as I miss him, he's surrounded by people who love him, and I know they're doing a wonderful job looking after him. It's okay to take a few days, maybe even a week." She looked up at him. "The most important thing right now is to make sure you get what you need."

He opened the door to their suite, set a flattened hand at the small of her back and ushered her inside. Biting a nail, she watched him explore the rooms, discovering for himself where everything was. Silently, he disappeared into his walk-in closet for a few moments, then he strode into the bathroom. A moment later, she heard the sound of water running.

If the situation had been normal, he would never have let go of her hand. She would have gone with him and offered him comfort and sex. They would have shared healing intimacy in that shower. They had certainly done so several times before.

Now everything was so strange. He advanced on her and made no secret of his sensual interest, and yet he had barriers that remained in some deep, fundamental way. It confused her and made her question her own instincts.

He acted like Dragos, but he didn't act like *her* Dragos.

Eyes filling with tears, she went to the balcony doors, opened them wide and stepped outside for some fresh air. He didn't know about the healing, intimate times they had shared in the shower together, and she didn't feel confident enough to go into the bathroom to join him, even though she wanted to. She didn't know how to act, and she was afraid of doing something wrong, something that might send him away.

She didn't hear him step out onto the balcony. Not only was he fast and light on his feet, but he was also extraordinarily quiet when he chose to be.

Something else alerted her, a huge, fierce Power brushing against her senses.

Wiping her face, she kept her gaze fixed firmly on the shadowed mountain range in the distance.

"You could leave, you know," she said. "Be free,

start a completely new life. You have an out like nobody has ever had in the history of Wyr mating."

Also, just because they had mated, that didn't mean they had to live together. Several different species of Wyr chose not to live with their mates. Solitary by nature, they kept their lives separate and came together only when they needed.

She didn't want to live that way. She couldn't imagine adapting to that after the wealth of what they had shared, but you never knew what you could live with once you didn't have any choice. If that was what it took to keep him in her life, she would do it.

His hands clamped down on her shoulders, and he spun her around.

He was naked, his inky black hair and dark bronze skin still damp. His clean, male scent wafted over her. She got only a blurred impression of his muscled body before he jerked her toward him, bending over her upturned face.

His expression had turned murderous, and the gold in his eyes glowed bright and hot.

"Fuck that," he hissed.

Aw, he said the sweetest things to her.

Patting his hair-sprinkled chest, she said unsteadily, "I didn't say you *should*, or even that I wanted you to. I said you *could*. I only meant to point out this situation is really bizarre."

He thrust that deadly face into hers, growling, "I keep what is mine. I don't leave it. I don't lose it, not ever, and I go after anyone who tries to take it from me."

She knew that quite well, which was one of the major reasons she had chosen not to tell him that she had once stolen from him. That, in fact, him chasing after her had been how they had first met.

Being that it was another one of those complicated concepts and all, and best appreciated in context.

She should say something to lighten the mood. She should reach for the gentle, pragmatic way with which she had responded to his traumatized reaction at the site of the accident.

But her pragmatic side was worn out. It had gotten its ass kicked over the last two days. All of a sudden, she didn't have any more coping ability left, and even though she tried to stop the tears from coming, her damn eyes sprang a leak.

Her voice wobbled, and her mouth shook. "That's just it—you don't have any of those memories anymore that make me yours."

If anything, he looked even more furious. "What happened to 'I'm in your bones'?"

"Well, I want it to be true, but I don't know that it is, do I? And I'm t-tired."

"Stop that," he demanded. "Stop."

He cupped her face. Despite the roughness of his tone, his hands were infinitely gentle as he wiped the paths of her tears with both thumbs.

Belatedly she realized he was ordering her to stop crying, and a hiccup of laughter broke out of her. It quickly twisted into something else.

"I thought you were dead," she sobbed. "I stood in front of that horrible pile of rock and thought you were dead, and all I wanted to do was crawl under that pile to join you."

His hard features turned stricken. The world tilted as he scooped her into his arms and carried her into the bedroom.

He laid her on the bed and came down over her, pinning her with his heavy body. She craved his weight. Gripping the back of his head, she dug her fingers through his silky black hair, holding on to him tightly.

His mouth came down on hers, stopping her uncontrolled flood of words.

Hardened lips slanted over hers, and his tongue plunged into her mouth. There was no finesse, no coaxing. This was a taking, and she reached for it with all of her greedy heart, kissing him back with everything she had inside of her. All the love, all the desire.

Bunching his fists in the bedspread on either side of her head, he thrust a heavy, muscled thigh between hers. The hard weight of his erection lay against her pelvis, and she reached for it, caressing the broad, velvet head with one shaking hand.

He hissed into her mouth, and his hips pushed against hers rhythmically.

She pushed back, matching his rhythm. Pulling his mouth from hers, he rose onto his knees and shredded the clothes from her body.

When she was completely naked, he froze. The quality of his stillness made her pause, and she searched his expression.

He was staring at her.

Their bedroom lay in shadows. The only illumination came from the moonlight shining in through the windows, and from her.

The pearly luminescence shone from every inch of her. It had been a part of her since birth. It served no purpose. Like the color of her hair, or her eyes, it simply was. Often she had been exasperated with it, and sometimes fearful for what it gave away about her nature.

It was the most dangerous fact of her existence, the most likely thing to betray her. She could never let down her guard or relax her cloaking spell, unless she was absolutely sure she was in a private, safe place.

All of that melted away in the face of the wonder in Dragos's expression. With one hand, he touched the swelling curve of her breast, circling the pink jut of her nipple with the tips of his callused fingers.

With the other hand, he stroked the curve of her slender waist and the swell of her hip. The golden curls at the juncture of her thighs grew damp with the full, sharp ache of desire.

She never realized how empty she was until she was with him. Then the emptiness pierced her, and he was the only one who could ease the ache.

"You're the most gorgeous thing I have ever seen." His words were barely audible.

Grasping his large, hard penis in one glowing hand, she stroked his length and whispered, "You're the most gorgeous thing I've ever seen too."

His powerful frame was bound with heavy muscles. He was a dark, shadowy figure in the moonlit room, the bulk of his body defined by even darker shadows—the silken black hair sprinkled across his broad chest and arrowing down to his groin, the ripple of his abdominals and biceps as he crawled over her, the long indentation of flesh at his hips.

He didn't stop until he caged her with his body, pausing on his hands and knees over her. It was a dominant, possessive posture, and she loved it. Running her hands hungrily over him, she touched his flat, male nipples and petted the sprinkle of hair on his chest, following the path it made down to his groin.

His heavy, thick erection hung down to her, and underneath it, his sac had drawn tight. She circled the base of his penis and stroked his testicles, intending to slide down the bed between his legs and take him in her mouth, but he had other plans.

Taking her by the chin, he tilted her face up to his, making her look at him as he parted her legs and settled between them. His gaze burned with incandescence.

He said softly, "You are mine. You are always going to be mine. It doesn't matter what came before, the only thing that matters is what is now and going forward. There will never be anyone else for you. Only me. *Me.*"

A part of her marveled at the strange emphasis he put on those words, but it was overwhelmed by the huge tide of other feelings. Gladness, fierce joy and gratitude were foremost among them.

"Of course I am. I always have been, I always will be."

Until death might call an end to their lives, but even then, death couldn't part them. They were Wyr, mated for life.

One or the other of them might linger to finish their affairs. When she thought Dragos might be gone, she had made that commitment, silently, to Liam. She cherished the fact that her mother had done that for her before leaving this earth, and she would do no less for her son.

But in the end, she would always orbit around Dragos, always look for him, always reach for him. Whatever bridge he crossed, whatever journey he might make, she would always follow.

His rough-hewn features and body clenched tight, as he focused on some internal landscape only he could see. Sprawling over her, he burrowed his face into her neck and sought her skin with his mouth, while he reached between her legs to finger the plump, delicate folds of her sex.

He sucked, licked, bit at her, his sharp teeth causing a light, erotic sting. "This is mine," he muttered into the curve of her breast before he suckled her nipple. "This, and this."

Gripping his shoulders, she jerked and shuddered under the sensual onslaught.

"Yes," she told him.

Yes, and yes.

Breathing heavily, he rested his forehead against her

breastbone. "What lies inside this body is mine."

He was claiming all of her.

She lifted her head off the bed. "Dragos," she said, even as he probed and stroked her slick, private flesh.

He paused and tilted his head to look up at her. His brilliant gaze was jealous, secretive. For the love of all the gods, what on earth was going on in that convoluted mind of his?

She so adored this difficult, arrogant man.

In a strong, sure voice, she told him, "You are mine, too. You always will be. I'll never give up or let go, no matter how many times you get bonked on the head, or how exasperating you become."

She could say some pretty sweet things too, when she put her mind to it.

Satisfaction flashed across his face, along with triumph, and his reaction caught her attention, confusing her all over again. After all, it wasn't as though she had made any secret of how she felt about him.

She didn't have time to puzzle over it for long. Holding her gaze deliberately, he penetrated her with two fingers. She was so ready for him he didn't need to draw out any moisture.

The sensation of his fingers gliding into her felt so good, so necessary, she braced her heels against the mattress and lifted her hips up to his touch.

It caused him to growl underneath his breath. He fucked her with his fingers, intently watching every nuance of her expression. When the ball of his thumb came in contact with her clitoris, she shattered into a million pieces.

Her eyes dampened. When she could talk again, she murmured, "I guess there were some other things you didn't forget."

"It must be like riding a bicycle." He hesitated with a frown. "Except I don't think I ride bicycles."

At that, she burst out laughing and wrapped her arms around him. "No, darling, you don't ride bicycles."

He lunged at her, a quick, predatory swoop, and captured her mouth. Kissing her so deeply, he pushed her into the mattress, while at the same time he gripped his penis and rubbed the thick, broad head against her fluted opening. She lost her laughter in anticipation.

He pushed into her, and it was everything she knew and needed for it to be. Familiarity and recognition only made it sweeter and stronger, and she had room enough to ache for him that he had lost that deep, strong experience.

Then that thought fled, as he filled her to the brim, not stopping until he had sunk all the way into her, to the root. His hips flexing at the bowl of her pelvis, he clenched his teeth and muttered, "I can't get deep enough."

She knew that pained intensity. She had felt it so many times herself.

There was only one way she knew to make it better. Putting her mouth to his ear, she whispered, "Try."

Growling, he started to move. With an instinct that went deeper than thought, she picked up his rhythm and matched it, lifting her hips for his thrusts.

Hauling her up briefly, he angled one arm underneath her torso, his forearm sliding up between her shoulder blades as he sank his fist into her hair. With his other hand, he gripped her by the hip as he fucked her harder.

So possessive. She embraced all of it, the slight awkwardness of the position, the tight grasp he had on her body.

The tension was building again. Raking her fingernails down his back, she egged him on. "Harder."

He responded immediately, pistoning in deliberate thrusts. Their bodies dampened with sweat. This wasn't sweet, slow lovemaking. It was fierce and desperate.

Greedy, she was so greedy. She was frustrated she didn't get a chance to climax again. He plunged ahead of her to the finish, arcing up with a gasp as he spurted into her.

Letting go of her own need, she embraced him and focused on his pleasure. She felt every gorgeous pulse of his penis. Trying to make it last for him, she gripped him as tightly as she could with her inner muscles.

He came to a halt, breathing raggedly. She stroked the back of his neck.

His fingers loosened in her hair, and he came up onto his elbows. He looked agonized, desperate.

He said roughly, "I'm not done."

She stared. Before she could respond, he hauled her up bodily and flipped her so that she came onto her hands and knees. Incredulously, she complied, arching her back and tilting her ass in primal invitation.

Always when he penetrated her from behind, he felt bigger, and he seemed to get deeper. He entered her with a growl that vibrated down her spine. A nearly inaudible whine came out of her in response.

Oh God, oh God. This was a miracle she didn't even know to hope for.

Pleasure and emotion rocketed through her body. It was her turn to clench fistfuls of the bedspread. His hands clamped down on to her hips, and as he fucked her, she buried her face in the material to muffle the sound of her sob.

He was mating.

Maybe he didn't remember their life together, but he was mating with her.

That was the last true coherent thought she had before the swell of her own mating frenzy took her over. Her climax came over her like a steamroller. She flung back her head, gasping at the intensity of it.

Just when she thought the peak had passed, he wrapped an arm around her and found her clitoris with his fingers, and she exploded again. Clawing at his thigh, she urged him on.

This time his thrusts sent her against the headboard. She tried to brace herself, but she wasn't in control. Neither of them were. As he came again too, an animal sound wrenched out of him.

Silence stole into the room, and stillness. It was a chance to catch her breath.

But only for a moment.

He came down over her, spooning her so that his

chest pressed against her back. She could feel his heart pounding against her skin, a powerful, rapid force.

Meanwhile, he remained planted deep inside of her, his erection as hard as ever.

She knew this dance. They had been through it before.

Dragos buried his face in her hair, as he whispered, "I'm still not done."

Chapter Nine

b E DREAMED OF being buried, lost in darkness.
Beyond his grave, a splendid, graceful creature of shining, ivory light waited for him. She had delicate hooves and legs, and the single, slender horn on her forehead pierced him sweetly through the heart.

Come back, she called. *Come back to me.*

Yearning toward her, he struggled to free himself. Dust filled his nostrils, choking him. From an immeasurable distance across the starry night, Death, whose name was Azrael, turned to face him.

Azrael whispered his name.

Dragos was well acquainted with that old bastard. They were, after all, brothers. Azrael, also known as the Hunter, was a part of the dragon's nature, as Dragos was a part of his.

He said to Azrael, *You will not have me.*

Azrael gave him a pale, elegant smile. At times Death could appear quite alluring. Green eyes glittering, he said, *One day I might, brother. You are immortal, not Deathless, and nothing in this universe lasts forever.*

Opening his jaws wide, the dragon let out a furious roar, and Death vanished in a blast of heat and light.

DRAGOS WOKE WITH a start.

Sunlight poured through the large windows of the bedroom. Pia nestled against his side, her head resting on his arm. She was deeply asleep.

Shaking off the dream, he lifted his head and let his gaze roam down her nude body. Her luminescent glow was not quite as apparent in the bright light of day. Instead, her skin retained a faint, pearly sheen. While the effect was subtle, it was still all too obviously inhuman.

Her current position accentuated the hourglass shape of her body. She had marks on her skin, faint smudges of bruising and reddened scores of bite and scratch marks. She was already healing, and by midafternoon the marks would be gone completely.

A more civilized man would care that he had marked her. Perhaps *the other Dragos* would have cared. He touched one fading bruise lightly with his finger. Being neither of those two men, and intensely possessive, he would be sorry to see them disappear.

Then he regarded his own body. He was so much bigger than she, harder and more calloused, and yet he had marks on his skin too. As he shifted lazily against the sheets, the scratches she had made on his back reminded him of her own passionate response to him.

Carefully, so as not to wake her, he leaned over her sleeping form and mouthed, "You are so very much mine."

He was a fierce creature at the mildest of times. Now, the intensity of his feelings for her shook even him. And so, she was still a fool to have allowed it, let alone to have welcomed it as she had.

He eased her head off his arm and replaced it with a pillow. She never awakened. They had not stopped making love until well after dawn, and clearly he had worn her out.

Slipping out of bed, he went to the bathroom to sluice off quickly in the shower. After a few moments of searching in his closet, he located faded, cutoff jean shorts that he slipped on. He didn't bother with any other clothes, or with shoes. The summer day was already acquiring heat, and besides, they were alone on the estate.

He left her to search for food in the kitchen. The refrigerator was well stocked with both carnivore and vegan dishes that could be consumed with a minimum of effort. Someone had planned well for them.

Standing at the counter, he ate most of a roast chicken. Once the sharpest edge of his hunger had been satisfied, he went exploring.

The office—*the other Dragos's* office—drew him. He took his time discovering all the different components, glancing through file drawers, reading the first pages of contracts, studying building plans strewn all over a round, mahogany table. The construction site by the lake would be quite a compact complex when it was completed, combining both offices and living quarters.

Without having to be told, he knew that nothing left out in plain view would be vitally important. Any sensitive materials were either locked in the recessed wall safe he found hidden behind a paneling, or password protected on his computer, or hidden in the inaccessible recesses of his mind.

Raging against his lost memory was an exercise in futility. He clamped down on the emotion as he tried several combinations on the computer, yet failed to discover the right password.

What would *the other Dragos* use as a password? He would not fall into the trap of using personal or obvious information.

When another log-in attempt failed, his self-control slipped. Snarling, he swept everything off his desk and threw a stapler with such force it shot through a window.

The glass shattered and fell out of the window frame, just as Pia walked around one edge of the doorway, talking on a cell phone.

Stopping in midsentence, she came to an abrupt halt. Then she said into her phone, "I'll have to call you back later. I just wanted to let you know we'll need a few days here."

"I'll arrange everything," said the man on the other end of the call. "You concentrate on yourselves. Don't worry about a thing."

Graydon, the man's name was.

"Give Peanut all my love," Pia said.

All her love? Dragos's rage acquired a new focus. Who was this Peanut?

"I will," Graydon promised. "This is fantastic news, honey. I'll talk to you soon."

Her face calm and movements unhurried, she

turned off her cell phone. She had showered too, Dragos saw, and had dressed in a cheerful outfit of yellow shorts and a light summer top splashed with big, bright sunflowers. Her hair was still damp, and she wore pretty flip-flop sandals with tiny yellow flowers etched into leather straps.

She looked like a happy creature of sunshine and light, while he was still seriously considering smashing the desktop computer to bits.

"You love someone called Peanut," he growled, his fists clenched. "Who the fuck has a name like Peanut?"

She flinched. Somehow, he had managed to strike a nerve. Tucking her phone into her pocket, she said quietly, "That's our son's nickname. I started calling him that when he was just a little bundle of cells. You know, because for a while he was just the size of a peanut. Anyway, it stuck. His real name is Liam."

He sucked in a breath. Pivoting away from her, he stared sightlessly out the window he'd broken.

She came up behind him and stroked his back. As soon as her fingers touched his bare skin, the last of his rage died. He bowed his head.

"What happened?" she asked gently.

He rubbed his face. "I can't figure out his password."

She paused, and when she spoke next, her voice had gentled even further. "*His* password?"

Tilting his head toward the sound of her voice, he realized what he had let slip.

His emotions surged again, a powerful cocktail of

anger and frustration. All at once he let it go.

"Yes, *his* password," he snapped. He shrugged away from her calming touch and rounded on her. "*The other Dragos.* The one who has a closet full of handmade suits upstairs. The one who reads contracts and negotiates treaties, and who debates the difference between Wolf and Viking appliances." He gestured violently at the appliance manuals that had been resting on the desk, and now lay scattered across the floor.

She bit her lip. It was not in laughter. She said softly, "You wanted to buy the best things for my kitchen."

The walls of the house closed in on him. Grabbing her hand, he snarled, "I've got to get out of here."

Moving rapidly, he dragged her out of the house. She didn't try to stop him. Instead, she trotted willingly at his side. As soon as they reached the open air, he let go of her hand, shapeshifted into the dragon, scooped her into one paw and launched.

Some flights are lazy, long spiraling glides through the air. This fight was a battle. His wings scything through the air, he flew as fast as he could back to the mountainside where he had rested the day before.

The ledge by the stream was just as they had left it, with the pile of his gifts, her pack underneath the trees, and the stack of firewood and partially burnt wood in the fire ring.

He landed, not gently, but caught himself up before he set her on her feet, which he did with deliberate care. Then he whirled away from her to pace.

She said nothing. Out of the corner of his eye, he

watched her walk to her pack and settle in the shade of the tree, with her back braced against the trunk.

Tilting his head toward the sun, he considered leaving her and taking a solitary flight. But if he had truly wanted to be alone, the dragon would have left her back at the house, and she was clever enough to let him find his own way through his uncertain, surly mood.

At last, he gave in to the summer sun and stretched out his great length on the hot stone.

He said into the silence, "I am well aware of how crazy I sound."

He glanced at her sidelong. She had curled onto her side, knees tucked to her chest and head resting on her pack, watching him. Her expression was accepting, even compassionate. How could she look at him in such a way? She, of all people, should know that he was dangerous.

He demanded, "You do know that I am not that man, don't you?"

Finally, she spoke. "I believe that you are not the man you think you were."

Scowling, the dragon snapped, "What does that mean?"

"If you look at the details of his life without having his memories, I think it would be easy to get the wrong impression of who *that* Dragos is," she told him. Sitting up, she crossed her legs and toyed with a blade of grass. "The handmade suits, the contracts and negotiations… He didn't do all of that because he was civilized. He did it because he was playing the game." She met his gaze.

"And you are very, very good at it."

Tapping his talons on the stone, he considered that. Playing a game. Yes, he could understand that.

Rising up on his haunches, the dragon crawled over to her, bringing his head down until his snout came close to her face.

"I snapped at you," he whispered.

She cupped his snout and smiled up into his gaze. "I'm drawing a line right now. We have to agree to get over that. I know you're dangerous. I've always known you were dangerous. I was not naive about your nature when I mated with you the first time, and I am certainly not naive about it now. You never broke faith with me. *You* would never hurt me. What you did when you were injured and you couldn't recognize me is not anything we are going to worry about again."

A sense of peace threatened to take away his bad mood. He whuffled at her.

"I'm not ever going to be a good man," he warned.

She pressed a kiss to his snout. "We talked about that once, and I told you then—maybe you're not a good man, but you make a truly excellent dragon."

He muttered, "Maybe over time I can make peace with that other Dragos."

"If you give it a serious try, I think you'll be surprised at how well you do." She lifted a shoulder. "And if you can't adjust, maybe we'll go somewhere else and do other things. We're going to live a long time together, and things change."

The last of his tension eased away. Heaving an immense sigh, he shapeshifted and laid his head in her lap. She stroked her fingers through his hair, and for the first time since the accident, he fell into a truly deep, restful sleep.

✧   ✧   ✧

THE SUN TRAVELED across a blue, cloudless sky as Dragos slept.

After a while, she grew sleepy too, until finally she couldn't keep her eyes open any longer, and she nodded off, her hands laced protectively over the back of his head.

Sometime later, he began to stir, and she came awake with a jerk. She rubbed her eyes and looked around. They had dozed the afternoon away.

After nuzzling her thighs, he yawned and rolled onto his back. She gave him a smile as she flicked bits of grass off his skin.

He never got sunburned, no matter how long he stayed out in the sun. Instead, the dark bronze of his skin grew more burnished and rich. After a moment, all the bits of grass were gone and she gave up on that small excuse to touch him and simply stroked his bare chest.

He watched her, his expression more peaceful than it had been in some time. It would always break her heart a little to look at the new white, jagged scar on his brow. She touched it with a finger, swallowing hard.

He's mated with me, she thought, not once, but

twice.

I am so lucky. I am the luckiest woman in the world.

The smile she gave him twisted, because it was simply too small of a gesture to contain the enormity of the emotions inside her.

"I love you, you know," she told him.

He cocked a sleek, black eyebrow at her. Coincidentally enough, it was the same brow that now carried the scar. "You surely must, woman."

She chuckled. "Yeah."

Stomach muscles flexing, he sat up and twisted to give her a lingering kiss. "One of the craziest things that has been running through my head," he muttered, "is how goddamned jealous I've been of that other Dragos."

She put her arms around his neck. "Maybe I tried too soon to make you feel better about him. I could have used the threat of him to keep you under control."

Maybe that wasn't a very funny joke, but she was pleased with the effort. Every time they talked, every joke, every revelation, meant they put one more step between them and what had happened.

He must have agreed because he smiled briefly against her lips. Putting a hand at the back of her head, he deepened the kiss, and it escalated swiftly—a hot, explosive flash fire of emotion.

Coming up on his knees, his face taut and flushed with need, he yanked her clothes off. She was a willing participant, wriggling out of her top before he could figure out the complexities of undoing the buttons.

When he kicked off his jean shorts, his hardened penis bounced as it came free of the material. He pulled her down onto the grass and covered her with his body.

They could find time for foreplay and finesse later. Much later, after the first wave of the mating urge eased, or perhaps, for her, after the memory of the fear and pain over the last two days faded.

They weren't there yet. For now, he took her in a blaze of heat, and they coupled like the animals they were. Words tangled with motion, and it all became one thing.

I love you, love you.

I'll never let you go. You're mine. You're my mate.

They burned each other out, until at last they could rest quietly in each other's arms.

At last, he pulled away from her. She watched as he went to the pile of wrapped gold and jewels. Unceremoniously, he dumped the sapphires into her pack, took the cloth that the jewels had been wrapped in and dampened it at the spring.

When he returned, he washed the inside of her thighs gently. She stroked his arm as he did it, marveling at his intent expression. Sometimes he wanted so desperately to get something right, the sight of it shot like an arrow right through her.

After he finished, they dressed. The sky was darkening by the time they packed the rest of his treasure into the pack. He shifted back into his dragon form, invited her into the curve of his paw, and after she had settled comfortably, they flew back to the estate.

Once the buildings came into view, he banked and wheeled overhead, not suspiciously, as he had the day before, but in a more leisurely fashion, as he took a good look in the last light of day.

She glanced without much interest over the scene. They had flown over many times, just like this, as they talked about plans for renovations and the new buildings. Most of her attention remained on him, as she gauged his reaction to the things he saw.

Which was why she noticed the small hitch in the rhythm of his flight.

He said, curiously, "We never talked about that building."

She looked down again at the focus of his attention.

It was the house of the estate manager, some distance away from the construction site, along the curve of the lake.

A pang struck. Although she wouldn't trade her memories away for anything, it was hard to remember their time together all by herself.

She told him, "It's the estate manager's house. His name is Mitchell. He used to live here full-time when the main house was empty, but he's taking a vacation right now, as we figure out how to restructure his job."

Dragos folded his wings and descended. Even though she knew he would never drop her, the abrupt change in altitude made her clutch at one of his talons.

Landing on the shore of the lake in front of the house, he set her down and shapeshifted. He wore a strained, listening expression.

Watching him, she said, "We spent our wedding night in that house."

He whispered, "You gave birth there. In that room, with the big window, while we looked over the lake. We were all alone."

Her breath stopped, and her heart began to race. "Yes."

He turned on her, with the swiftness of fresh outrage. "You stole one of my pennies!"

She wasn't sure what pure joy looked like.

But she knew what it felt like, shining out of her own face.

Chapter Ten

WHILE HIS FIRST breakthrough was nothing short of miraculous, his recovery was not quite so simple or easy.

They took two more days together, partly so that he could gain some control over the volatility of his mating urges, and partly to see if he might regain more of his memories before they began to deal with the outside world again.

After hours of patiently talking between long bouts of lovemaking, he recalled most of their time together. A few odd bits and pieces still remained missing, but he lost the sense of competing with *the other Dragos*, especially when he recalled the intensity of mating with her the first time.

She was right. She was in his bones. One morning, as they lay exhausted and entwined, he whispered into her hair, "I'll always mate with you."

He could hear the smile in her voice as she whispered back, "I believe you."

Pia managed to convince him that he should have at least one consultation with Dr. Kathryn Shaw, the Wyr surgeon who often treated sentinels when they were injured. Because of that, the doctor was privy to certain confidences.

Although he finally agreed, Dragos was reluctant to do even that. Secretive by nature, it went against a very strong instinct in him to reveal to anyone the fact that his memory still remained impaired.

The morning of the consultation, Graydon brought Kathryn to the house. She was another avian Wyr, a falcon, and they flew in to land in the clearing, shapeshifted into their human forms and stood talking together for a few minutes before walking up to the front door.

They were the first people to return to the estate. Their arrival had been carefully choreographed, with nothing left to chance, so that Dragos could observe both of them from a distance.

When he laid eyes on Graydon's brawny figure, Dragos said immediately, "Of course, I know him. He is a good friend of mine—one of my best friends—and we've worked together for centuries."

Pia's expression lit up all over again. "You absolutely have."

When Dragos switched his attention to Kathryn, his frustration returned.

Like most Wyr falcons, the doctor had a nervy, slender form. Her large, honey brown eyes were sharp with intelligence, and she had thick chestnut hair, which she wore pinned away from her narrow face with a plain tortoiseshell barrette.

At Pia's inquiring glance, he said, "I'm supposed to know her too."

She responded as though he had actually asked a question. "Yes. She's part of our extended inner circle, and she's one of the few people who knows what my Wyr form is. Between her surgery skills and my healing ability, we managed to save Aryal's wings after she'd been badly hurt earlier this year."

Aryal was one of his sentinels, the contentious one. He and Pia had gone over everything she knew about the sentinels the night before.

His mouth tightened. "I've got nothing."

"That's okay." Pia laid a hand on his arm, and he calmed. He always calmed when she touched him. "Will you still let her examine you? Please?"

If the doctor knew about Pia's Wyr form, Dragos could deal with her knowing about him too. "Yes."

She leaned out the front door and waved her arm in invitation, and Graydon and Kathryn approached.

As they drew close, they slowed. At their uncertain expressions, Dragos said to the doctor, "Not you." He looked into Graydon's familiar gray eyes and smiled. "Yes, you."

A broad, relieved grin broke over Graydon's rugged features. As the other man stepped forward, Dragos pulled him into a quick, hard hug.

After letting him go, Graydon made as if he might hug Pia too, but she stepped away nimbly with a warning smile, at which he caught himself up with a sheepish expression.

Dragos had room to be grateful for her quick thinking at maintaining some distance between her and the other man. Wyr could be dangerously volatile when they were in the middle of mating, and in so many ways, he was still a stranger to himself.

Dragos and Pia had cleaned up the broken glass in his office and taped the open window with a covering of thick plastic, so the doctor examined him there.

Graydon went to the kitchen to wait, while Pia remained close by Dragos's side as Kathryn shone a bright penlight into his eyes, tested his reflexes and balance, and asked him a series of questions.

She took care to ask before she did anything, which helped. After getting his assent, she also examined him magically.

Gritting his teeth, he endured the sensation of alien magic sweeping through his head. She was clearly adept at handling injured Wyr with uncertain control over their more violent impulses, and she finished that part of the examination quickly.

Afterward, the doctor perched a hip on the edge of the nearby mahogany table and regarded them with calm, intelligent eyes.

"You already know I'm a surgeon and not a neurologist," Kathryn said. "So my first advice is, we should find you someone who specializes in treating patients with amnesia."

"No," Dragos said. Beside him, Pia stirred. They held hands, and he clamped his fingers tightly over hers. He told her again, "No. It's hard enough for me to trust Kathryn with this. I will not consult with a total stranger."

Pia's shoulders slumped, and she sighed, although she didn't look surprised.

Neither did Kathryn. "Let me know if you revisit that decision," the doctor said. "In the meantime, treating memory loss is as much an art as it is a science, but we do know some things. For example, different types of memory are stored in different ways. Your procedural memory, which involves skills and tasks, appears to be undamaged. You know how to take a shower, how to fly, how to get dressed, etc."

Unexpectedly, one corner of Dragos's mouth quirked. He said, deadpan, "Or how to ride a bicycle."

He felt, rather than saw, Pia's attention flash to him. An exhalation of laughter escaped her, as she shifted in her chair.

"Exactly," said Kathryn. "Then there's declarative memory, which has two parts—semantic and episodic. Semantic memory contains facts and concepts. Episodic memory contains events and experiences. From what you've said, most of your semantic memory appears to be undamaged, but not all of it. You retain many concepts and facts, but the more closely those are tied to your episodic memory—or your events and experiences—the more likely there might be some impairment."

As wordy as that was, it was starting to sound a lot like Pia's *complicated concepts*.

"Explain," he ordered.

"Okay." Kathryn's reply was easygoing enough. She exchanged a glance with Pia and shifted into a more settled position. "You know there is the Wyr demesne here in New York."

"Yes, but I didn't recall that a few days ago." He thought of the wounded dragon resting on the ledge while waiting for a suicidal fool to climb up to him. "I was pretty deep into my animal nature."

"You've done a lot of healing since then." Kathryn hesitated and glanced at Pia again. "I'm going to ask you a question, and I want you to respond quickly, without giving it too much thought. How is the relationship between the Wyr demesne and the Dark Fae demesne?"

"Not bad," he said instantly, then he paused and frowned. "But that wasn't always true, was it?"

"No," Pia said. "It wasn't."

He looked at her from under lowered brows. "What happened?"

Her expression turned wry. "You and the Dark Fae King Urien didn't get along. Urien kidnapped me, and you killed him. But we love the new queen, Niniane."

Kathryn held up one slim hand. "So, on the one hand, you have the semantic memory, or the facts and concepts—which is, the Wyr demesne and the Dark Fae demesne haven't always gotten along." The doctor held up her other hand. "Here, on the other hand, you have episodic memory, or your events and experiences— which is, you killed the Dark Fae King. Both of these are housed in the declarative part of your memory. The damage you've sustained is in that area."

Frustration welled again. Letting go of Pia's hand, he raked his fingers through his hair. He said, "What you're really saying is I might not remember certain facts and concepts if I've got some sort of personal event attached to it?"

"Yes," replied Kathryn. "I think that's likely."

Which meant he might not remember old enemies or secrets that had been hidden long ago.

Inside, the dragon roused as he realized the world around him had gotten that much more dangerous.

Clearly thinking along the same lines, Pia muttered faintly, "Dragos has lived for millennia. He's witnessed and interacted with so much history."

The doctor said again, "Well, yes." Kathryn looked at Dragos. "If it's any consolation, I'm not sure how much a specialist could help you anyway. You have a… unique and capacious mind."

"I've got to get those memories back," he growled. "All of them."

"I'm sorry." Kathryn frowned. "There's no easy way to say this. You did sustain brain damage. It's real and discernible, and I could sense it as a shadowed area when I scanned you. It's very possible the only reason why you've made as much progress as you have is because Pia is the one who healed you. I've seen the kind of miracle that can come from her healing."

He lowered his hands and gave Pia a grim look. She whispered, "We're lucky you're alive, and you remember as much as you do."

Lucky.

Slipping an arm around her shoulders, he leaned his forehead against hers.

Early that morning, in the first blush of dawn, he had speared into her body as she cried out his name, and he had been incredulous at the newness, the raw magnificence of it.

Yes, he was so damned lucky. More lucky than he ever deserved.

After a moment, Kathryn said, "There's another important aspect of memory—emotion. The most vivid memories tend to be tied to emotion, so it's possible those might come back the easiest. Imagery can also be used to stimulate further recall."

As Dragos turned his attention back to the doctor, his eyes narrowed. "Pia told me about Graydon, but I didn't remember him until I saw him."

"That's a great example," Kathryn replied. "I suggest you go through all the photo albums you own. I can also put together some exercises that might help. Just remember, having someone remind you of an event—like killing the Dark Fae King—won't stimulate true recall. But, now that you've started to remember some things, I think you can hope for more periods of spontaneous recovery."

"Yet there's no guarantee I'll get it all back," Dragos said.

Kathryn smiled. "No, but life doesn't come with any guarantees, does it? Your recovery has already been pretty astonishing. Try to be patient and give your brain time to reroute new pathways. You never know what you might be able to achieve."

There was truth in that. He had a mate and a son.

And he remembered a time when he never thought he would have either.

He met Pia's gaze.

She mouthed at him, "Lucky."

His lips tightened, but then he smiled and nodded.

AFTER STAYING FOR another half an hour or so, Kathryn left, with a promise to return for a follow-up exam the following week.

Graydon sent for the rest of the sentinels, and afterward, the two men went out to the patio area, while Pia wandered off to make another phone call.

Graydon carried two bottles of cold beer from the kitchen. They had begun to sweat in the heat of the day. He handed one to Dragos, who inspected the label.

Oh, yes. He liked this beer.

He took a long pull, while Graydon sat forward and leaned his elbows on his knees. "They'll be here in a few," Graydon said. "They were hanging out at a dive bar in town."

Dragos tested out a few words. "Who... got the short straw?"

Graydon's head came up, a smile lightening his craggy features. "Grym stayed in New York."

Grym.

Scowling, Dragos tried and failed to recall what that sentinel looked like.

Graydon promised, "Maybe you have to see him, like you did with me. We'll Skype with him later."

His jaw tightened. "Kathryn said I might not get

everything back. That means you and the others need to be extra vigilant, because the gods only know what I won't recall."

Straightening, the other man took a long, deep breath. "Okay," he said. "We'll handle it. We'll teach you everything we know."

"And we need to keep this quiet," Dragos said. "The last thing we need is for this to leak out."

Graydon rubbed the back of his neck. "A lot of people were at the construction site, and news of the accident has already gotten out to the public. But the only ones who know you lost your memory are the sentinels, and the doc." His frowning gray gaze met Dragos's. "It might take some fancy tap dancing, but we can keep this under wraps."

Pia came into sight, and both men paused to look at her. She had her head bowed, as she concentrated on the person on the other end of the phone.

Graydon said in a quiet, telepathic voice, *When you disappeared, she handled things like a boss. She got a plan in place that covered everything—she coordinated the search for you and even drew up a will. Just in case. Then she climbed up that mountain and healed your ass. It was a good thing she was around to save the day.*

As she glanced toward them, Dragos smiled at her.

He said aloud, "Pia saves me every day."

"Amen to that," said Graydon.

They clinked bottles.

Pia hung up and walked over to them. She looked both excited and worried at once.

Dragos stood. "What is it?"

"Liam's going to be here in a few minutes." She bit her lip. "They're driving in with the sentinels. Eva said to be braced."

"What does that mean?"

Her worried expression deepened as she lifted her shoulders. "I don't know! All she would say is that he went through another growth spurt."

Together, they both turned to stare at Graydon, who winced at them apologetically. "Nothing's wrong." He held up both hands. "Liam is fine. So we decided it was best to not disturb you, until you had the capacity to deal with it."

"Deal with what?" Dragos demanded.

His sharp hearing caught the sound of approaching vehicles, so without waiting to hear a reply, he strode through the house, Pia close on his heels.

Two SUVs pulled to a stop, containing Eva and Hugh, and five tall, strong-looking people, all of whom Dragos knew immediately.

Aryal and Quentin. Bayne, Constantine, and Alex.

All his sentinels, except for Grym, who had drawn the short straw and stayed in the city.

Pushing past him, Pia ran down the steps toward the SUV that carried Eva and Hugh. Belatedly, Dragos realized that what he had taken for a space in the backseat was actually filled with a car seat.

Of course it was.

Eva leaped out of the passenger seat, one hand held out toward Pia. "He's all right, it's all right. Aw, shit, there's no way to make this easier."

"What the hell?" Pia exclaimed at her angrily. She pushed past Eva and yanked open the rear door to look inside.

Silence fell over the group, as they stood watching, all except for Dragos, who strode rapidly toward the SUV. His stomach clenched as Pia whispered, "Oh, my God."

She reached into the backseat and lifted out a smiling, tow-headed boy.

A big, beautiful boy. A much bigger boy than the toddler Dragos remembered. He was no expert on children, but Liam looked to be twice as big, maybe four years old.

"What the fuck?" he whispered.

Pia sank to her knees, hugging Liam tight, and the boy threw his arms around her neck. "What did I miss?" she cried. "What did I miss?"

"I missed you," Liam told her. "Bunches and bunches. Hi, Mom."

The boy *talked*.

Reaching their side, Dragos sank to his knees beside them.

"Look at you," Pia breathed. She ran her hands compulsively over Liam. "How did this happen?"

Liam beamed. "I'm being a big soldier."

Her eyes went wide, and she looked as if she'd been punched.

The boy cocked his head, and his smile started to dim. "Isn't that what you wanted?"

Immediately she snatched him tight, kissing him all

over his face and hugging him fiercely, as she sobbed, "Of course it is. You're such a *good, good boy*. You're the most amazing boy I've ever seen. It's okay to stop growing now. It really is. You can stop for a while. Dear God, you're big enough."

Liam kissed her back then turned his attention to Dragos and grew still.

Sensing Liam's change in focus, Pia looked at Dragos, too. With obvious reluctance, she let her arms loosen and let Liam stand on his own.

Dragos wanted to reach for him, but Liam hung back, leaning against his mom.

Dragos asked, "Are you afraid of me?"

Shaking his head, the boy asked a question of his own. "Do you remember me?"

"I do," he said, a little hoarsely. "I remember you so well, and I really don't want you to be afraid of me."

Liam pushed away from Pia and stepped toward him. Holding very still, Dragos watched many expressions pass over that young face.

Liam looked into his gaze. It was an old, deep look from those violet eyes, a look that did not seem to come from a child.

Then Liam smiled and patted him on the cheek.

He said in a gentle voice, "You're a good dad."

Astonished, broken wide open, Dragos felt something slide down his face. He touched his cheek and discovered wetness. Feeling a fullness and depth of emotion he had never felt before, he watched as Liam slipped around him and skipped toward the house.

Peanut Goes To School

To School

Thea Harrison

To my copyeditor, Luann, who makes every story better.

Chapter One

T
HE TRICKY THING about using a cloaking spell is that cloaking spells are tricky.

Liam snickered to himself as he tiptoed around the patio furniture and changed into his dragon form. His dragon had grown to the size of an adult lion, and he had to be careful not to knock over the furniture as he shapeshifted.

He also managed to hold on to his cloaking spell, which was a big fat win. Dad had said Liam's cloaking ability was one of the best he'd ever seen, although it was difficult to stay hidden while changing forms.

But since his dad could do it, Liam felt sure he would be able to do it also. Eventually. Sometimes. If he kept practicing, pretty soon he should be able to stay cloaked all the time if he needed to.

Liam was playing his favorite game, Spy Wyr, which he had totally made up himself. When he grew up, he was going to be a secret sentinel. Uncle Graydon would send him out on missions, and when he returned after saving somebody, or maybe even after saving everybody, Mom and Dad would be really proud of him.

Of course, because it was undercover, Dad would have to give him medals in secret. Sometimes they might be silver and bronze ones, or when he did something amazing, they might be gold. Or maybe when he did something really outstanding, Dad would give him a sparkly medal with diamonds on it. Then Liam would have to find a super-secret place to hide them.

His dragon side liked the sound of that. It made him feel growly and fine.

By day, Liam would be, oh, maybe a basketball player. Basketball players traveled a lot, so it would be a good cover, and besides, it would be fun to play ball all the time, so that would be a big fat win.

Hi, my name is Cuelebre, Liam Cuelebre. My code name is Double Oh Peanut, but you can call me Rock Star for short.

Snickering again, he started climbing the house. It was a big house and there was a lot of brick on the outside. If he had been in his human form, he wouldn't have been able to climb it, but in his dragon form, he could get a good grip by digging the tips of his talons into the brick.

One of his favorite things to do was sit on the roof and look around. Hugh said it was his perching instinct. Dad said he would have to get the roof reinforced, because Liam was going to get a lot bigger before he finished growing.

It was mid-August, but the day was nice and cool for a change, so lots of windows were open. And even though it was Sunday, there were always plenty of people about. Hesitating as he clung to the side of the house, he tried to decide who he wanted to spy on next.

Mom and Dad were hanging out in their rooms. . . . They had been relaxing a lot since Dad got hurt the month before.

If Liam could sneak past Dad's superpowers of detection, he was pretty sure he could sneak past anything. That might go a long way toward convincing Uncle Graydon to hire him for spy missions when he got bigger.

Once the idea occurred to him, he couldn't shake it loose. Giving into temptation, he climbed sideways to the end of the house, around the corner and up to Mom and Dad's balcony. It was a lot more work than he had anticipated, so he got tired, and he was glad to reach the point where he could cling to a support beam on the underside of the balcony.

From overhead came the sound of quiet rustling and the creak of furniture. Mom and Dad were outside on the balcony. They sounded like they might be cuddling.

Liam loved to cuddle with them and sprawl in a big heap to watch movies or football games. As he thought of joining them, he started to lose interest in playing Spy Wyr.

Then Mom said in a quiet voice, "I feel like it's all my fault."

"You know that's not true," Dad replied. "He was growing quickly before you said anything to him."

Liam started to get a hot, tight feeling somewhere in his middle. Were they talking about him?

"I know, but I'd give almost anything to turn back time and take back what I said."

Liam's wings and tail drooped. He knew exactly what she was talking about. They *were* talking about him, and Mom sounded really sad.

Last month, when Dad had gotten hurt so bad, Mom had said to Liam, *You need to be a big soldier now.*

And Liam had thought, I can do that.

He had *pushed* to get bigger, because Mom needed him to be strong.

Getting bigger wasn't hard. It was kind of like shapeshifting, and his dragon form wanted him to be big anyway. He could feel it inside, straining to encompass all of his Power. And, as Dad had said, he was growing awfully fast anyway. But for some reason, when he had gone through that growth spurt, it had hurt Mom, and the last thing in the world Liam wanted to do was hurt her.

For the first time ever, he thought, Am I bad?

Asking that question made the hot, tight feeling in his middle worse.

"I can't believe I'm going to take him to school in the morning," Mom said. "Even though he's taller than most first graders, he's only six months old."

"We've talked about this," Dad said. "We agreed that he needed school."

"I know and I was even the one who argued for that, but I have to ask—are we going about this the right way? He's already far past what a normal first grader knows anyway. He's read through a third of our library, he writes in complete sentences, and he's been learning high-school algebra from Hugh." She muttered, "*I* don't even remember how to do high-school algebra."

"Never mind the academics," Dad said. "You were right. He needs the socialization. The only people he interacts with are adults. He has to learn to relate to other children too, while he's still a child."

"I agree," Mom told him. "I'm just fretting. Dragos, he's so innocent."

"I know, but that innocent boy is also a dangerous predator. He can already take down animals that are more than twice the size of his Wyr form."

It was only one cow, Liam thought. He hadn't thought it was that big of a deal.

Dad was still talking. "When he killed those cows, Hugh said he went into a complete frenzy."

Okay, Liam might have forgotten about the other cows. His snout itched, and he rubbed it on one forearm.

"He needs to learn how to control himself," Dad said. "And for that, he needs to develop social ties. Relationships will be the only real check on him when he grows to his full size. He has to care enough about other people so that he controls himself, for their sake."

Mom whispered, "Like you?"

"Yes," said Dad. "Exactly like me."

They fell silent. Liam suspected they might be kissing, which they liked to do a lot.

From around the corner, in the direction of the

kitchen, Hugh called out, "Liam, come on in. It's time for lunch."

He heaved a sigh. He didn't want to leave. He wanted to listen to Mom and Dad talk until they said something that made everything better. He wanted that hot, tight feeling to go away.

"Liam!" Hugh shouted. "Don't make me come after you, buddy."

He could tell Hugh was too cheerful to be mad. Hugh almost never got mad, but Liam also didn't want Hugh to find out where he was, because then Mom and Dad would find out too, and what was the point of spying if you couldn't keep it a secret?

Releasing his hold on the support beam, he let himself fall. Like a cat, he twisted in midair so that he landed in a crouch, right side up. Trudging around the corner of the house, he shapeshifted back into a human boy and went inside for lunch.

The rest of the day seemed to go on forever. Desultorily, Liam played Spy Wyr some more, but his heart wasn't in it.

He was starting to feel nervous about school. What if the other kids didn't like him? How was he supposed to learn to socialize, if that happened? From the way Dad was talking, it sounded pretty important.

And besides, what if he didn't make any friends?

For supper, Mom cooked his favorite meal, spaghetti with meatballs, and Liam, Mom and Dad ate together in the breakfast nook off the kitchen. Mom had meatballs with her spaghetti too, but hers were the fake kind. Liam wasn't like Dad about food—even though he liked real meat a lot better, he liked fake meatballs just fine too.

For some reason, tonight his spaghetti noodles were hard to swallow, and he pushed the meatballs around his plate, until Mom frowned and asked, "Are you feeling all right, sweetheart?"

He wasn't sure. All his feelings were tangled up in a knot, and he didn't know how to untangle them, or how to answer her. So, he shrugged and said, "Sure."

She looked at him for a long, thoughtful moment. "I've never seen you without an appetite."

After thinking about it for a moment, he shrugged again. "Me neither."

Both Mom and Dad laughed, and then it was Dad's turn to study him. Dad's keen, gold gaze seemed to see everything, and Liam squirmed in his seat. But all Dad said was, "Maybe you'll be hungry later, or in the morning."

"Sure, maybe," he mumbled, fiddling with his napkin.

"Why don't you go upstairs and take your bath?" Mom suggested. "I'll be up soon to tuck you into bed."

Liam looked outside. It was still plenty light outside, but Mom had already talked to him about how he would have to go to bed earlier on school nights. At the time, he hadn't minded, but now it kind of sucked.

"Do I have to?" he asked. "It's so early, and I'm not tired."

"Yes, you have to." She smiled at him. Mom's

smiles were the most beautiful thing in the world, and they almost always made things better. They almost even made an early bedtime okay, but not quite.

He thought about arguing, but he could tell by the calm look on their faces that Mom and Dad were going to team up on this one.

He heaved an aggrieved sigh. "Okay, fine."

As he slid out of his seat and stood, Dad swept a large arm around him and pulled him in for a hug. Liam leaned against him. Dad was so big and strong that when Liam leaned on him, it was hard to be afraid.

The problem was, he couldn't lean on Dad forever. He had to go to school by himself.

As he straightened, Dad kissed him on the forehead. Mom said, "See you in a few minutes."

Upstairs, he gave his bath toys some consideration, but he didn't feel like playing anymore, so he took a shower instead. After drying his hair and putting on some underpants, he went to his closet and pulled out a pair of tan khaki shorts and a yellow and blue plaid shirt. The shirt had a collar, and it buttoned down the front. The yellow and blue colors reminded him of the sky.

It was his favorite outfit. He slipped on the khakis and shrugged into the shirt. He was just beginning to button it when Mom walked into his room.

Her eyebrows went up. "What are you doing?"

"I'm getting dressed for school," he told her.

The beginnings of a confused smile tugged at the corner of her mouth. "Sweetie, you do realize you don't go to school until the morning."

He gave her a serious look. "I know that."

"So why are you putting on your school clothes?"

He toed the carpet with one bare foot. "I don't want to be late. I thought it might be better if I got dressed now."

Her smile faded, and she gave him a completely serious look back. Then she went to sit in the rocking chair where she would rock him when he was a baby. Since he had gotten so big, they had taken out the crib and put in a real bed, but they had kept the rocking chair.

Actually, he might still like it when Mom rocked him in the chair. Sometimes. As long as she didn't tell anyone, and she had promised she wouldn't.

Mom had to move Bunny out of the way. Leaning forward, she rested her elbows on her knees as she held the stuffed toy in both hands.

"Tomorrow's a pretty big deal," she said. "I understand if you need to wear your school clothes tonight, just to be sure. But what if I cross-my-heart promise that you will have plenty of time to get dressed in the morning, and eat a good breakfast too, and you will still be on time for school? Does that help?"

Lifting one shoulder, he admitted, "It might."

"You can still sleep in your school clothes if you want, but if you do, they'll wrinkle, and you might not want to wear them in the morning."

He frowned. He wanted to wear this outfit tomorrow, not something else. "Okay, I'll put on my pjs."

"I think that's a smart choice. You'll be a lot more comfortable." As he changed into his Superman pajamas, she petted Bunny between its floppy ears. "Can you tell me why you're so nervous about school?"

He gave it some thought.

He couldn't ask her if he was bad, because what if he was? And what if other people could tell that he was?

What if Mom didn't know he was bad until he asked her, but then she found out? The hot, tight feeling came back. He had never thought of loss before Dad got hurt, but now he had. And he couldn't lose his mom. He just couldn't.

When she spoke again, her voice was quieter, gentler. "Liam, are you okay?"

Ducking his head, he mumbled, "I dunno."

"Would you like to rock with me for a few minutes?"

He nodded. She sat back in the rocking chair, and as he climbed in her lap, she wrapped her arms around him. He put his head on her shoulder, and she rocked him. After a while, she handed Bunny to him, and he smiled as he looked down at the toy. He was much too big for it now, but he still liked having it around.

"Look at those legs of yours," she said. "Look at those big feet."

She poked him in the thigh until he squirmed and laughed. They took a moment to look at his legs. They were too long, and his feet dangled almost to the floor, but he didn't care.

"Pretty soon you're going to be too big to ride on

my back," she said softly.

A pang struck. He loved, loved, loved her Wyr form, and he was never happier than when she took him for rides in the forest that summer.

He whispered, "I can't stop growing."

Immediately, she clasped him in a tight hold. "Of course you can't," she told him in a strong voice. "Nor should you. We're just going to have to flip things around. When you get big enough, I'm going to ride on *your* back instead."

He started to smile. "Really?"

"Absolutely. And I will love it every bit as much. Pinky swear." She pressed her lips to his forehead. "There aren't any words big enough to tell you how much I love you."

Well, space was pretty big. In fact, it was the biggest thing he knew of. He told her, "I love you bigger than space."

Tilting her head, she smiled into his eyes. "How perfect. I love you bigger than space too."

They rocked until gradually the tight, hot feeling eased, and he felt better. When she suggested he climb into bed, he didn't argue, and after she tucked the covers around him, she gave him one last kiss and turned the lights out as she left.

Rolling over, Liam fell asleep almost immediately and dreamed of how delicious the warm, fresh blood from the cows had tasted as it gushed down his throat.

Chapter Two

MOM KEPT HER promise and woke him early enough so he could put on his favorite clothes and sit down to a big breakfast of scrambled eggs and steak with Dad.

Dad was dressed for work too, but he didn't wear suits as often in their new home as he did when he was in the city. Today he wore jeans and a black T-shirt, although he had a stack of business papers with him at the table.

Liam bounced in his chair and waved his fork around as he talked around mouthfuls of food. Sometimes he pretended to conduct an invisible orchestra. The third time he asked what time it was, Dad got up from the table and left the kitchen area.

After a few moments he returned with a portable alarm clock, which he set directly in front of Liam's plate with such a look at Liam that he had to giggle. Out of the corner of his eye, he could see that Mom was laughing quietly too.

"Sorry, not sorry," Liam said. He had picked that one up off the Internet.

"So I can see," said Dad, with one black eyebrow raised.

Mom went to the kitchen for more coffee, which was when Dad turned to look him in the eye. All the humor was gone from his face, and it made Liam sober too.

"You're going to be stronger than anyone else today, including the teachers," said Dad in a quiet way that said he meant business. "Hugh and a few other guards will be nearby to keep an eye on things, but they won't be on school grounds. I want you to promise me you'll watch your temper, and you'll do as your teacher says."

"Yessir," said Liam. He sat up straight.

Dad gave him a smile. "Good boy."

But what if he wasn't? What if he wasn't a good boy?

The hot, tight feeling returned, and he had to put down his fork. He asked, "May I be excused?"

Dad's gaze went to the food that Liam had left on his plate, but he didn't say anything about it. Instead, he said, "Sure. Go brush your teeth and get your backpack."

Liam's new backpack was full of everything on his school list, like glue, scissors, and crayons. He dashed off to do as he was told, and all too soon, Mom, Eva and he piled into one of the SUVs and headed for school.

The trip seemed to take forever, but all of a sudden, Eva made a right turn, and he realized they were pulling into the school parking lot.

He stared curiously at the large school playground, which was located behind a tall, chain link fence. Big trees offered lots of shade, and there were two jungle gyms, along with a swing set.

He watched as Mom slipped on a baseball cap and dark sunglasses. She wore the cap and glasses a lot when they went out. She called it her incognito look. Turning to him, she gave him a bright smile. "Are you ready?"

No. "Yes!"

"Okay, let's go."

As they climbed out of the vehicle, he realized that other parents and kids were going into the school too. Most were either human or Wyr, but he also noticed one girl who looked Dark Fae. Her black hair had been cut into a bob at her chin, and her pointed ears peeked through the shining cap. Like Liam, she was taller than a lot of the other kids, and her large gray eyes darted everywhere.

Mom offered her hand, and he took it. She switched to telepathy. *Don't forget, you're registered as Liam Giovanni, not Liam Cuelebre. The principal knows who you are, but nobody else does.*

I didn't forget, he told her. He liked using Mom's maiden name. It made him feel like he was undercover.

She pulled her sunglasses down her nose to look at him over the top of the rim. *You have so much Power, sweetie. . . . Make sure to keep your cloaking tight around your body, okay? Otherwise you might make someone nervous.*

Okay, he said.

What about your cell phone? Do you have it with you?

Yeah. He patted the pocket of his shorts where the phone rested.

Who do you get if you rapid-dial number one?

He looked up at her. *You.*

That's right. Who is number two?

Dad. He kept staring at the Dark Fae girl when she wasn't looking in their direction. He liked how she looked. She looked sassy.

And number three?

Hugh.

Her fingers tightened on his. *Remember to dial Hugh first, if you need somebody right away, because he'll be just outside the school grounds.*

I won't forget, he told her.

"You're going to have a great day, I just know it," Mom said out loud. Her voice sounded kind of clogged up, like she might be getting a cold. "It's hard to believe that only last year you really were the size of a peanut."

He said, out of the corner of his mouth, "Mom, you promised you weren't going to call me that in public anymore."

"Right! Sorry, sweetheart."

As they reached the doors, he turned to her. "I remember how to get to my classroom. It's okay, you can go home now."

"Sounds good. I'll meet you right here after school." She gave him a smile that looked a bit strange, but he was too busy to question it for long.

"Okay." Pulling his hand free, he hopped to reach up for her kiss.

Usually he was an optimistic guy, and as he darted inside, last night's nervousness became a thing of the past, because Mom was right.

He was going to have a pretty great day.

✧   ✧   ✧

PIA STARED AFTER Liam as he disappeared into the school building.

Over the last couple of months, his hair had darkened to a honeyed gold, and it wouldn't be long before he stood as tall as her shoulder. Whenever she looked into his eyes, which were the same midnight violet as her own, she caught a glimpse of the Power contained in his tall, young body.

It wasn't the same as Dragos's Power. It didn't boil with quite the same fiery heat. But it was every bit as strong, every bit as vast.

She was so proud of him, and more than a little scared for his future, and she loved him so much, sometimes it squeezed the air right out of her lungs.

And look at how strong and brave he was. He ran into the building without giving her a single backward glance.

Well, that was *good*. Good for him.

As she turned to walk back to the SUV where Eva waited, tears spilled out of her eyes and ran down her cheeks.

Climbing into the passenger seat, she slammed the door and looked straight ahead. "Don't try to talk me out of this. I need to cry it out."

Eva put one dark brown hand on her knee in a

gentle pat. "Your baby just went off to school. You go right ahead, and cry all you want to, sugar. Today you get a free pass on anything you want."

Pia nodded, wiped her eyes and stared out the passenger window as Eva drove them back home. The majority of work was finally done on the house, and the focus of construction now centered on the office complex by the lake.

The site where Dragos had been so badly injured last month.

Pia didn't intentionally set out to avoid the area, but for one reason or another, she never went down there after Dragos's accident. She kept telling herself that things would be different once the complex was completed. For now, whenever she stepped through the trees and looked at the scene, all she could remember was the horror and terror she felt when she thought Dragos might have died.

After they parked, Eva gave her a tight hug. "Let me know if you want to talk anything over."

"I will. Thanks." Returning the hug, she went inside to find Dragos.

He was in his office, sitting at his desk and conducting a meeting via the secure telecom system he'd had installed. After days of fierce concentration as he had tried to think of what *the other Dragos*—the Dragos before his accident—would have done, he had finally managed to recreate the password on his computer. As she heard the voices, she recognized two of his sentinels, Graydon and Constantine.

That was how he approached anything to do with his injury and subsequent memory loss. He treated it like a battle and brought all of his formidable attention and tactical skills to the field with the intent to win. Pia found it both exhilarating and exhausting to watch.

Reluctant to interrupt, she hovered in the doorway, but as soon as he caught sight of her, Dragos said to his screen, "We'll have to talk more later. I've got to go now."

"Sure thing." Constantine's voice sounded clearly over the speakers.

Graydon said, "Text me when you're ready to pick this up again."

Then Dragos strode around the corner of his desk, wearing a look of concern on his hard features. He frowned. "You've been crying."

She gave him a twisted smile. "Yeah, I got emotional after I watched Liam go into the building. He didn't want me to come with him, and he ran in without a backward glance, and I was so glad that he was strong and secure enough to do that. . . . Then I cried like a baby all the way home."

He pulled her into his arms, and she went gladly, soaking in the feeling of his fierce energy as it wrapped around her protectively.

She found her favorite spot, the slight hollow of breastbone in the middle of his chest where she could rest her cheek. They stood like that for moment and then she said, "I don't want to be a helicopter parent, but you know, if he keeps growing like this, he's going to be . . . What, like a twenty-eight-year-old when he's actually two? That bends my head, and it makes me worry."

She felt Dragos shaking his head. "Tough as it is to adjust your thinking, we're never going to be able to judge him by normal standards. He's too much of a prodigy."

"I know, but my own past was so human, I don't understand how he knows the things he knows."

His fingers threaded through her hair. "The first-generation of the Elder Races were all fully formed when they came into being at the birth of the world. Magic has long since settled into balance, but in the beginning, it was nowhere near as defined. It ran hot and wild, and crazy things happened. It's possible the only reason Liam is having any kind of childhood experience at all is because he was conceived, and he didn't form spontaneously as the first generation did."

She thought back to her shock when she first found out she was pregnant. She muttered, "His conception seemed kind of spontaneous to me."

She could hear the smile in Dragos's voice as he continued, "He's also the product of two very rare and magical parents, and the combined Power he has inherited from each of us is quite unique. If he had been conceived at the beginning of the world, he might have sprung into existence fully formed too. As it is, he has to contend with the laws of nature as they are now."

As she listened to him, she calmed. He was always so much warmer than her. She reveled in his body warmth, in the hard strength of his arms resting around her, in all the sensual evidence of his presence. "I love listening to stories about how things were in the beginning. It sounds fascinating."

"It was a dangerous and unpredictable time," he told her. "And, yes, it was fascinating too." He rested his cheek on top of her head. "At any rate, all this talk about Liam is pure speculation, as we have virtually nothing else to compare him to."

"We'll just have to accept whatever the future brings us, and it's okay," she murmured. "I'll adjust. The main thing is that he's healthy and happy." Tilting back her head, she gave him a wry smile. "One thing's for sure—it's never dull around here, is it?"

His sexy mouth widened. "No, it never is."

"Anyway, I'm sorry I interrupted your meeting."

He cupped the back of her head in one big hand. "You should always interrupt me. If I'm in the middle of something urgent that can't be put on hold, I'll let you know."

Her gaze slid over to one corner of his office. Crates and stacks of books dominated that area of the room. The large round conference table was piled high with even more books, and there were more crates waiting his attention in the library.

Since July, Dragos had spent a virtual fortune on a variety of books on history and politics, both human and Elder Races, and the subject of each cluster of books focused on the gaps he had discovered in his memory.

Along with reading obsessively late into the night, he spent long hours talking to each of the sentinels, while major corporate decisions had been put on hold. His businesses, along with the Wyr demesne itself, were treading water but not making any forward strides.

Thankfully, they had the most active time of the political season behind them for the year. Dragos's assistants, especially Kris, were dedicated to the point of obsession, and with the sentinels' help, Dragos could afford to take time to concentrate on his own healing.

She asked, "How is it going?"

"Nothing new." He growled, "I'm learning a lot."

The frustration was evident in his voice. During the first few weeks of his recovery, he'd had several strong episodes of spontaneous memory retrieval. Now he recalled almost everything from the last few years, but since then, he had discovered that he'd lost entire centuries, and it had been at least ten days since he'd had his last breakthrough.

And, as he was quick to point out, so much of what had really happened in history had never made it into any book. Most of Dragos's life, in fact, including any number of private wars, feuds, pacts, and betrayals.

Closing her eyes, she rubbed his wide, muscled back. "I'm so sorry."

And she was. She was terribly sorry about his frustration, and she understood how the whole experience contributed to him looking at the world through even more distrustful eyes. He believed that they were more vulnerable now, and what he didn't know could possibly hurt them one day.

But in a way, she couldn't relate. She didn't care about what had happened that far in the past. All that really mattered to her was that he was hers again, that he remembered her, that he had regained his physical health and he loved and needed her as much as he ever had.

The Wyr demesne was strong. They had all kinds of help and protection, and they could rebuild anything else.

She asked, "Is there anything I can do to help?"

He buried his nose in her hair, took a deep breath and sighed. "You help just by being here."

"Well, that bit is easy," she told him with a smile. "Because I wouldn't be anywhere else." After a pause, she added more gently, "I do get concerned sometimes at how hard you're working. It's only been a month since you got hurt, so you might very well have more memories return. But I hope you can come to terms with the fact that you might not, either."

"I'll cross that bridge when I come to it," he said. The tone of his voice had turned dark and edged. "But I'm not there yet, and in the meantime, I won't let go of a single moment of my life without a fight."

That ferocity of his was one of the very things that had drawn her to him in the first place. He wouldn't let go of anything of his without a fight. And he was the meanest, nastiest fighter she knew.

Drawing comfort from that now, she lifted her head, and he responded readily, cupping her chin and covering her mouth with his, until everything else fell away in the brightness of the fire they created together.

Chapter Three

SCHOOL WAS EVERY bit as interesting as Liam thought it would be.

Well, actually the *schooling* bit wasn't very interesting, but Mom and Dad had already warned him that he would know a lot more than other first graders. Be patient, they had said. Your school experience is going to be different from everyone else's.

Everything else was awesome.

His teacher's name was Mrs. Teaberry, and she was pretty old. He couldn't tell what exactly Mrs. Teaberry was—he wasn't very good yet at identifying other peoples' natures—but she might be part Fae. Her hair was gray, and she had interesting lines on her face that moved around as her expression changed.

There were twenty kids in his class, and he watched them with fascination. Some were boisterous and excited, and others seemed timid and shy. One of them cried quietly for a few minutes, hiding it behind one hand. He felt bad for her, but as he sat across the classroom from her, there was nothing he could do to help.

There was no sign of the Dark Fae girl, so she must be in another class. He was sorry about that, as he liked how her eyes sparkled.

The teacher talked a lot, and he got bored and stopped paying attention. His gaze wandered over to a collection of books she had on a bookcase in one corner, behind her desk. Those weren't kids' books. Those were adult books, with titles that contained words like *learning methodology*, and *first-grade literacy*.

He had never read anything like those books before, and they piqued his interest.

When morning recess came, he slipped out of line, doubled back into the classroom and went to explore the teacher's books. He had flipped through almost all of them when Mrs. Teaberry walked back into the empty classroom.

The wrinkles on her face shifted into an expression of surprise. "Liam," she said. "What on earth are you doing? You're supposed to be outside with everybody else."

He closed the last book and slid it back on the shelf. "I wanted to read your books first."

She laughed. "You mean you're done looking at them. They're a bit too old for you."

Turning, he cocked his head at her. "No, I read them. I'm done now."

Her eyes narrowed, and her smile faded into something much more stern. "I don't appreciate someone who tells tall tales. You didn't read all of those books in just a few minutes. You should have said that you were just looking at them."

Confused, he blinked. He wasn't telling any tall tales.

Was she . . . calling him a liar? He wasn't sure. Nobody had ever called him a liar before.

"No," he said again, patiently. "I read them."

He waited for her to ask him questions about the books, which was what Mom and Dad would have done.

Instead, her expression turned cold, and her voice sharpened. "Go outside, young man. We'll talk about this later."

Talk about what later?

More confused than ever, and growing a little angry, he did as he was told and went outside.

There were so many kids, many more than just from his classroom. All the classes were out, including the older ones. He stood still, absorbing the scene.

The morning had turned sunny and hot, and puffy white clouds floated around in the sky. Tilting his face up to the sunlight, he wanted very badly to join the clouds in flight, but that wasn't what he was supposed to be doing.

Somewhere, just off the school grounds, Hugh and other guards kept watch, but they were well hidden from sight. He thought about calling Hugh to say hi, but his phone was supposed to be for emergencies only, and he didn't think feeling lonely was an emergency.

In the playground, some kids were running and shouting, and others climbed on the jungle gyms. Still others were swinging on the swing set, and he noticed a few squatting and digging at the base of one of the trees.

Late as he was in joining recess, he wasn't exactly

sure how to participate. Was he supposed to run around and shout, or climb on the jungle gyms? He didn't feel like doing any of that, so he went in search of the Dark Fae girl instead.

It took him a while, because she wasn't easy to find, which made him curious and even more interested. His hunting instincts engaged, he started to look in less obvious, more out-of-the-way places.

There were a surprising number of places that were less obvious and out-of-the-way, such as behind trees, or down a bare concrete stairwell. Rounding the corner of the building, he found the Dark Fae girl in the middle of a tense scene.

He took everything in at once. There were four boys, along with the girl. One boy knelt on the ground, sniffling.

The Dark Fae girl shoved one of the three boys. "Leave him alone!"

The boy shoved her back, hard, making her stumble, while the last two boys closed around her in a circle. "I've told you before to stay out of this," the first boy hissed. "Stop sticking your nose in where it doesn't belong."

Liam felt his eyebrows go up. He didn't have a clue what all that was about, but the predator in him instinctively recognized how the three boys were acting. They were trying to act like the Dark Fae girl was prey, but clearly she wasn't having any of it.

The fourth boy though, the one on the ground, was acting quite a bit like prey. He was smaller than the others, more delicately built, and fear poured off him in waves.

Liam looked at him for a long moment. While he might act like prey, he wasn't a wild animal or a cow. He was a person. Liam thought he might be human, while the other three boys were some kind of Wyr.

The Dark Fae girl balled her hands into fists. Violence hovered in the air, an invisible and yet very real presence.

Hands in the pockets of his khaki shorts, Liam touched the tip of his phone with one finger but left it alone.

He said, "Hi, guys. What's up?"

The boy that the Dark Fae girl had shoved spun around, angrily. He said, "None of your business. Butt out."

Liam gave the human boy another thoughtful glance. His cheek was reddened. It looked like somebody had hit him.

Liam's attention went back to the boy who told him to butt out. Was he a ringleader? Liam always wondered what it might be like to meet a ringleader.

He said, "I don't think so. I think you need to stop what you're doing."

Ringleader Boy stared. "Are you stupid?"

"No." He darted a glance at the Dark Fae girl. "I don't believe I am."

The expression on her face, he had to admit, was a bit skeptical.

Ringleader Boy stepped forward, his posture aggressive and the expression in his eyes flat. The other two boys flanked him on either side. Liam recognized what they were doing. Dad had talked about it before. He called it pack behavior.

Ringleader Boy said, "Yeah, well, I think you're pretty stupid."

Interesting things were going on in Liam's body. He felt flushed and twitchy, at once angry and very alert.

He felt like violence might be a good thing.

Pulling his hands out of his pockets, Liam walked up to Ringleader Boy. He didn't stop until his chest bumped the other boy's chest hard enough to knock him back. Astonishment took over Ringleader Boy's face. His fist flashed up, shooting toward Liam's face.

Liam realized he was a lot faster than the other boy, and he had plenty of time to do something. As he watched Ringleader Boy's fist coming toward him, he tried to decide what he was supposed to do.

In the meantime, everything inside him seemed to be racing harder, faster. He felt his heart pounding as if he had been running, and he liked it. It felt good.

He brought up one arm and blocked the punch on his way to taking Ringleader Boy by the throat. The other boy's expression turned shocked, and he coughed.

Around them, the Dark Fae girl and the two other boys shifted. One of them swore. The human boy crawled several feet, stood and ran away.

None of that mattered. Liam looked Ringleader Boy in the eye. You, he thought. You're prey.

You're my prey.

Ringleader Boy's eyes widened, and fear crept in to join the ugliness.

Liam's cell phone rang, splintering the moment.

For a moment, he didn't move. It felt too good to have a grip on Ringleader Boy's throat. Then his phone rang again, and only three people in the entire world had his number—Hugh, Mom or Dad—so he let go of Ringleader Boy to reach inside his pocket.

As he did, the other boy's face twisted. Rubbing his throat, he snapped, "You're not supposed to have a cell phone in school."

As Liam watched, Ringleader Boy skipped backward to join his two friends, and they all raced away, disappearing around the corner of the school building.

Pulling out his phone, he answered it. "Hello?"

Hugh asked in a gentle, easygoing tone of voice, "Hi, Liam. What are you doing, buddy?"

Just the fact that he asked that question made Liam think Hugh knew what he was doing. Liam lifted his head and looked around. He couldn't see Hugh, but that didn't mean that Hugh couldn't see him.

Rubbing the back of his head, he said, "It's kind of hard to explain."

"Everything all right?"

"Sure, I guess." Turning on his heel, he looked around. Everyone was gone except for the Dark Fae girl, who watched him with large, wary eyes. He told Hugh, "I got really mad at somebody, and I almost lost my temper."

"But you didn't."

"No." But he could have. He had been awfully close. Did that make him bad? Honesty forced him to admit, "Not this time anyway."

Hugh didn't sound shocked or worried. In fact, he sounded as mild as ever. "Good job, sport. You okay?"

"Yeah. I think so."

"Call if you need to."

"I will."

He hung up and said to the Dark Fae girl, "Hi, my name's Liam."

He kind of wanted to add the Double Oh Peanut and Rock Star stuff, but he didn't think she would find it as funny as he had the first time.

She didn't say hi back. She said, "I'm Marika." She pointed to the phone. "First, that's gonna get you into trouble. You're in Mrs. Teaberry's class, right?"

"Yeah."

"She can be really mean if you get on her bad side. She's made kids cry before."

He pocketed it. "I'm supposed to carry my phone at all times, so it's gonna have to be okay."

Shaking her head, Marika said, "Second, those boys? They're not going to forgive or forget what you just did. You're pretty big for a first grader, and you're really, *really* fast. In fact you might be faster than any kid I've ever seen, plus you look strong. But they're third graders, and now you're on their shit list, and that's not a good place to be." She scowled and muttered *damn it* under her breath. "Sorry. I know I'm not supposed to swear at school."

Starting to feel entertained, Liam put his hands in his pockets again and rocked on the balls of his feet.

"It's okay," he told her, thinking of the sentinels, and of Hugh and Eva. And of Mom too, on occasion, but especially Dad. "I live with a bunch of people who swear a lot."

Marika looked at him sidelong again, as if she wasn't sure he had all his marbles. "Look, I'm trying to tell you something. You made some bad kids really mad at you just now."

Actually, he wasn't sure how to respond to that. He was running into a lot of new situations today. Rubbing the back of his head again, he thought about it. *Cool* didn't seem like quite the right thing to say, so his mind wandered off on a different tangent. "Who were they, and why were they bullying that other boy?"

She paused as if he had surprised her. Then she said, "Andrew is the guy who tried to punch you. He's the leader."

Oh yes. Ringleader Boy. He nodded.

"Joel and Brad are tools. They just do everything Andrew says, but that doesn't mean they do nothing. Perrin is the kid they were picking on. We're all in the same class. Perrin did something really stupid last year—when he saw them breaking into the teacher's lounge, he told on them. They got in major trouble and they weren't allowed to go to the end of the year picnic, and now they won't leave him alone."

"What did they do?"

Her face tightened. "I told you, they're really bad.

They stole money and ruined his lunch several times. They tore up his homework, and beat him up a couple times. Once his mom had to take him to the hospital for stitches. I told Perrin he had started something he had to finish, and he needed to tell his mom and dad who had hurt him, but he got too scared and stopped talking. Summer break is a long time. I thought they would have moved on to something else by now." Then her wide, gray gaze locked onto him, and her expression changed. "Since you've butted in, they probably have."

"You mean they'll start picking on me," he said.

She looked exasperated. "That's what I'm trying to tell you."

"Okay, thanks for the warning," he told her. He still liked her, but he had to admit, she seemed pretty grumpy. "What about you? You stuck up for Perrin too."

She looked angry and a bit lost. "I have to. He's my neighbor, and we've sort of grown up together. We had to play together when we were little. And he doesn't have a clue about how *anything* works."

So she recognized Perrin as prey too. Liam blew out a breath. "So, they don't leave you alone either?"

"Like I said, that's probably changed, thanks to you crashing their party. It's hard to believe you found so much trouble in your first recess."

It didn't seem like the best time to tell her he'd been looking for her.

Her head turned in the direction of the larger play area. "Look, I gotta go. Try not to be too stupid, will you?"

That sounded like some great advice. As she ran off, he called after her, "Thanks, I'll try."

The recess bell rang, and everybody ran to get in their line for class. For a few minutes, the playground swirled with confusion as kids pushed past each other, searching for the right place to get in line.

Something hit Liam between the shoulder blades, hard enough to send him down on one knee. Coughing in surprise at the sharp pain, he went forward, splaying his hands on the asphalt in front of him.

Then a blaze of energy shot through him. Breathing hard, he leaped to his feet and whirled, looking around. He couldn't see Andrew or either of the tools, Joel and Brad. Other children surrounded him. The babble of their voices seemed too loud and shrill. Nobody was paying attention to him, or looked like they thought anything was odd, but he knew what happened.

That hadn't been an ordinary shove. Someone had hit him, hard.

Nobody had ever hit him before.

He rotated his shoulders to ease the ache, while blood pounded through his body. It was another good lesson.

As strong and fast as he was, someone could still strike him in the back and hurt him bad, and if he didn't keep his guard up, he might never see it coming.

The rest of the morning dragged on. Mrs. Teaberry didn't smile at him or call on him, no matter how many times he raised his hand when she asked questions. She always picked somebody else to answer, until finally Liam stopped raising his hand altogether.

Perplexed, he studied her. She almost acted as if she were mad at him, or as if she didn't like him. He didn't know quite what to make of that. Usually, people liked him, but school had turned out to be much trickier than he had expected.

He was happy when lunchtime came. He would have gone to look for Marika, if he could have, but they were supposed to stay in line as they got their trays and went to sit at the long tables. Hungrily he ate all of his food, even though some of it was unappetizing.

After the meal, they went outside for another recess. The day had turned hot, and some of the other kids gathered in the shade of the large trees, but he liked the warm sunshine and basked in it.

The area between his shoulder blades, where somebody had hit him, still ached, and he rotated his shoulders. Sally, the girl he had sat by at lunch, asked, "Wanna play hopscotch?"

Just then, he caught sight of Andrew, Brad and Joel. They hung on the metal railing that bordered the concrete stairwell. As they talked, all three looked at him.

Andrew met his gaze. The other boy's eyes were narrowed and cold, and the sore spot between Liam's shoulders throbbed.

He said to Sally, "Thanks, but not right now. Maybe tomorrow."

"Okay." She walked away.

He watched as Sally joined a couple of other girls,

and they started a new game of hopscotch. Then he looked back at Andrew and the tools.

While he had been looking away, one of the tools, Brad, had disappeared. Andrew and Joel leaned their elbows on the railing, still watching him.

Liam's heart kicked. On reflex, he spun in a circle, but Brad was nowhere in sight. Andrew smiled at him, and it wasn't a nice expression.

It was obvious they were planning something, but what? Liam didn't know. He was starting to feel twitchy again, and after giving that first big kick of surprise, his heart kept pounding, only this time it didn't feel good. This time, he didn't have any idea what he should do or where he should go.

Was this how Perrin had felt, when the three other boys had bullied him?

As Liam stared at Andrew, a slow, wild anger started to burn through his uncertainty.

I'm not prey. *I will never be prey.*

But he could still be hurt.

They could still hurt him. They could still hurt other kids.

When Andrew crooked a finger at him in unmistakable invitation, he started forward. He glanced around at the buildings and the open land on the other side of the school fence. He still couldn't see Hugh or any of the other guards.

Moving toward the other boy, he slipped one hand into his pocket.

And turned off his phone.

Chapter Four

THE SUN FELT hot on his head and shoulders as he crossed the asphalt expanse toward the other two boys, and he burned with energy.

He also had plenty of time to think things over, just as he had when Andrew had tried to punch him at morning recess.

What am I going to do? What should I do?

Maybe those were two separate things.

Other questions occurred to him. What would Dad do? Or Uncle Graydon, or Hugh? Or Mom?

Trying to figure that out was much trickier than trying to hold on to a cloaking spell. They were all very different people, which meant they might make very different choices from each other.

Maybe that meant there was more than one right way to deal with something, and maybe . . . more than one wrong way to deal with something too.

To be sure he dealt with this in the right way, he might have to grow up some more. His dragon side liked that idea and tried to *push* to get bigger, but he managed to stay in control of that for now. Eventually his dragon side would win and he would go through another growth spurt, but he could postpone it for a while.

The only thing he knew for sure was that dealing with cows was easy compared to dealing with Andrew and the tools. As Hugh had said about the cows (or hunting any other kind of prey), take only what you need, kill them quick and don't let them suffer.

When he reached the stairwell the other boys straightened from the railing and started over to him, both walking with a bit of a swagger and darting glances at each other.

Were they egging each other on? Where had Brad gone?

Giving the area outside the playground one last glance, Liam jogged lightly down the bare, concrete steps in the stairwell. There was nothing at the bottom of the stairs except for a few dried leaves, and a metal, locked door that led into the school building.

Nobody would be able to see what happened down here, unless Hugh or one of the other guards flew directly overhead, which they might choose to do, but he hoped not. He wanted to figure this out on his own.

Turning, he put the concrete wall at his back and looked up at the other two boys who stood at the top of the stairs. Then the predator in him went quiet and waited.

Come on, he thought. I was fast earlier, and that surprised you, but I'm just a first grader and you guys are third graders. There's only one of me, while there's two of you.

Andrew and Joel must have arrived at the same

conclusion, because after exchanging a grin, they bounded down the stairs after him.

Okay, then. He got ready.

Andrew said, "How's your back? I heard you fell down earlier and got a boo-boo."

Joel snickered.

"Maybe you'll fall down again someday soon," said Andrew. The expression in his eyes had turned hectic, and he looked excited. "Maybe you'll get more than just a boo-boo. Maybe you'll lose some real blood."

Anger flared, bright and hot like the summer sun. Liam leaped at the other two boys, and before they could do anything, he shoved them against the wall, one hand around each of their throats. Shock bolted over their faces, as they slapped and kicked him.

He was too mad to really feel the blows. Leaning his weight on his arms, he held them pinned in place, and he felt the flutter of their pulses in his hands.

"I don't know why you need to bully other kids," he said. He thought of the teacher's books he had read that morning and some of the potential causes for disruptive behavior. "Maybe you're going through a rough time, or maybe you're just plain nasty. I don't like any of you, so I don't really care."

Andrew hit at Liam again. "You're making a serious mistake," he growled. "There are three of us and only one of you, and I will *hurt you bad* for this."

Liam's anger burst into outright rage. Leaning harder on his hands, he stuck his face into Andrew's and hissed.

Heat boiled out of his mouth, along with a lick of flame. It startled him so badly he stopped doing it.

Did I just breathe fire in my human form?

The other two boys quit struggling and stared. Andrew breathed, "What kind of Wyr *are* you?"

"Uh," said Joel. Tears ran down his cheeks. "Uh, uh, uh. I never meant any of it. Swear to God. *He* made me do it." He jerked his head toward Andrew.

Liam started to feel bad that he made someone else cry, but he forced himself to toughen up. None of them had gone easy on Perrin, or, he suspected, Marika either.

"Swear you'll stop," Liam told him. "Leave Perrin and Marika alone. Don't pick on anybody else, ever again."

"I swear," said Joel.

Letting him go, Liam wiped his hand on his shorts. As Joel raced up the stairs, Liam turned his attention to Andrew, whom he still held pinned.

He told the other boy, "You can try hitting me in the back again or hurting me some other way, but I know to watch out for you now, and anything you try is only going to make me mad. If you don't stop hurting people, I'll come find you. I'll hunt you down. That's what I'm made for, hunting things. And when I find you, I'll pound your face into the sidewalk."

Joel had gone red, but Andrew's face turned chalk white. His eyes darting around the stairwell, he whispered uncertainly, "You wouldn't dare."

"I can start now, if you want," said Liam.

Moving too fast for the other boy to stop him, he

flipped Andrew around. Bracing one hand at the back of the other boy's head, he pushed Andrew's face hard against the concrete wall.

Andrew cried out, "Okay, okay—I believe you! I swear, I'll stop! *I'll stop!*"

Breathing hard, Liam listened closely to what Andrew said. Like his ability to identify a person's nature, his truthsense wasn't very well developed yet, but he could still hear the ring of truth in the other boy's voice.

The thing was, Liam still didn't believe him. He thought Joel would probably keep his word, but Andrew seemed different from Brad and Joel. There was something wrong with Andrew, something really bad that ran deep. He might stop for a while until he stopped believing that he would get caught, but sooner or later Liam thought he would hurt somebody again, because he liked hurting people too much.

But Liam wasn't old enough to fix anything like that. The only thing he could do was scare Andrew badly enough to make sure that future stayed far away.

Leaning forward to put his lips near Andrew's ear, he tried another hiss. Heat boiled out between his lips again and singed the ends of the other boy's hair. Crying out, Andrew cringed against the wall.

That would have to do. Satisfied, he let him go, and Andrew bolted for the stairs.

Turning to follow the other boy, Liam climbed the stairs, and as he looked up he discovered Marika hanging over the railing and staring down at him. She wore a solemn expression, and her gray eyes were huge.

He reached the top stair and sat down, stretching his legs out and looking at them. He had collected a couple of bruises on his shins where the other boys had kicked him. They would fade quickly enough, hopefully before the end of the day.

The angry energy was leaving him. He felt his dragon side straining to get bigger again, and this time he had to struggle to stay in control. After not having much of an appetite for a couple of meals, he felt hollow and empty. He wanted some meat, but he wouldn't get a snack until after school, so he resigned himself to feeling hungry for a few hours.

Marika came to sit beside him. She tucked sleek black hair behind one pointed ear, as she said, "That was hella awesome. Excuse my French."

His cheeks warmed. "They needed to be stopped."

"Yeah, I know, or one of these days, they were going to hurt somebody really bad." She studied him for a moment. "You did a good thing. And dude, you breathed fire!"

"I guess I did, didn't I?" He gave Marika a sidelong smile. She smiled back. On impulse, he said, "Hey, would you like to be my girlfriend for a couple of days?"

A startled wash of color stained her pale cheeks. She stared at him. "Only for a couple of days?"

He had forgotten—she didn't know who he really was, or anything about him. "Or maybe a week. It's kind of hard to explain," he told her. "I'm not going to be a kid for very long, so I can't make any long-term commitments."

She laughed. "You really are strange, you know that? What kind of Wyr breathes fire?"

There was a pebble stuck in the sole of his shoe, and he reached down to pick at it. "My kind, I guess."

"Seriously, are you keeping it a secret?"

As he opened his mouth to tell her he didn't know if it was a secret or not, a tall, strange girl ran up to them. She was one of the older kids. She asked, "Are you Liam Giovanni?"

He nodded.

"Mrs. Teaberry said to tell you to come into the classroom now."

Disappointed, he glanced at Marika, who might or might not be his girlfriend. "But recess isn't over yet."

The strange girl lifted one shoulder. "Not my problem. Teacher wants to talk to you."

Sighing, he stood, and Marika did too. She grinned at him. "Yes."

It took him a moment to realize what she meant. Then happiness made him grin back. "Really?"

"Yes, weirdo. Really. See you later." She punched him lightly on the shoulder and took off.

He said to the strange girl, "I'm dating an older woman now."

Not bothering with a verbal reply, the strange girl curled a nostril at him before she took off too.

Cheerfully, Liam made his way back to the classroom. It was funny how everything had been so strange at the beginning of the day, but he knew where he was going now, and the hallways and the classrooms seemed familiar.

When he walked into his classroom, it was empty except for Mrs. Teaberry, who was in one corner stacking plastic tubs filled with supplies on top of each other.

He asked, "You wanted to talk to me?"

Straightening, she turned to face him, and the lines on her face didn't look friendly at all. "Yes, I did," she said. "We have two issues we need to settle. First, you need to know that liars won't do very well in my class. They won't do very well at all."

His cheerfulness faded into confusion. More than a little disturbed, he cocked his head. "Are you talking about me?"

Looking exasperated, she said, "Of course I am. Surely you haven't forgotten that you claimed to have read my entire bookshelf in a matter of minutes."

Clenching his hands, he said through his teeth, "But I did."

She pointed at him. "You need to tell the truth right now and admit you were lying."

His mouth dropped open, and he stared at her. "You want me to do what?"

"You have to change your behavior, or I promise you, you're going to have a very tough first year, which leads me to the second issue we need to address. I heard you have a cell phone, and you were taking phone calls during morning recess. That's against school policy, and you'll have to give it up." She walked toward him, holding out her hand.

His mind flashed back to earlier, when Andrew and Joel had been watching him with such satisfied smiles, while Brad had disappeared from sight. Marika had said his phone would get him into trouble, and it looked like the other boys had made sure of it.

As Mrs. Teaberry approached, he backed away. "I can't. I'm supposed to keep my phone with me at all times."

"Unacceptable. Give it to me right now." She wiggled her fingers at him demandingly.

Shaking his head, he said again, "I can't."

Her expression turned incredulous and angry. "You're in big trouble, young man. This is my classroom, and in here, other rules don't apply. You do as I tell you. Hand it over."

Nobody had ever said such a thing to him before. And anyway, he didn't believe it. Dad's rules applied everywhere.

His body turned very hot, then cold. This felt completely unlike what had happened with the other boys. With them, he had acted on instinct, a certain amount of predatory cunning and on snippets he had heard about how the sentinels handled problems, but Mrs. Teaberry was an adult and his teacher.

He was supposed to mind her, but he also couldn't go against the safety rules. Starting to tremble, he shook his head. "No."

Mrs. Teaberry's eyes flashed. Lunging forward, she grabbed him by the shoulder.

Shocked, Liam tried to twist away, but her grip on

him was too strong. "If you won't give it to me," Mrs. Teaberry said, "I'll just have to take it."

She rammed one hand into his pocket, searching for the phone. He struggled against her hold. "Stop—you can't do that. I'm supposed to keep it with me."

Her fingers dug into his shoulder like claws, and she shook him. "Everybody always thinks the rules don't apply to them," she snapped. "But they do. They apply to you too, mister."

He couldn't let her take the phone, and she was hurting him. She was scaring him too. He couldn't call Hugh. He had turned his phone off. He couldn't call Mom or Dad, either.

Feeling invaded and trapped, he felt his fingers change and his teeth lengthen into fangs. He rounded on Mrs. Teaberry with a snarl.

She recoiled from him. Almost immediately, she straightened until she stood very erect. Her tight mouth bit out words. *"Don't you dare bite me, you little animal."*

Trembling more violently than ever, he swiped at his face as he looked at her hands. She clenched his phone in one fist.

Breathing hard, he angled out his jaw and said, "Give it back."

Astonishment took over her expression. She shook the phone at him. "I said you can't have it in school."

Growling, he walked toward her. She retreated until her back came up against a wall. Dimly, he was aware that his face was still not right. He had too many teeth, and they felt sharp against his tongue. When he held out one hand, palm up, he saw that it was tipped with long, sharp talons.

Cautiously, her eyes wide, Mrs. Teaberry set the phone in his palm.

As he turned it on, he thought about calling Hugh, because he wanted to see a friendly face as soon as possible. Then he thought about calling Mom, because he needed her to love on him and tell him everything was going to be okay.

But really, he had screwed up in so many ways that day, the only thing to do was to take it straight to the top.

He pressed rapid-dial number two.

Dad answered before the first ring had ended. "What's going on, Liam?"

Taking a deep breath, he said, "Can you come pick me up? I think I'm about to get expelled."

Chapter Five

DRAGOS CHANGED INTO his dragon form, since flying directly to the school was much faster than driving on the winding country roads. Pia rode on his back, muttering worriedly. She asked, *Did he tell you what happened?*

No, Dragos said, which was the strict truth.

He didn't mention what Hugh had already told him about Liam's two confrontations at recess. While Dragos planned on telling Pia everything, he still hadn't figured out what to say about those incidents.

He was proud as hell of how his son had handled the bullies, and he was both surprised and intrigued at Liam's newly emerged talent for breathing fire in his human form, but Dragos wasn't sure that Pia would feel the same way. Sometimes family dynamics were an interesting puzzle.

He also planned on having Andrew and his family investigated. As Hugh pointed out, the boy might need counseling or even special schooling.

Dragos kept his cloaking spell tight around them until after he had landed and shapeshifted back into his human form. Taking Pia's hand, they strode quickly into the school building and to the administrative offices.

The school secretary escorted them into the principal's office. Inside, the principal, Doreen Chambers, waited with an older woman, and with Liam.

Dragos took in everything about the older woman at a glance. She was of mixed race, part human and part Dark Fae, and she wore a tight-lipped, self-righteous expression. He turned his attention to his son, who sat with such quiet dignity that it took Dragos a moment to realize Liam was trembling. He clutched his phone tightly in both hands and didn't look at either the principal or the older woman.

A silent snarl built at the back of Dragos's throat. As Pia rushed to Liam, Dragos rounded on the other two women. He said in a quiet, rigidly controlled voice, "Explain this."

As the older woman had caught sight of him and Pia, her expression had changed. Clearly she recognized them. Instead of looking self-righteous, she started to look worried.

She should.

Doreen Chambers walked around her desk, hand outstretched to Dragos. She said, "Lord and Lady Cuelebre, this is Liam's teacher, Elora Teaberry. I owe all of you a profound apology. You see, we have a policy that children aren't allowed to have cell phones at school. . . . And with everything involved with the start of the school year, I simply forgot to tell Elora that we would make an exception in Liam's case."

Dragos ignored the principal's outstretched hand. Instead, he focused on Liam's teacher. Not only had her expression changed, but she was starting to smell nervous too.

On its own, that wouldn't be enough to pique his interest, because people smelled nervous around him all the time. However, when he combined her nervousness with Liam's upset, he didn't like the picture that was starting to emerge.

Elora Teaberry's chin came up. "Mr. and Mrs. Cuelebre," she said stiffly. "Had I been told that your son would be in my class, things might have gone very differently. As it was, I insisted he give me his cell phone, and he growled and snapped at me. I'm sure I don't have to tell you that this is not acceptable or safe behavior—"

Tuning her out, Dragos turned to Pia and Liam. Whispering soft words of comfort, Pia squatted by Liam's chair. His head lowered, Liam turned in his chair to lean toward her. Pia slipped an arm around him, cupped his shoulder and squeezed.

With an indrawn hiss and a grimace, Liam pulled away from her hug, and everything in the room changed drastically.

Frowning, Pia asked him sharply, "What's the matter, sweetheart—are you hurt anywhere?"

Liam muttered, "Not really. It's okay."

Pia's eyes flashed to Dragos. Shifting so that she crouched in front of Liam and blocked him from the rest of the room, she went silent. Liam looked at her, nodded then shook his head. They had gone telepathic. She eased the neckline of his shirt to one side to reveal bruises in the shape of fingermarks on one slim shoulder.

"Oh my God," said the principal, blanching.

Dragos's silent snarl turned audible. Pia whirled to face Elora Teaberry, her expression blazing with incredulous rage. "You put your hands on him. *You shook him?*"

The teacher's nervousness turned to outright fear, and her gaze darted around the room. "Everything I did was in self-defense. Your son snarled at me—he acted like he would bite me. He had partially shapeshifted, and he had claws and teeth—"

Liam said in a clear, strong voice, "You're a liar. You're lying."

Sliding out of his chair, he stood beside Pia's crouching figure and put his arm around her. To Dragos's eyes, it looked like a protective stance. Liam was guarding his mother.

Reining in his own rage so that he could at least appear calm, Dragos asked Liam, "What really happened?"

Liam said, "Well, first she said, you couldn't have read all those books, you're a liar. And I said, I did too read them, but she never asked me about learning methodology or first-grade literacy, or anything about what was really in the books. Then she said, it's against the rules to have a cell phone, so you give it to me right now, young man, and I said no, I can't do that, it's against the rules. So she grabbed me, and I tried to fight her off, and she shook me, and that's when I got toothy, and she said, *Don't you dare bite me, you little animal.*" He was breathing hard, and his eyes flashed with dark violet fire. "And she got my phone out of my pocket, so I said, give it back. And she gave it back. That's when I called you."

When he finished, a stark silence fell as everyone stared at Elora Teaberry, who stood with her back pressed against the wall. "That's not what happened," she said faintly. "He growled first. He snapped at me. He thought the rules didn't apply to him!"

Dragos could hear the lie in her voice. It was so apparent he felt sure the other two women could hear it too.

The principal's expression was appalled, while Pia looked more murderous than Dragos had ever seen her, and he knew fully well that he had the teacher's death stamped in the lines of his own face.

"This is so far beyond anything appropriate or acceptable, I have no words," breathed the principal.

"Well, you'd better come up with a few," Pia snarled as she surged to her feet. "And 'I'm so desperately sorry' and 'We're going to press charges' better be some of the first words out of your mouth."

It was so charming how Pia's thinking went straight to the justice system, while he thought of things like vivisection and dismemberment.

Dragos's gaze dropped to Liam. Now that he had told his story, the boy looked completely calm, even analytical, as he regarded Elora Teaberry. He had stopped shaking, and all signs of his previous upset had vanished.

What was going on in that brilliant, unpredictable, dangerous young mind of his?

Dragos decided to find out. He asked telepathically, *What do you think should happen to Mrs. Teaberry?*

Liam's gaze lifted to his. *Other kids warned me she would be mean. I want to know if she's hurt anybody else.*

Dragos lifted his eyebrows. *That's an excellent point*, he said. *I think we should find out, and if she has, we need to contact those children's parents.*

Liam nodded. He had slipped his arm around Pia's waist, and he leaned against her again. His expression was serious. *We need to make sure those kids are okay.*

Liam had been hurt, and he'd been upset and frightened enough that he had partially shapeshifted, but his first thought afterward had been for other children.

A powerful wave of pride conquered Dragos's rage. Already, his son was a far better man than he would ever be.

Walking over to Pia and Liam, he asked gently, *Are you all right?*

The boy gave him a faint smile, and Dragos got a glimpse of the older soul inhabiting that young body. *Yeah. I didn't let her keep my phone.*

He stroked Liam's bright, silken hair. *Good boy.*

"Oh, I almost forgot," Liam said aloud. He looked up at his mom and gave her a crooked grin. "I've got a girlfriend."

Dragos wished he could have taken a photo of that moment, because the look on Pia's face was priceless.

✧ ✧ ✧

MAYBE THINGS DIDN'T completely and totally suck after all.

A couple of the guards who had been watching over the school with Hugh came to take Mrs. Teaberry away, but not before Dad stood in the corner with her for a long time in silence. Liam never found out what Dad said to her, but whatever it was, it turned her skin pasty white and made her hands shake.

Briefly, Liam thought he might feel bad about that, but then he didn't. Sorry, not sorry.

After the guards took Mrs. Teaberry out of the room, Mom, Dad, Mrs. Chambers and he talked. Mom asked, "How do you feel about school now?"

"I like it!" he told her. It had been a busy first day, and going undercover was every bit as interesting as he thought it would be.

"Do you want to come back tomorrow?" Mom watched him closely.

"Yeah. Does that mean I get a new teacher?"

"It absolutely does," Dad said.

The adults talked for a while, and Liam lost interest. He wandered over to the bookcases that Mrs. Chambers had in her office, and he read a couple of books until they were finished. Mrs. Chambers said, "There'll be a substitute teacher in his class until I can hire someone else. Again, I can't tell you how sorry I am that this happened. Elora worked here for years, and I never heard a whisper of anything like this before."

Liam sneaked a look at Mom, who didn't look mollified. Her face set, she said, "Sometimes you only hear whispers if you listen for them well enough."

At that, Mrs. Chambers looked both terribly apologetic and rather offended, which Liam thought was a pretty hard expression to pull off. But she must have thought Mom had a point, because she didn't say anything.

Soon afterward, they left. Liam would have rather gone back into class, but Mom and Dad decided he'd had enough for one day. Outside, Eva leaned against the bumper of an SUV. Dad held out his hand, and Eva tossed the keys at him.

Dad said, "Thanks. Find your own way home, okay?"

"You got it," Eva said.

"I'm going to ride in the back with Liam," Mom said.

Dad smiled at them. "Good idea."

While he wouldn't have thought to ask for it, Liam was glad she did. They rode for a while quietly, and when he sneaked his hand into Mom's, she closed her fingers around his tightly.

Suddenly, she burst out, "I want to punch her evil, lying face."

Liam caught a flash of hot gold as Dad looked at them, narrow-eyed, in the rearview mirror. Dad said, completely seriously, "I can make that happen."

It wasn't really funny, and yet somehow it was. He burst out laughing, and after a few moments Mom and

Dad laughed too. Mom raised his hand and kissed it. He wiggled sideways in his seat belt so he could lay his head on her shoulder, and in that moment, he felt completely happy.

She said, "I'm so sorry you ever had to go through that, but especially on your first day."

"I'm not," he told her.

She turned to him with a look of surprise. "Really?"

"Yeah. I mean, she made me mad and she sort of scared me for a few minutes, but it didn't last long, and she shouldn't be a teacher."

"Out of the mouth of babes," said Dad.

"What do you want for supper?" Mom asked him.

He replied, "Lots and lots of spaghetti. I'm starving."

She chuckled. "Dad and I might eat something else, but you can have spaghetti every night this week if you want."

So, in fact, everything turned out to be almost perfect.

Almost.

That night he ate so much spaghetti, Mom said he was in danger of turning into a big noodle, which made him laugh so hard, he fell out of his chair. The rest of the school week went well. The substitute teacher was wonderful, a smart and nice man named Mr. Huddleston. After a few days, Principal Chambers came into the classroom to announce that Mr. Huddleston would be their permanent teacher, and all the kids cheered.

Dad told him Mrs. Teaberry went to jail. It turned

out she had been mean to other kids, and Dad said that lots of parents were pressing charges. Andrew, Brad and Joel stayed quiet at recess, and they left all the other kids alone.

Mom contacted Marika's and Perrin's parents, and one day, they came over for a playdate after school.

Liam had an awesome time. Perrin was an odd, nervous little nerd of a boy, but after he relaxed, he shouted and charged around with every bit as much energy as Marika did. They explored the woods behind the house and played pirates until the sun went down and the other kids had to go home.

So actually life could hardly have been better, except for one thing that weighed and weighed on his mind, until finally, on Friday evening, he couldn't take it any longer.

After supper, he and Mom made vegan rice crispy treats and together they ate the whole batch. Then, when Mom went upstairs to take a bath, he went in search of Dad and found him reading one of his history books in the library.

Liam wandered over to hang on the arm of his chair. Dad looked at him over the edge of his book. "Something on your mind?"

"Yeah. Maybe." Liam couldn't look into his dad's keen gaze, and he bent his head as he asked, "Can I talk to you in private?"

Dad glanced around the library, but instead of pointing out that the room was already empty except for them, after a moment he said, "Let's go for a walk."

Liam swallowed and nodded.

They went outside.

The sun had just set behind the nearby mountains, but it was still hot and plenty light enough. Overhead, the sky was streaked with rainbow colors. It would be a good evening to go flying, except Liam didn't feel like it.

Dad led him to the path that went to the lake, and soon they walked along the beach toward the half-completed office complex. It was the one place where Mom never came anymore.

Liam darted a thoughtful, uncertain glance up at Dad's face. While it was impossible to read Dad's expression, he felt pretty sure Dad hadn't picked the location by accident.

He said, experimentally, "I like the lake."

"I do too," said Dad. Stopping at a stack of concrete blocks, he sat on the edge of the pile and stretched his long legs out. He gave Liam a sidelong smile. "Don't worry, Mom will get over it. I think she'll come down here a lot once the building is completed and people move in. She doesn't let much hold her down, you know."

Liam nodded and turned to look out over the water, which reflected the rainbow colors in the sky. The lake blurred as his eyes filled, and his mouth wobbled as he asked, "Am I bad?"

In a very quiet voice, Dad asked, "Now, why would you think to ask such a thing?"

Squatting, he picked up a stick to poke at the ground, mostly to hide the fact that his tears had spilled over. "Last Sunday, when I was playing Spy Wyr, I heard you and Mom talking about how I needed school, so I could learn how to control myself."

Dad stayed silent a moment. He said, "We were on the balcony. Where were you?"

"I climbed up to the beams u-underneath."

From the corner of his eye, he watched as Dad closed his eyes briefly and said to himself, "I didn't sense a damned thing."

He guessed that meant he'd gotten pretty good at his cloaking spell. Ducking his head, he said, "There were some bad boys at school. I made one of them cry, and I scared the other one pretty good. And I meant to. I . . . liked it. Oh—also, I can breathe fire. Watch."

Holding the stick to his lips, he concentrated on pulling on his Power as he hissed. Heat boiled out of his mouth, along with a lick of flame, and the stick caught fire.

"That's something, that is," said Dad in a soft voice. "Can you put it out?"

"Sure." He started to bury it in the dirt between his feet.

Dad took him gently by the wrist to stop him. "No, not that way. Try to put it out with your mind."

Liam looked at him uncertainly then focused on the stick. After a few moments, he said, "I don't think I can do that."

"That's okay, maybe you can't do it yet, but I'm sure you will be able to. We'll practice at it." Dad passed his hand over the stick and the tiny flame died down.

"Okay, first things first. Come here."

As Liam stood up, Dad did something he didn't often do anymore. He picked Liam up like he was a little kid. Turning into the embrace, Liam wrapped his legs around Dad's waist and put his head on his shoulder.

Dad sat down again, holding him in a whole body hug. It felt good, like being surrounded by a hot, comforting fire. He rested his chin on Liam's shoulder. "Your mom and I already know about what happened with those other boys."

He mumbled, "You do?"

"Mm-hm. Hugh told us. After talking about it, we decided not to say anything unless you brought it up."

"Oh." After thinking about it, he whispered, "I'm not sorry."

Sorry, not sorry.

Dad rubbed his back. "You know what I think?"

He shook his head.

"I think you did an outstanding job."

Outstanding. He lifted his head. "Really?"

"Really. You spoke to them in their language. You backed them off, and you made them stop hurting other kids. And you controlled yourself, and you didn't hurt them in return."

He had to point out, "I scared them pretty bad."

"Yes, you did." Dad's face was calm. "If you were to talk to humans about this, they would probably say that things should be handled in a different way, and I respect that—but Liam, it's important to remember, we're not humans, and neither are those boys. They're stronger than humans, more dangerous. They're predators, and they crossed a line. You know what happens when Wyr go bad, don't you? They can hurt a lot of people before they're brought down."

"That's what the sentinels do," he said.

"That's right—that's part of what the sentinels do." Dad paused. "I also think it's important for you to remember, you have two sides to your nature. You have some of me in you, but you also have some of your mom too."

"That makes sense," he muttered.

"Your mom is much more peaceful than I am, so sometimes, you might find that those two sides are in conflict with each other. When that happens, you've got to give yourself time to think things over. You can always talk to either your mom or me. Between the three of us, I feel sure that we can sort things out. Okay?"

Blinking to clear his eyesight, he nodded. "Okay."

Dad looked over the water then back at him. "You know how old I am, right?"

"Yeah." It was actually hard to wrap his mind around the concept of just how old Dad was, but he had a general sort of idea.

Dad smiled at him. "In all of that time, you are the best thing I've ever done. You are the absolute best part of me, and I am so proud of you. Your mom is proud of you too, and she understands you better than you might think. You might be dangerous, but you could never, ever be bad. You just have to promise me one thing."

The weight lifted from his shoulders, until he felt light and free again. "What's that?"

"You've got to stop spying on adults, especially your mom and me. Sometimes we say things to each other that are private, and we say it in a way that the other person might understand, but nobody else would. It's called taking things in context. When you overhear stuff you're not supposed to hear, that's a good way to get your feelings hurt over nothing."

That made sense. He heaved a sigh. "Can I still play Spy Wyr with my friends?"

"Yes, you can."

"Okay. I promise I'll stop."

"Good boy. Are you ready to go back inside?"

"Yeah."

Dad hugged him tight then set him on his feet and stood.

As Liam looked up, his gaze caught on the thin white scar on Dad's forehead.

Dad was so big, so strong. He was stronger than anyone else Liam knew, but still . . . his dad could be hurt. As strong, old and fast as he was, someone could come at his back.

And Liam loved him so much it hurt. It was a good, deep ache.

When I finish getting big, he thought, I'm not ever going to let anything happen to you, or to Mom.

Not on my watch.

Dad held out his hand, and he took it. Together in the peaceful, deepening twilight, they walked back up to the house.

Thank you!

Dear Readers,

Thank you for reading A Dragon's Family Album! This is a collection of two previously published novellas and a short story—*Dragos Takes a Holiday*, *Pia Saves the Day*, and *Peanut Goes to School*.

While each of my Elder Races novellas can be read on their own, all of them expand on the world-building in the Elder Races universe. Many of them are a series of linked stories that are best enjoyed when read together. For example, the first Elder Races novella is *True Colors*, which is the beginning of four linked Tarot novellas, including *Natural Evil*, *Devil's Gate*, and *Hunter's Season*. If you enjoyed A Dragon's Family Album and you haven't yet read the previous stories, check them out!

Would you like to stay in touch and hear about new releases? You can:

- Sign up for my monthly email at:
  www.theaharrison.com
- Follow me on Twitter at:
  @TheaHarrison
- Like my Facebook page at
  http://facebook.com/TheaHarrison

Reviews help other readers find the books they like to read. I appreciate each and every review, whether positive or negative.

Happy reading!
Thea

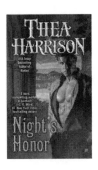
Formerly employed by a Djinn, Tess finds herself out of a job and running for her life. When she auditions to become a human attendant of a Vampyre, she catches the eye of none other than Xavier del Torro, the dangerous right-hand man of the Nightkind King. Now she must conquer her fear in order to receive the very protection she desires, even as her heart becomes vulnerable to desires of its own.

Turned during the Spanish Inquisition, Xavier del Torro has a violent history and reputation. But still waters run deep, and his true nature is far more complex than it first appears. When Tess catches Xavier's attention at the Vampyre's Ball, he is intrigued by her defiance, but her courage is what truly captures his emotions. Soon he vows to protect her by any means necessary – a promise that could put everyone in his life in danger.